BLOOD SISTERS

By

D. J. Bershaw

Book Four of Sisters In Arms

Published by Sucker's Junk Press
           P.O. Box 85
           Lafayette, OR 97217

First Printing, November 2019

ISBN: 978-0-9986796-4-8

Cover design by J. Kathleen Cheney
(jkathleencheney@gmail,com)

ALSO BY D. J. BERSHAW

SISTERS IN ARMS SERIES

———————————————

Other Blood

Blood's A Rover

Blood Tide

Blood Sisters

OTHER NOVELS

———————————————

Saving Sophie Scholl

Guardian Angel

Eco-Freak

Seen the Elephant, Heard the Owl

Damsel

Oral Wars

Our daughters were dressed to go to another world, wearing hiking shorts and boots, standing in the midnight darkness, kid-sized backpacks sitting by their sides. Tall for their age at four years old, they appeared six, with gaps where baby teeth had recently been shed. Little vampires mature quickly.

They looked hopefully up at me, trying to radiate innocence as I studied them in the lights of the fusion-powered truck which had delivered our group of ten to the Shift Point. A few feet away, ordnance bags were being unloaded, and the currency of our destination distributed. Conversations in both Gaelic and English swirled around us.

"What do you two have in your backpacks?" I asked casually, kneeling on one knee in front of my daughter. I spread the front of Quinn's light summer jacket so I could read her T-shirt. She flinched away from me.

On the ride here, both girls had been careful to keep their jackets covering their shirts. That usually meant nothing good. And Maren did her very best to position Quinn between her and me, which meant that her T-shirt was more parent-provocative than Quinn's. "I'm going to want to see yours, too, Mare," I said, as I examined my daughter's.

'Black Ops Brat,' hers read, black letters on olive drab. Not too bad, infinitely better than their favorites, 'Our Mommies Suck.' Which were probably in the bottoms of their tiny backpacks, come to think of it.

I sighed, crooking a finger at Maren. "Lemme' see, Mare."

"Now you're gonna get it," Quinn said, grinning at her sister and sticking out her tongue, certain she was safe. Having spent her first nine months in what I consider a more loving environment -- me -- Quinn is not quite as competitive and wild as Maren, but she's hardly anybody's sweet little angel, either.

I regarded her balefully. "Quinnie, *leave* Maren alone. I'm going to be looking in your *packs* next." That shut her up for the moment, and she blanched enough so the spray of freckles across her nose stood out against her tan.

Yess! Mommy still had the power. Even when you can heal almost instantly, move at something near light speed, and bench-press the average family sedan, it's always nice to be able to deal with your children.

I saw 'If You Can Read This, You're Probably Already Dead,' on Maren's shirt, and sighed again. I looked across the clearing. "Farrell! You want to get over here and help manage your monster?"

The shirt was not a hit with Maren's mother. Farrell glared down at her troublesome daughter. "Didn't I tell you that you could only wear that one around the house?"

"Yes'm," Maren replied in a low contrite voice, her head hanging. Quinn began to snicker, until I shushed her.

"Did you bring something else?" Farrell asked.

"Yes, Mommy," Maren said, continuing to keep her eyes down.

"Okay," Farrell said, "I want to see it on you when we've all made the Shift. We're going to go with Beckin and Brone. You two will come with Morag, Reen, and the others." She crouched down and hugged both girls.

Quinn looked up at me. "Can't we go with *you*?"

I gathered them to me, one little head on each of my shoulders. They squeezed hard, stronger than most adult normal humans. "No, my darlings," I said. "Children don't get to go with the first group, just in case something's wrong on the other side. You'll see us again in a few minutes. Don't worry."

We stepped to the center of the clearing, Farrell, me, Beckin Gilmer, and Brone, the big Berzerker Champion.

Beckin began to work her *Siog* trick, turning the walls of the worlds inside-out. The air around us seemed to thicken, and the familiar twisting sensation of the Shift enveloped our bodies. Light bent.

My last sight of the girls was of them waving, concerned expressions on their small faces.

Then we were across the Shift.

And the world exploded.

CHAPTER ONE

BLASTED

The iron tang of human blood, sharp and sweet, feathered up my nostrils and brought me back to consciousness.

Blood -- my good friend, faithful and true.

Crime and horror writers always say blood smells like copper. For blood that smells and tastes like copper, go kill a squid. Human blood is a bunch different.

Ask any vampire. We'll set you straight.

The blood smell originated from something lumpy pressed into my right side. Not my blood, not that of some other Changeling, and not *Siog* either. That was promising.

My head splitting, I bounced along a relatively flat trail, strapped onto something rough and seemingly wooden. I was sore all over. Particularly my back.

My bonds were loose, not intended to hold me captive, just to keep me attached to whatever I lay on. That meant our side won. Also promising.

But where were Quinn and Maren?

I remembered lights, shouting, thunderous blasts, being hammered violently sideways by a shockwave, then nothing.

I didn't remember our daughters being beside me then.

My pain and soreness was rapidly disappearing, but I must've really been thumped. Maybe even seriously broken. We vampires *do* heal. *That* part of the old legends *is* true, even though a lot of the other stuff is extremely bogus.

I cautiously opened my eyes. I lay on a travois. Pine branches arched high overhead in the night, stars winking through thin spots in the canopy. We'd made the shift shortly after midnight, so chances were good that I hadn't been out long. My internal bump of direction said I moved south, through younger trees, not the Shift Point giants.

They'd been waiting for us, whoever set off those explosions, but something had gone wrong for them. Some of us had survived, which meant that none of them had.

Worked for me.

CHAPTER TWO

SURVIVORS

I looked to my right. Beckin Gilmer lay beside me, her green eyes closed, the lumpy wrapped packet that stank of fresh blood wedged between us.

My Need surfaced, seeking the blood, sensing that I'd been injured, knowing it would restore my reserves.

I pushed the Need down and away, and lifted up on one elbow, trying to see if Beckin breathed. Her coal black hair was matted with blood, her narrow *Siog* face streaked with it. The jouncing prevented me from seeing any chest movement. She must be alive, otherwise whoever was towing us would have left her in an open meadow, her dead eyes on the stars, only bleached bones within a month. Tough to kill, the *Siogi*, almost as hard to put down as us vampires. Beckin must be expected to make it.

Arching my stiff spine, I stretched the bindings, and craned my neck to see who hauled Beckin and me through the night. A very broad back loomed above me, big hands holding the upper end of the travois as easily and lightly as most people would hold a baby bird.

Brone. The Monster Brone, a huge man, tall even for a Berzerk. Still wearing his custom black Nike jacket, silver swoosh shining in the starlight. And when I saw who walked beside him, carrying our ordnance bags and a pair of rifles, a line of ears strung from her web belt, I nearly cried out from relief.

Crying out didn't happen. "Farrell!" I croaked weakly. "Where're Quinn and Maren?"

She was instantly at my side, stroking my forehead, checking me over, smiling down at me. "They were in the second group. They didn't shift with us. You don't remember that? How *bad* do you feel?" she asked, her husky voice and copper gaze filled with both relief and concern.

10

Brone stopped and gently turned, shifting his grip on the travois to face us. Once he saw I seemed all right, his brown eyes were only for Beckin. They'd known each other since early childhood, growing up in the same village, Four Crossings.

"Okay," I finally answered, still taking stock. The Changed basically have only two states: okay or dead. And events were coming back to me, now, though I had to struggle some to remember. Our daughters were waving to us when we shifted. "Well, they've gotta be okay, you think?"

Farrell nodded. "Yeah, should be. The blast only affected this side of the point, I'm sure. As small as they are, they couldn't survive anything like the hit you took."

I let out a long sigh of relief. I was still groggy enough not to have realized that -- had the girls made the shift and been killed -- Farrell would hardly have left their
bodies behind. "Well, get me off this thing and give me some water. I'm a little sore, but I think I'm all right." I nudged the packet next to me. "What's this?"

"Provisions contributed by our late ambushers," Farrell said as she untied my ropes. "Flanks and thighs, mostly. A coupla fairly healthy livers. They were a scrubby lot. We left their bodies in a pile, cut their horses loose, trashed their poor-ass weaponry. *M-1s*, for shit's sake."

"Who were they?" I asked, standing shakily, grateful for the canteen she offered.

"Dunno. Locals needin' bucks, I guess, but two of 'em were well-fed and had decent survival gear, wore Mormon undies. Saints on a mission, maybe. *They* had M-16s, which we kept. Old Vietnam-era stuff, of course, but then *everything's* old here."

Farrell was right about that. Here, Richard Nixon had A-bombed Hanoi in the spring of 1970, and touched off a limited world-wrecker nuclear exchange that left much of the northern hemisphere very short on governmental centers and military installations. The east coast and California got severely whumped, but the south, midwest, and the western states outside California had mostly been spared.

Disney's 'Small World' had gotten a lot smaller, at least as far as people were concerned. Even in Oregon, population was down to about forty percent of pre-war, and a lot of those were refugees from California. That part's not so very different from our world, when you stop to think about it.

The *Siogi*, pragmatic as always, call this continuum 'Blasted.' Our timeline is the 'Crowded Lands.' Theirs is 'Eireann Mor,' or sometimes 'Tir na Nog,' -- the Land of Eternal Youth -- a name which we should find as perfectly appropriate as they do. To us, after all, they're the elves. Not the cute, squeeky-voiced variety, understand, with the curly-toed shoes and stuff, but rather the cold, scary, and lethal sort, who'll slit you open just to see what's inside.

"How long was I out?" My canteen was already nearly empty.

"Close to a half-hour. You bounced off one of the big Ponderosa on its way down. Smashed you up pretty good."

I glanced at Brone. His faint smile of reassurance didn't begin to erase his fears for Beckin. Oh, he was happy enough for me, but he knew Farrell and I could take care of ourselves. At the moment, Beckin -- unconscious and helpless -- was a different story.

I took my bag from Farrell, slung the strap over my left shoulder, put my right arm around her waist, and nuzzled her neck. "You think the girls will be all right?" I asked into the ear I tongued. Now that the Shift Point was destroyed, they couldn't come through, and we couldn't go back until we reached another operating Point.

She frowned. "They should be okay. They're with Morag and the Severers. Morag has at least one kid."

In my estimation, that's like saying "Hitler loved dogs and children."

12

However, despite what you might guess, 'Morag and the Severers' is not a rock group. Morag Timmerly -- 'Morag Death's Daughter' is her battle name -- is one of Beckin's more lethal relatives. Her jolly band of mercenaries -- the 39th Severers -- a couple thousand strong women strong, had served until recently in the Azteka Wars, down in the ass end of South Caledon. When things cooled off for the fruit harvest in SoCal -- they honestly call it that in English -- the 39th came north to Four Crossings for rest and refitment. Morag and a few of her more bored officers agreed to accompany us on a little jaunt to this timeline. A sort of extended playday for them.

And now it had gotten complicated. Shifting takes a *Siog* to manipulate the energies. Neither Brone nor Farrell nor I can do it. We'd lost the Point, and Beckin, our only *Siog*, had been injured. So, even if another point were nearby, we were stuck here until Beckin got healthy.

Maren and Quinn would be wanting their mommies, and their mommies couldn't be there and couldn't do anything about it.

Try explaining *that* to a pair of four-year-old vampires.

Good luck, Morag.

CHAPTER THREE

WE MONSTERS ALL

The Change giveth and the Change taketh away. One of the things it taketh away is squeamishness over diet. Maggot-ridden roadkill or our late enemies, it's all the same to us. As we walked through the high mountain darkness in heavy timber, pumice crunching under our boots, we nibbled on Farrell's human salvage.

Brone was not overly pleased with this, shooting us the occasional look of dark disbelief. Most of humanity has taboos against cannibalism, so his reaction wasn't overly surprising. Born and bred to wreak terminal havoc amongst any opposition, however, Brone might have been expected to be a tad more understanding than the average man on the street. Ten or so people had died swiftly back in that stand of stately old growth, and Farrell hadn't killed them all.

At six-and-a-half-feet plus, and three hundred pounds, the Monster Brone resembled former-footballer-turned-movie-actor Howie Long, an over-sized altar boy. Despite that, he couldn't be as sweet and good-natured as he looked.

Then I remembered my own open freckled features, grey eyes, and straw-blonde hair. For most of my life, for most people meeting me, I had conjured up visions of apple pie, ice cream, and motherhood. Well, at least the motherhood part was right. Now.

Anyway, my internal dialogue as to who was as innocent as they looked was small beer compared to Beckin's recovery and our reuniting with Quinn and Maren.

More than anything else, right now I wanted to sit down in a quiet, warm place, hold my daughter close, curl up for a nap, and just be Mommy Megan.

Not to be, at least not anytime soon, without Beckin.

A half-mile later, the wide trail began to break out into more open terrain, and we could see over the

14

myriad of moon-drenched finger ridges and down into what, in our world is the Umatilla River drainage. In this timeline -- Blasted -- all the names were the same as in ours, with only the last thirty years of diverging history.

Brone paused for a moment when the vista opened up. He set the travois handles down, and the three of us knelt and examined Beckin. He seemed to be able to see well enough, but my guess was that Berzerks didn't have our night vision.

"She's better," he said, standing. He allowed himself a small smile of satisfaction. "Her breathing was definitely shallower at the beginning." Brone's voice is not a big basso profundo, but a resonant baritone. He measures his words carefully, yet still manages matter-of-fact youthful enthusiasm. My mother would refer to him as a "very nice young man." She would be right, I suspect, only as long as he didn't get his hands on you when he was pissed.

"Beckin said something about a 'cache?'" Farrell asked.

Brone's satisfied expression moderated. "We need to get there as fast as possible. Somebody will come looking for the ambushers. They had radios. The Cache's about a half-mile away. Regardless of the timeline, if the line is visited frequently enough, the Cache is always in the same spot." He picked up the travois again.

"What's there?" I asked, as we trudged off down the trail.

"Food, clothing, medication, a place to clean up and sleep. Probably a few vehicles, and cans of fuel laced with fuel extenders. A popular timeline, like yours, will have residents on site, but this one doesn't."

"How obvious is this place?" Farrell asked. "Would anybody know what it was?"

"No," Brone replied. "It's within what appears to be a lava outcropping situated in a fairly flat lava flow. The remote that opens it will be in Beckin's pack."

15

I whistled. "Pretty sophisticated and expensive."

Brone just grinned and shook his head. "I have a cousin who wasn't suited for the arena. He became an accountant. The *Siogi* have more wealth than they could ever need. Every timeline has its own short list of technology unique to that particular history. The *Siogi* have cross-pollinated every significant invention they've come across into the other timelines. It's been pure profit. The zipper, the razor blade, the bottle cap. Name it, and it's been sold somewhere else. You've seen the Starcore fusion units. What would that be worth to your people?"

"Name your price," Farrell said.

"Exactly," Brone answered, nodding again, "so they can put together a multiplicity of sophisticated facilities and never grumble at the cost. It doesn't matter to them."

"Must be nice to bounce around realities," I said, "and grab all the great inventions." Looking ahead, I could see the edges of a big lava field, and the trail began to curve downward. Scrubby trees protruded intermittently from the folds and crevices of lava, spindly pine with pipestem branches poking up here and there.

Brone grinned outright. "We all benefit from it."

"Plus *you* have your Nike contract," Farrell put in teasingly.

"Amalgith is a hard bargainer," Brone replied, but he clearly enjoyed the thought of income gained on his own, and Amalgith Straight-tongue was the Nike distributor for all of Eireann Mor. Rumor was that Amalgith secured the Nike rights on a handshake with Phil Knight himself, which fits right in with some of the stories about Knight that circulate around *our* Oregon.

"For Amalgith, though," I said, "signing you is a license to print money." There could be only one Berzerker Champion, and that was Brone, a big, affable kid from the sticks. He was enormously popular, the

16

Eireann Mor equivalent of Tiger Woods, Picabo Street, and the WWF rolled into one.

"Not to mention your stud fees," Farrell added.

Brone regarded her bleakly, reddening, apparently not expecting us to have that particular tidbit of information. Once individuals are mature, *Siog* society is free-wheeling and sexually permissive by our standards, but I suspected Brone was uneasy with the procreative aspects of his new fame. He stuck his chin into his chest and looked acutely embarrassed. "It's all Artificial Insemination," he muttered, "not Live Cover."

"He's jesting, of course," a voice from behind us said. "Every third one is live in every sense of the word."

We all turned, Brone's embarrassment vanishing in an instant as his eyes brightened.

Sitting up, Beckin Gilmer busily sliced the bonds holding her to the travois. In the moonlight, her green eyes glowed. Her smile was grimly amused. "I *do* hope you killed each and every one of those who tried to kill us," she said, in her soft rasping voice.

CHAPTER FOUR

OBITUARY EYES

How to describe the *Siogi*?

A feather-edged knife gleaming in a clear mountain streambed, a brittle wind in hard, high places, and arterial blood jetting raggedly onto a bright winter snowfield. All those things and more.

Their wardeeds stretch back to the birth of years. Their bones bleach in uncounted battlefields along a hundred timelines.

The mortal servants of Lady Death, they serve her well. They study, quantify, and worship her until she finds them. It is their way, their truth, and their light, consuming and subsuming every element of their existence. Their gift to themselves and the world at large, as it were. A one-word resume', a curriculum necrae.

And how to describe Beckin Gilmer?

Beckin Black-and-Silver. Her Guild Name, given when she finished her training at Death School, First In Class, the best killer of the lot. Cute name. Nice kid. Pure of heart, quick of hand, single of mind. At nine, she killed for the first time, erupting out of a trailside pile of autumn leaves and driving an eight-inch blade up under a beating heart. By the time we met, she knew more ways to serve Lady Death than can be named.

To her, we -- Majors Farrell Gray and Megan Connolly -- are something like big sisters. Quinn and Maren are little sisters, and Colonel John Tierney, the Commanding Officer of our NCD -- *No Collateral Damage* -- Unit, is a revered elder. It may sound goofy, but such is the stratified mindset of the young *Siog*. They simply have to have some pigeonhole to stick you in. Beckin's moderated her worldview in the five years since we met, but she's been unable to shake the categories she first assigned us.

18

The fact that Farrell took her virginity and I've shared my body with her *has* helped, though. Plus, she was present at the girls' births, so we have that bond, too.

Physically, however, the first thing anyone notices about Beckin are her green eyes, luminous against her golden skin and framed by sharp cheekbones, a short, slender nose, and a wide, serious mouth. And, unlike Farrell's, which has red highlights, Beckin's black hair is so solidly dark it seems to swallow light.

But it all comes back to her eyes. "Obituary Eyes," Farrell says, green death looking out at the world, ready to come for you at any moment.

Farrell and I have a couple of inches on Beckin's five-eleven, and probably twenty pounds of additional muscle apiece, but when you start knifework at five, and study weaponry for the next fifteen years, your skills accumulate to the point where death is only a flicker of thought away.

Now we sat inside the Cache, warm, clean and dry, the travois and its grisly cargo abandoned over the side of the ridge about a half-mile beyond the Cache. Farrell and me propped up on cushions, Brone on a sturdy three-legged stool, and Beckin resting on crossed legs, maps unfolded before her on an Oriental rug.

Beckin sipped hot chocolate as she let her thoughts spin out between her lips. *Siogi* love chocolate, all the more because the chocolate trade route is generally blocked by the Azteka. There are no airplanes in Eireann Mor, but they do have huge airships not unlike zeppelins. Occasionally, between campaigns, either *Blood Harvest* or *Skyhammer*, the primary west coast *Siogi* war vessels, will make a run into South America for raw chocolate -- and raw profit, of course -- but the demand for the sweet product is never fully met.

At the moment, then, with her cup of hot chocolate, Beckin seemed as happy as I'd ever seen her with her clothes on. All the more so, because she had a challenge: getting our asses to safety. Our casual overnighter to Pendleton and its bazaar with the kids had turned suddenly serious.

"The nearest dedicated Shift Point is on the North Cedar River, on the other side of the *Dromlach Iairrtha* -- the Western Spinals," Beckin said.

Farrell laughed. "Which we call the Cascades, right?"

Beckin's answering grin was more a nano-second's grimace. "Yes, of course. And, according to these maps, we are slightly over two hundred and fifty miles from North Cedar. Morag will go there, also." Her smile warmed and expanded to include both of us. "I expect she will keep Quinn and Maren with her, rather than return them to Four Crossings. That would be like Morag, thinking to give the little ones experience." Beside her, Brone gave a thoughtful nod.

I shot Farrell a questioning glance. Just what I wanted, the girls in the care of a homicidal maniac, albeit a genial one. Farrell lifted an eyebrow and shrugged, but her expression held a tinge of like concern.

Beckin saw that, and shook her head, reaching over her maps and touching our hands. "Don't worry. Morag or any of her followers would die protecting them. They will provision in *Crosbhothar* -- your Pendleton -- then head west across the high plains to the mountains. And remember, the girls are in company with some of the greatest fighters in our world, traveling across *our* lands." She sighed. "Any of our children would consider it a great adventure. I know I would have, at their age."

"They may even get to kill," Brone added, with a sunny smile, taking a long swallow of his own chocolate. Then, at Beckin's withering look, he coughed and raised his left hand, palm outward. "Just animals, of course."

"They'll doubtless be in a truck marked with the insignia of the Severers," Beckin continued, "and not even some petty warlord with an eye to expand her or his own power would ever be fool enough to cross Morag and her dread companions. To irritate Morag is to court a painful end. Not for nothing is she called 'Death's Daughter.'"

I leaned back in the cushions and took Farrell's hand. "Well, I'm certainly reassured, Gray. How about you?"

"Hey, I was never worried, Megs," she replied, squeezing my fingers.

"Bullshit," I said. "You were taken aback there for a minute, thinking of the girls with Morag." I remembered all too well the first time I'd seen Morag Timmerly, a few years ago, at a gaming table in the *Cloch fhola Rua* -- The Blood Red Stone -- a tavern and wayhouse in Four Crossings.

The place had gone absolutely dead silent during the first thirty seconds after we walked in with Beckin. The only significant sound came from the sixty-inch Sony flatscreen hanging against the wall, along with the intermittent tinkling of glasses being cleaned behind the bar.

Even in a society of slender, graceful, black-haired, green-eyed people -- only the very rare redheads can have blue eyes -- Morag stood out. Tall for a Siog, about six-three, with her hair buzzed to a uniform quarter-inch, her monastic appearance was accentuated by the dark loose clothes her people favor.

Siogi youngsters, like Beckin, tend to be nearly humorless, and many of the adults are serious as hell. At something over eighty, Morag Timmerly had long ago shed any vestiges of somberness. Her green gaze lifted to ours, she laid her hand of cards face-down with a warning look at her gambling partners, and stood, smiling.

"Greetings, Cousin," she said to Beckin, inclining her head. "And greetings to you, the first *Nos* I have ever seen." Her eyes raked us up and down, frankly curious. The rest of the patrons more or less did the same. We were exotic, definitely something new under their sun. No Siog has my white-blond hair and freckles, and

21

Farrell's copper eyes are unusual enough in our world, let alone here.

Her brief examination finished, still smiling widely and gesturing at the table, Morag asked, "Do you drink and gamble, then?"

"Depends on the drink," Farrell replied, grinning up at her.

"Depends on the game," I said, doing the same.

Morag gave a guffaw that shook the rafters and -- as I look back on it now -- more or less defined the mood of our evening. "You *are* indeed military, cagey and cautious," she said, shaking our hands. "I'll buy the first round."

Even Beckin found it impossible to resist Morag's infectious nature, and Beckin was far more serious in those days. As the evening wore on, I even responded a time or two to the occasional inquisitive warm knee under the table, nudging Morag back and grinning. And the Stone did a brisk business, half of Four Crossings coming in to see the 'The *Nos*' -- a term we supposed must have its roots in the German 'Nosferatu.' Most of them wanted to buy us a drink, too. Farrell, Beckin, and I were never without glasses of something during the entire four hours.

And of course I watched Morag, trying to see the famous and revered killer in this gregarious and charming woman, who seemed to treat everyone with equal parts teasing and easy camaraderie.

The killer was there. I had only to look. Morag's back was always to a wall, never to the open room, and when she moved, the outline of handle, holster or sheath could be momentarily glimpsed through her garments on upper arm or thigh. On her trips to the john, she always paused and briefly studied the room before rejoining us.

And that had been among friends and comrades.

So, no, I wasn't particularly worried that something awful might happen to the girls.

I just wanted them with us.

CHAPTER FIVE

TRAVELING ORDERS

"We have roughly two days' travel to get to the other side of the Warm Springs Reservation," Beckin said, as she moved her right index finger over a zig-zag route between Pendleton and the Cascades. The Reservation is just northeast of North Cedar. "We have a one-and-a-half ton canvas-top Army truck at our disposal. I suggest we go into Pendleton this morning, discover what we can concerning the route west, purchase foodstuffs and drink, then drive to Condon, which is just over a hundred mile journey." She looked at each of us in turn. "Does this seem practical?"

Farrell yawned. "How soon can we expect somebody to come looking for our ambushers, I wonder?"

After thinking about that for a few moments, Beckin said, "The Shift Point is a sacred place to both the Umatilla and Nez Perce, and is on -- here -- what used to be federal lands, equidistant between the two tribal territories. While we can come and go much as we please, most others, if discovered, are at least questioned by tribal law enforcement. To the tribes, those who awaited our arrival have desecrated holy ground."

"They couldn't have known when exactly we would arrive," I said. "They must've been waiting for weeks."

"And someone informed them of the spot," Brone added.

I looked at Brone with new respect, even though I knew from experience that most berzerkers are thoughtful, considerate, pragmatic souls. Someone that big and, in Brone's case, amiable, it's hard not to think they're all muscle and no brains. Big, blindingly fast, killer galoots.

Preconceived notions'll get you into trouble, like folks assuming all vampires are nasty blood-sucking killers. Which we are, of course, just not all the time.

Brone was right about there having been an info-leak. It didn't take a berzerker brain to figure that out. Perhaps the leak came from an individual looking for a buck, or maybe just checking up on an old legend. Didn't matter, really. The cat was at least partway out of the bag, unless the only people who knew were the deaders back at the shift point.

And that might be wishful thinking, since apparently two of them were Saints, which did not bode well. Like ants following an ant scout's formic acid trail, where one Mormon went, others were sure to follow. That's how the Empire of the Saints operated. They'd lost thousands of men to the radioactive hells of California, just to salvage what military hardware had survived the war. For them, it must have seemed like a good trade-off. The highest birthrate on the planet quickly replenished those lost, and all those lost were official sure-nuff top-drawer martyrs.

The end result was that the Empire had enough armaments to take down most of the United States west of the Mississippi. One of these years, conventional wisdom said, they'd come marching out of Utah and southern Idaho, and the fat would be in the fire.

In our timeline, Mormons are a conservative, hundred and fifty year-old, male-dominant aspect of Christianity who baptize the dead of other faiths and breed like the dickens. And Christ was in South America after the Resurrection, and their sacred golden tablets got misplaced. Weird by any standards, it's like they tried to pack a couple millennia of theologic oddness into their short church history. Then there's the women's rights thing and those darn minorities. It's not easy being Mo.

Of course, us good Catholics dote on human sacrifice and ritual cannibalism, so who am I to criticize?

Here, however, when Utah found itself in a bit of a nuclear-caused power vacuum, Hosea Gregorson -- the 'Man From Manti' -- stepped forward and claimed the reins of authority. Give the man credit, in the face of uncertain church leadership, he understood what needed to be done to preserve his faith's homeland, and did it.

Things did get a little messy during the transition, I understand, according to the very few survivors of the old leadership who got out alive. That's how those things go, I suppose, which is why one of the Changed - - Lieutenant Colonel Africa Brown -- sits in the Black Ops section of the Pentagon, looking out for *our* welfare. We had our own little bloody palace coup back in the fall of '93. Since then, we've had very few problems with our bosses in D.C., so I can sympathize with the aggressive Mister Gregorson -- to a degree, anyway.

It's a bit more personal here for the folks in northeastern Oregon, with the Triskelon flag of the Empire waving just on the other side of the Snake River.

Farrell broke into my little reverie, as she frequently does. "You're thinking about the Saints, huh, Megs?"

I grinned sheepishly. "Yeah. They're probably as persistent here as back home. Unless this was just a low-profile limited effort, with just those two hoping to unearth something big, then someone else will come looking."

"In our world," Beckin said, shaking her head, "scavengers would already have finished the bodies."

Brone nodded. "Slashcats and wolves."

Eireann Mor never lost the macrofauna that mankind wiped out in our timeline. No humanity developed, so there was no one to make it over the Alaska landbridge. Slashcats are sabertooths, and Eireann Mor wolves are two or three times as large as ours. I think they have hyenas, too, and bear the size of oxen.

Maybe I shouldn't have thought of that, what with Quinn and Maren rambling over Eireann Mor in a truck. But Morag would protect them. I knew that. I just wanted to be part of it. Being a mom means that you want desperately to look out for your young, and it's no different for vampire moms.

"Do any of you find a flaw with my thinking on our route or timetable?" Beckin asked. "The sooner we arrive in Pendleton, the quicker we can disappear into the crowds of Market Day in the Bazaar. Four hours sleep now will replenish our energies. If we leave after a short breakfast, we should be away from here by seven o'clock." She turned her pale lime gaze on me. "Do you feel fully recovered, Megan?"

"I think so," I replied, shrugging. No aches or pains remained, not that much lasts with our bodies, and twenty thousand calories of food and fluid had put me back on line. "Find out at the next crunch, I guess."

Farrell snorted and Beckin chuckled in her dead-pan way. "I could say the same," Beckin said. She stretched her long arms in the air, "and we can only hope there will be such."

"Just as long as it's in this timeline," Farrell said, "and not the one Morag and the girls are in."

"I seem to remember," Beckin said, her expression bemused as she folded up her maps, "that Morag killed for the first time when *she* was Quinn and Maren's age."

"You are just so damn helpful," Farrell said.

"Next," I said, "you'll be telling us that the mastodons are migrating along the east flank of the Cascades, and that slashcats frequently confuse covered trucks with older, ailing mastodons."

Beckin shook her head, her brow furrowing for an instant. "No, I don't believe so. Did Morag tell you that?"

For a moment I thought she was serious, then I caught a glimmer of amusement in the depths of her green gaze. Sly little shit. Five years ago, she *would've* been serious, but she's learned too well from us, primarily from Farrell.

I looked up at Brone. He was tending toward bland and non-committal, but obviously having some difficulty holding it in. Although we'd met him several years before he'd become Champion, these past few days were our first prolonged contact with one another,

26

and his initial uncertainty over people well outside his experience still showed.

Just before we left for this timeline, hoping to get him more at ease, I'd asked Brone to go into the practice arena with me -- his own turf -- and had quickly learned just how fast and precise someone his size could be. I also learned some physics. Though I was several times stronger than Brone, and a fair amount quicker, he still weighed three hundred pounds to my one-seventy-five.

In the arena, the only thing to hold onto was one another, which largely negated my strength advantage. Particularly since I was unwilling to grab Brone and try to crush limbs or take him apart, and the simple *size* of the guy made him tough to get a grip on. Plus he wasn't the Berzerker Champion for nothing. The kid knew his stuff.

In front of the girls and Farrell, he threw me twenty feet within the first second we established contact. Quinn and Maren didn't utter a sound, but their eyes and mouths went round with astonishment, having thought their mommies invulnerable, and I heard Farrell cover a snicker.

I landed on all fours in the sawdust, my nose about six inches off the floor. Brone didn't grin, or even change expression, merely stood waiting. Not so serious elsewhere; damned serious here. I relaunched at him. This time, using my momentum, he tossed me thirty feet, nearly to the edge of the circle.

I eventually got smarter; I'm not sure I ever wore him down much. Farrell said afterward it looked like a leopard fighting a lion. A fair analogy. My Dad spent a season coaching eighth grade wrestling, though, and I remembered watching the videos at home. So I knew there was no way, with the weight difference, that I could pin Brone. I just tried to get underneath him and get him in the air.

That proved difficult. He wasn't that much slower than I was, and all his movements were totally efficient, nothing wasted. At times, it seemed as though no part of his body got more than three inches off the floor.

Eventually, I faked him down to his right, looped over him to his left, and got my right hand under him and levered him up with my elbow. A split-second later, I held him over my head.

Then Brone discovered how ticklish I am.

Fortunately, he was, too.

We ended up on our backs on the sawdust floor, laughing like idiots. Quinn and Maren ran over and jumped on me, being careful to keep well away from Brone, glaring at him defiantly, wolf cubs with their mother.

"They're *protecting* you," Brone said, smiling at the girls, wheezing with laughter.

"You're right," I agreed, pulling the girls down to me and hugging them. Twin sets of hazel-brown eyes regarded me with concern while they hugged me back fiercely. They might know that their mommy and Mister Brone weren't really fighting, but their gut instincts still told them to be careful of the big man.

Smart little vampires, I'd thought, stroking their short brown hair. Keep that attitude foremost in your heads, and you'll stay alive long after you leave your first home.

But I had found out that Brone was definitely one of the good guys. Even if our eclectic dining habits bothered him a bit, he was still solidly on our side.

And I could hardly wait to quiz Farrell about the confrontation at the Shift Point, find out just what Brone had done.

"So there's absolutely no nearer point?" Farrell asked, ignoring Beckin's sly humor.

Beckin sighed. "In fact, there *could* be, but frankly, this timeline doesn't have enough financial base to interest us for anything other than the occasional visit, so no one uses more than the three or four convenient ones. Even in your world, Oregon has only *five* points that we maintain, so we're lucky to have what we have here. Morag *will* go to North Cedar."

"There could be other shift points, couldn't there?" I asked, knowing that any intersection of the old natural ley lines could create a node that permitted passage between the timelines. Even in our world, churches, mosques, temples, convents, monasteries, and important government buildings tend to be sited on the nodes, their builders sensing at some level the emanations of power the nodes produce.

"To be sure," Beckin replied, nodding, "there are hundreds, many of which could be turned to our use. And while even I could sense a powerful node situated in a stable isolated location, my youth and inexperience prevents me from actually following a line to its intersections. At close to ninety, Morag can almost certainly do so, but since I cannot, North Cedar is it for her and us." As she spoke the last few words, Beckin gave one of her cute little shrugs, her shoulders barely moving.

"Can the destroyed point be restored?" Farrell asked.

"Yes. Our elders will find a nearby lesser node, bring a crew through to remove and repair the damage, recreating stability. Likely they will interdict this line for five years or so, until interest dissipates." Beckin grinned. "As you two would say, 'not our problem.'" Slipping her maps back into their case, she rose gracefully to her feet. "And now, my friends, we need to rest."

Rest. That sounded good.

Maybe then I could quit fretting about the girls for a few hours.

29

CHAPTER SIX

INTERLUDE

I got back to our overnight quarters a few minutes after Farrell, pulling aside the door curtain and stepping into the room.

"What happened to you?" she asked, looking up from where she examined the contents of her ordnance bag. Most of her clothes were neatly folded on the floor beside what passes for a bed in Eireann Mor, a kind of cross between a futon and one of our beds. Our beds, with legs, strike the Siogi as impractical, since an assassin could hide underneath.

"Talking to Brone," I replied, peeling off my T-shirt. "He wanted to assure me that Beckin's remark about him doing live cover was in jest."

"He's a virgin, then?"

"Yeah, I think so. He didn't exactly *say* that, of course. If true, he'll be a father before he has sex."

"Wow. That's weird." Farrell ran the fingers of her right hand through her short hair, sending ripples of red flashing over the black. Seeing her move did what it always does when we're together. An instant lump developed in my throat. She's just so *damn* good-looking.

She cocked her head at me, and put down the Beretta ten millimeter she'd been holding. "You're gettin' your sappy look, Megs."

I nodded. "You realize that this is the first time we've been so utterly separated from Quinn and Maren?"

Zipping up the bag after tucking the automatic away, Farrell pursed her lips briefly before saying very softly, "I know, believe me, I know." Her copper gaze was about as troubled as I've seen it.

"Morag will kill anything or anyone who tries to harm them."

She heaved the bag against the wall almost angrily. "I *know* that. And I trust Morag. This was just supposed to be a *holiday*, for shit's sake!"

"You're stealing my lines, Gray. Bein' sappy."

Now she looked rueful. "No shit."

I heard the curtain rustle behind me, and turned to see Beckin -- spectacularly nude -- slip through the doorway. "You okay?" I asked.

Her smile was wider than usual. "Certainly. I thought you two might like to reaffirm our still being alive."

Farrell chuckled. "This would be the 'vampire love' thing, then?"

"Yes," Beckin answered, licking her lower lip, regarding us from behind long lashes, "this would be exactly that."

Vampire love. Cute.

We pounced.

CHAPTER SEVEN

CABBAGE HILL

Though thunderstorms can still form up in the Wallowas at any time during summer, mid-June is beyond the spring cavalcade of storms in off the Pacific or down out of Canada. The sun rose early in the cold, clear air of the high mountains, warm against my back where I sat in the bed of the truck as we trundled over the lava toward the road.

And, no, we don't wither in the sun, writhing and screaming as we crisp into dust. Instead, after the Change, for the first time in my life, I tanned, to a nice golden-brown. Not as dark as Farrell, a true mahogany, but definitely better than burning and peeling continuously.

So Beckin and I rested our butts on the hard parallel seats on the edges of the truck bed and clung to the uprights as Farrell whipped down the gravel to the southwest, toward Meacham, on Highway 30, at the top of Cabbage Hill.

We were probably two miles away from the cache when the faint sounds of a helicopter came from the north. As I listened, the distant 'whup-whup' changed pitch, then settled into an softer idle. The chopper had clearly landed, and very near last night's confrontation site.

It could be from one of a couple sources. What remained of the Pacific Northwest's air power had reopened the old Pasco Naval Air Station in the Tri-city area, and used that location to counter the Saints' threat from Salt Lake City. It might be from Pasco. The number of warbirds there wasn't all that great, but they had the advantage of limitless supplies of aviation-quality gasoline and J-series jet fuel, so a lot of missions got flown, and many of those were variable-wing aircraft.

I thought I remembered that Boeing was turning out planes again, too, so the Saints' superiority might be slowly eroding. And the Saints might be getting more desperate.

The Alaska oilfields still produced petroleum in serious quantities, and all the refineries were along the coast, a long, long way from Utah. The Saints, even though they had more hardware, had to beg and borrow fuel to get their birds up.

On the other hand, stories of people appearing out of nowhere in the middle of a pine forest might tempt the Saints to use some precious air/fuel-hours and sneak over their borders. Even if Pasco might bring a jet fighter or two down on them, which could easily happen. Moderate chance of death, maybe a big pay-off down the line.

Sounded Saintly.

Beckin heard the chopper, too. A little frown creased her brow, and she lifted one eyebrow at me.

"Maybe not good," I said, shaking my head, "and I wish we knew more about just what we're getting into here."

Brone turned slightly in his seat, partially facing us. He didn't have a lot of room. Every time we hit a pothole, I thought his knees would take out the truck's dash. "I know a few facts," he said, his left arm wrapped around the back of his seat, "but not many. The Saints fly into La Grande, to the east of Pendleton, with some frequency, but rarely to Pendleton itself, and no ships' weaponry is allowed. In the past, there have been incidents where unauthorized Saint incursions have resulted in Saint planes being blown out of the sky."

"So this is the edge of the Saint envelope?" I asked.

Brone smiled and shrugged. "Apparently. The United States is beginning to come back together into some sort of a cohesive entity. There may be more regional governmental divisions, and the federal capital may end up in Kansas City, but the end result is that the Empire of the Saints is on shaky ground. The power

33

vacuum which Gregorson saw and exploited is filling around him. The Saints are being pressed, and they are growing frustrated and desperate."

"You think that's a Saint helicopter, then?" Farrell asked, from behind the wheel, glancing at the big berzerker as we hauled ass toward the pavement.

Brone only shrugged again, and smiled his sunny smile. "I hope not," he replied, and settled back down into his seat. As much as space permitted, he was so damned big. I was extremely glad he was with us, though. Although he would draw attention to the four of us, any direct personal threat to us would initially focus on Brone. Leaving Farrell, myself, and the incredibly competent Beckin to do our little dances of death. Seconds always count, and Brone would provide that distraction.

Other possibilities presented themselves.

Were there intelligence pros and black ops folks in Pendleton? An interesting thought to consider. The answer, of course, was "yes." When that question needs to be asked, there's only the one answer.

"Who's the boss in Pendleton?" I asked Brone.

"The Mayor, I think," he answered, without looking back. "Operating on the advice and consent of the City Council."

"Just like our Pendleton. What about the law?"

"Police."

I shook my head. "So the city really wasn't too affected by the nuclear exchange? Not like Portland." Portland had taken years to shake down into its current stability. There had been riots, fires, and unchecked disease. What passed for authority in Portland and environs still didn't extend much beyond the city's southern borders, either.

"No," Brone continued, "Pendleton has remained a cattle and agricultural town. Each fall, the Roundup has continued without interruption, and things probably aren't so very different from your timeline."

34

When we were still about two miles from the pavement, the idling pitch of the helicopter changed again, to lift, and then the sound faded away almost entirely, as the craft moved north. Beckin didn't say anything, only made a sour face. I silently agreed with her. The chopper had been at or near the pile of bodies, and they had to have known exactly where to look.

They weren't from Pasco, almost certainly. But they *had* headed north, so we couldn't rule that out.

Then the faint noise changed direction, to the west, then south, and came closer, the sound building again. They must be running some sort of search pattern.

We'd reached the pavement and turned west toward Meacham, when the helicopter whizzed loudly by overhead, just above tree-top level, whipping the pine branches wildly. A white UH-1D from the late sixties, its cargo bay doors closed, carrying no visible weaponry, with only a nose-mounted FM antenna marring its front end.

"Mormon," Brone said, looking up, shielding his eyes against the glare with one big hand. "They're always white." The rest of us didn't look up.

"They won't know we aren't coming in from La Grande," Farrell said, from behind the wheel. The chopper had swung back over the road about a half-mile ahead of us, and accelerated rapidly in the direction of Meacham.

"They may be going to the Checkpoint," Brone said.

"Checkpoint?" I asked.

"Umatilla County Sheriff," Brone replied. "The highway passed out of Union County a few miles back. They tend to keep loose track of travelers from the east."

"They still won't know we're not from La Grande," Farrell said, referring to the helicopter, "and we were on the highway before they saw us."

"What're they gonna do?" I asked, "open up on us in front of the Sheriff's people?"

"I didn't see any weapons," Beckin put in quietly.

From behind the wheel, Farrell guffawed. "Almost anything that Huey might carry could be out of sight in the cargo bay. Probably an XM-6 weapons system, with four M60 machine guns and XM-157 2.75 inch rockets. Ten minutes to install it -- tops -- if they know what they're doing, and the internal supports are already in place."

"Really?" Beckin said, grinning, her curiosity piqued. She sat more upright now that we were on the smoother pavement. I couldn't see her eyes through the B&L Shooters she wore, but it was all too obvious that she found the prospect of danger intriguing.

"Don't get too eager," I cautioned. "All we've got are rifles. That was a pretty hot little gunship in its day, and it's more than enough now to take us out without breaking a sweat."

"But they have to *land* to fit their weapons, don't they?" Beckin asked, and her sly grin turned wicked.

"Yeah, probably," I replied. Her meaning was obvious, the always-practical *Siog* warrior mind at work. If a chink existed in any kind of defensive armor, a *Siogi* wedge would find it.

But when we arrived at the Checkpoint a few minutes later, the Saint gunship sat silently on a wide turnout, its rotors motionless, a couple hundred yards beyond the check itself.

Waiting.

For us.

Shit.

CHAPTER EIGHT

CHECKPOINT

Meacham consisted of a small grocery store and gas station, with flats of local produce displayed in the shadows of the steep roof overhang, next to the front entrance. Two older pickups and an orange Chevy Suburban crummy were parked beside the grocery. A larger building sat to the rear, big enough to be some sort of boarding house.

Two large hardened concrete bunkers comprised the Checkpoint, one on each side of the pavement, wide gunports up eight feet off the ground. Twin snouts of paired
50-caliber machine guns protruded out the ports, one of each set trained on the helicopter, and the other two in our general direction. One guy talked into a field telephone, on the horn to Headquarters probably, presumably Pendleton.

The Saint chopper clearly had the seven brown-uniformed checkpoint personnel -- two of which were women -- on high alert, to put it mildly. They were almost negatively interested in us, but still took the time. The lanky, weatherbeaten guy who sauntered over to talk to us actually tipped his campaign hat, once he saw we were women and that Brone looked unthreatening at the moment. He did raise an eyebrow at our jeans, T-shirts, and black forage caps.

"Mornin, folks," he said, and smiled, his thumbs hooked in his belt as he looked us over. He had a toothpick in the corner of his mouth. "I don't suppose you ladies have any connection to our other visitors?" He seemed more interested in our sunglasses than us. His Ray-Bans looked Vietnam-era. And I had my first eerie realization: None of them were smoking. Tobacco must be rare or absent here.

"Not really," Farrell answered. She tilted her head at the chopper. "I've never seen one of those up close."

The sheriff assumed a hurt expression, and snorted, then let his grin widen. "Yeah, I'll just *bet* you haven't, M'am." He held out his hand. "Name's James Runkle. I'm kind of the lead man here." His tongue transferred the toothpick to the opposite corner of his mouth.

"You're County?" Farrell asked, shaking his hand as she introduced herself.

"Yup," Runkle replied, leaning over to shake Brone's hand, then to Beckin and me. His hand was dry, leathery, strong. When he was done with introductions, he eyed the truck. "Nice rig. Good shape for her age."

Then he turned his attention to Beckin, and his whole demeanor changed. "If I was to ask, M'am, for you to lift up your shades, what color would your eyes be?"

"You know what color," Beckin answered, without changing expression, and I heard Brone's seat creak.

"Thought so," Runkle said, nodding and looking slightly pleased. "Which means that those godly folk behind me in that Huey *might* just be lookin' for you. Somethin's got their attention, and I know you ain't runaway Saint maidens. Plus, the Saints don't regularly tempt fate and Pasco without reason, even if they are crazy damfool bastards. Beggin' your pardon."

Runkle tipped his hat again, then glanced at the chopper. "Now why don't you just drive on out? We'll keep the guns on 'em. They won't get too spunky." He turned back to Farrell. "What branch, if you don't mind my askin'?"

"Army."

This time, Runkle's grin was a kid's. He shook his head. " *Women* in the Real Army." Now his gaze included all of us. "Must be quite a place you're from. You get back through here, I wouldn't mind hearin' the story."

He tipped his hat again, and walked away, his final words coming back to us as he waved us through. "*An rath.*"

Gaelic for "Good luck."

Farrell put the truck in gear, and we eased forward.

38

I looked across the truck bed at Beckin.
At the moment, a very smug Beckin.

CHAPTER NINE

CONTACT

We drove between the machine gun muzzles and down the highway past the parked Saint helicopter, trying to look only curious as we peered off-handedly through the tinted lexan, barely able to see outlines within. The side facing us sported the thick black triskelon of the Empire, a sort of three-pronged swastika with the hooks to the left instead of the right. A potent symbol of power hereabouts, as Runkle probably would have put it.

"At least four in there," I said, when we were safely out of earshot, moving rapidly toward Deadman's Pass.

"That means probably five or six," Farrell added, as she worked her way up through the gears. "How long to get to town?"

"Half an hour or less," Beckin replied.

I did some quick math. "So, maybe ten minutes for the chopper. And fifteen minutes to get their armament in place -- tops."

Farrell laughed. "Less for the weapons, if they don't set up everything, or if they have some sort of modified Sagami gun mount that just swings out. Land, pop the door on that side off, then catch us on the switchbacks."

"They'll want us *alive*," Beckin said. "It might be personal to them because of their dead, but they need information. Now they have only dead comrades, and they can't be sure of our origins."

I thought about that. She was right, and I should have realized it before she did. "We'll be down into the steeper part of the hill before they can catch us," I said, "if they give us another six or seven minutes. From the bottom of the hill, we'll be in pea farms and wheat fields. Too many witnesses. Anyway, our friend Runkle may call in a couple of jets from Pasco, and save us the speculation."

40

Beckin leaned back into her bench, pulled her forage cap down over her eyes, and crossed her arms over her chest. "No," she said, sounding as smug as she looked. "Were I the Saints, I would take off to the east to try to fool the checkpoint people, swing north into the Umatilla canyon, and fly west along the bottom of the canyon to Pendleton. Land there, then try to follow us and see where we go. They've seen us; we haven't seen them."

"Do they dress funny?" Farrell asked. We all looked at Brone, our Saint 'expert.'

He shrugged and shook his head. "I'm not certain."

We were nearly to the top of the switchbacks when we heard the Huey take off back at the Checkpoint. Just in case, I slid my ordnance bag out from under my bench, unzipped it and brought out my La France A16K Assault Rifle and Beretta ten-millimeter automatic. I tossed the pistol to Beckin, and snapped a filled magazine into the La France, then checked it over carefully. I'd cleaned it just prior to heading to the Shift Point, so it should be in good working order.

It seemed perfect. Safeties off, Beckin and I sat on our respective sides of the truck, keeping our weapons low and out-of-sight, scanning the sky. The chopper sounded as though it was heading east, as Beckin had suggested.

Then the sound changed, and drifted to the north. Beckin looked at me, smiled, and gripped her right wrist with her left hand, ready to swing up into firing stance.

I wasn't quite ready to believe that the Huey would pop around the descending ridge in front of us, but I still held the rifle as though I expected it to.

We were virtually out in the open, seriously exposed. The timber had begun to thin out a few miles back, and now only occasional groups of tall pine marred the grassy ridge sides. At this elevation, the wild grasses were still green, and the light morning breeze played over them in short, bursting waves.

41

Very beautiful, very bucolic, and very nerve-wracking. We started downslope into the switchbacks, Farrell keeping the truck as close the right side rock wall as she could.

I heard the Huey clearly about fifteen seconds before it roared around a rock face and swooped in on us.

By the time the absence of fitted weapons on the chopper registered, I'd blown out the left side nose panel, and Beckin had holed the cheek window door -- and subsequently the roof -- at least five times.

Pieces of plastic from the nose panel rattled down the side of the cliff and smashed on the road behind us as the Huey whipped by.

The pilot -- whoever he was -- was damned good. He stood the little craft on its side, the main rotors no more than ten feet from the rock wall, and got the hell out of Dodge. I barely managed to punch two additional holes in the aft section assembly, and they were gone in a cloud of dust and smaller rocks.

They didn't come back.

Farrell whooped. "No weapons! The *dipshits* were only bluffing! Tryin' to scare us. *Morons*."

"Mormons," I corrected, totally pumped, our modified adrenaline singing in my veins.

"They felt our teeth," Beckin said, her raspy voice heavy with satisfaction as she tracked the blue sky with my Beretta.

"They won't make that mistake again," I said.

Farrell pointed down into the flat valley, still laughing. "By the time they recover, we'll be getting close to Pendleton."

"And the Bazaar," Brone said, speaking for the first time since the confrontation. He adjusted the bill of his cap. "They have wonderful ice cream."

Suddenly the sound of distant jets rose from the northwest, and two tiny dots appeared just above the horizon.

Farrell stopped the truck, and we watched the dots grow swiftly into sixties-era F-102A Delta Daggers with

U.S. Air Force stenciled on their fuselages. They were beautiful. I'd never seen one in flight, only in a museum, and found a lump developing in my throat. While we watched, enveloped by their sound, they screamed by overhead in parallel wide turns and boomed off to the east in pursuit of the Huey.

I made a mental note to salute James Runkle with my next beer.

Or maybe with a bowl of ice cream.

And wished Quinn and Maren would be there to share it with us.

CHAPTER TEN

BAZAAR

Highway 30 goes right through downtown Pendleton, after traversing the farms and ranches east of the city. The core area looked no different than I remembered from the one or two family visits when I was a kid.

Vehicles were all older, of course, nothing newer than 1970, with cars much larger than in our world, and the number of Japanese or European cars or trucks nil. Still, traffic was significant, with a fair number of produce trucks and pickups loaded with goods, mostly heading toward the Bazaar, which had opened close to an hour earlier.

Men and women with briefcases and tote bags filled the sidewalks, most dressed for work, in styles that seemed fairly old-fashioned, and ran heavily to wool. Cotton might well be a thing of the past here, but the Pendleton Woolen Mills must still be up and running. The few skirts I saw on women certainly looked woolen. Nobody seemed to wear hats, except folks who were obviously farmers. Might even be a thriving hemp industry somewhere around, too. I thought I caught a whiff of it.

As we drove slowly along Court Street in the light morning traffic, I smelled coffee, which surprised me some, and herbal tea, which didn't. Even here, there were no cigarettes, although there might be pipe tobacco.

All in all, it wasn't the things that were different that were so surprising, it was the things that were the same. Shopkeepers rolled out awnings, carried signs out on the sidewalks, and hailed their fellow townsfolk. Some people bustled to work, others sort of meandered, stopping to chew the fat, or just savoring a nice bright morning in late June.

There were few kids on the streets at this hour, but those that were wore shorts not much different from our timeline, and just as drab. Bicycles -- virtually all of them fat-tired -- threaded their way alongside the other vehicles. There was a motorcycle about a block up ahead of us, a four-stroke, but I couldn't see it well enough to know what it was for sure. I wondered where they got tires and inner tubes. Most of the tires I saw on four-wheelers looked like re-caps.

As we left the business area, we began to go past markets and the occasional service station. All of the latter seemed to have repair facilities. My guess was that every competent shadetree mechanic and blacksmith did a thriving business keeping the wheels of commerce turning. I did wonder where they got their electrical components, but of course, for all we knew, General Motors and Ford sources might still be turning out replacements. Nearly thirty years, after all, had passed. For a while, though, scavenge and black market operations must've been interesting.

As Beckin had said earlier, not our problem. The urban scene in Pendleton wasn't going to occupy us for more than a few hours. We stopped at Ron's Texaco on Court, fueled the truck, and filled the four five gallon gas cans we'd stuck in the bed. More than enough to get us to North Cedar. I didn't see any new Texaco signs or the usual little airplane and truck piggybanks, though the place was clean and neat, and there *were* cans of Texaco oil for sale.

Our nearly-new gas cans did create quite a stir among the staff, however, and a guy with a loaded GMC hay truck stopped and tried to hire Brone, who "looked like he could do a day's work." Brone graciously declined, and we headed -- laughing at the big lunk -- for the Bazaar.

The Bazaar was to have been our exotic little trip with the girls, and I became momentarily depressed as the high walls of the Round-Up Arena appeared on the right, surrounded by tents and trailers separated by sawdust-covered paths. Livestock pens and horse stables were filled with animals, and it was clear that a fair number of people actually arrived by horse.

At least, I thought, reunion with Quinn and Maren was only a couple of days away, now that Beckin was back in good shape. All we had to do was make it to North Cedar, provided we'd shaken the Saints. Certainly we'd shaken them up, and hopefully, that would be enough. We parked the truck under a huge spreading willow, close by the banks of the Umatilla River, and started slowly across the grassy parking area toward the stalls and tents. Brone stopped two small boys, gave them one of what passed for a five-dollar bill in this society, and asked them to watch the truck for an hour.

"Where'd you learn that down-home accent?" I asked, elbowing him in the ribs, as we walked away from the two awe-struck kids. Like the *Siogi*, Brone's English had been unaccented.

"Shucks, M'am," he said, smiling humbly, "I'm just tryin' to fit in, so's the local folks don't fret none."

Beckin snorted. "Brone has every episode of *Bonanza* on disc. When we were small, before I went to Death School and Brone began training, it was always cowboys this, cowboys that. Even now, he has a John Wayne poster in his workout room."

"Want me to do his walk?" Brone asked. He began to lurch slightly.

"No," Beckin replied, "and I don't want to pretend to be a wicked Indian girl ever again, either." But she smiled warmly when she said it, and I wondered, not for the first time, if she knew how much Brone cared for her. Probably. Beckin is incredibly sharp. She'd set herself up as something like a free-lance trouble-shooter after spending two years with us. For her society, an unusual activity. Most young Siogi ally themselves with one group or another after their education is complete, a kind of internship of death.

Instead, her mother's older brothers -- whom we'd met exactly twice -- had foisted her off on us, since she was, as they put it, "very, very serious." Our CO, John

46

Tierney, Irish to the core, being enamored of the whole concept of "wee folk," and that sort of shit, had thought it a "grand idea." We'd done our best to lighten Beckin up. The sex was really secondary, but there are extremely good reasons why elves are so attractive to humans in the old stories. Oh, my, yes.

"So, what was this naughty Indian girl's name?" Farrell asked, putting her right arm around Beckin's shoulders. "And why have *I* never heard it?"

"'Little Weasel,'" Brone said quickly, before Beckin could silence him.

"Hey, that's appropriate," I added, and Farrell whooped with laughter, loud enough so that the few people walking ahead of us turned to look back and smile.

"Hush, the lot of you," Beckin growled, "or I'll have you on my blade." She wasn't really angry or irritated, though she sounded it. When truly upset, Beckin never spoke. She acted, and heaven help who- or whatever might be the focus of her displeasure.

We entered the first aisle, inhaling the fresh scent of the pine sawdust strewn everywhere. The booths and tents seemed to have no pattern, but as we walked around, it was obvious that many families' positions in the maze were nearly hereditary, that the larger trees and the high walls of the rodeo arena seemed to shade older folks or larger families.

Pendleton had probably always been like this, friendly and bustling, filled with decent people harkening back to what is referred to as 'a simpler time.' Probably the people who say that so piously don't think of nuclear war as the cause of the 'simpler time,' but there you go.

We needed to buy dried fruit and meat, maybe a few fresh things to snack on today. I wanted some strawberries, and Brone hadn't shut up about the ice cream. The Arts and Crafts stuff shouldn't have caught our attention. Since every third display seemed to have toys or games, though, it was hard to avoid seeing things

47

the girls might like. That we would give to them the day after tomorrow, I reminded myself, examining little wooden carvings of animals.

That persistent nagging concern about Quinn and Maren somehow became less when I passed a particularly elegant juniper horse to Farrell to examine, or felt a wooden puzzle move under my fingertips.

In the end, we bought a half-dozen things from a short, stocky woman of indeterminate age, who might herself have been carved from a dark myrtlewood burl. Native American, I thought, seeing her teeth flash white against her skin, and watching her nimble fingers make change.

We drifted down the next aisle over, casually looking at the stock in other booths, Quinn and Maren's presents in small sacks. Beckin, meanwhile, had been methodically collecting the amounts of foodstuffs we'd need for the next two-and-a-half days. Doing the "real work," as she put it.

Up one aisle and down the next, the crowds around us growing thicker as the morning wore on. Brone had gone off to find his ice cream some time ago, and I kept a eye cocked for his large presence. I'd already found a pair of corndogs, Farrell had joined me in that guilty pleasure, and Beckin had purchased some candy for later in the day.

We naturally drew some stares, three tall women wearing black forage caps, their eyes covered by sunglasses. Never impolite stares, only curious. This was something like the heartland, after all.

And it was greatly comforting to know that in this place, in this America, life went on in all its important ways. We could walk through an outdoor market day crowd, through its familiar sights and smells, and feel at home. Only the absence of the girls cast any shadow on my peace.

Then I saw the five young men walking through the crowd, all dressed alike in muted tans, staring hard at the three of us, and that peace dropped away like mercury off a slanted tabletop.

Guess the Mormons *did* dress funny.

CHAPTER ELEVEN

SAINTS ALIVE

I poked Farrell, whose brief glance at the advancing Saints told her all she needed to know. She started to grin. Beckin had already seen them and sized them up. Now she purposefully ignored them, pointed us toward a display to our right and steered us in that direction.

"Are there only five?" she asked, under her breath, then exclaimed over a particularly bright patchwork quilt which hung in the sunlight with several less gaudy versions of itself. She fingered each one carefully, exclaiming to the two women who owned the booth.

"Yeah," I replied, "but I don't think they're just gonna walk by."

"Just so," Beckin said, and her hooded gaze roved swiftly around us, darting left and right, checking spaces between displays, where people were, and the placement of tent pegs and ropes. "There are police here somewhere. We mustn't kill anyone openly." A cough sounded behind us.

I nodded. "There were two cop cars around the side of the bleachers."

"Then I shall be nice," Beckin answered softly. "These are simply lovely," she said in a louder voice to the quilt women, giving them her best incandescent smile. They simpered and smiled back, heads bobbing on turkey necks, pleased that this oddly-dressed young woman liked their work. I could tell that they knew we were wearing cotton. Their quilts were cotton, salvaged from worn garments or hoarded stores of fabric, but their clothes were woven hemp.

Another cough came from behind, and this time we turned. "Oh, my," Beckin said, and covered her mouth.

The five Saints stood in a tight knot, their zealots' gazes burning through us. Their slacks were tan, their long-sleeved shirts cream, and their neatly-knotted ties navy blue. The one in front was the obvious leader, maybe five-ten, his hair slightly shorter than his companions, and his anger more obvious. The guy immediately behind him was large, muscular, and reeked of steroids. The others were normal-sized. Two of them watched the crowds more than they watched us. Smarter lads, I thought, and watched them back.

Beckin was only faking surprise, I attempted a neutral expression, and Farrell flat refused to be intimidated. "What is *this*?" she asked, looking the Saints up and down, laughing, "the Beige Brotherhood?"

"My name is Richard Gregorson," the leader said in a rather high, haughty voice, his features twisted in anger. He paused for effect, for his last name to be recognized.

Twenty feet behind Gregorson, I saw a medium-sized, slender man with grizzled grey hair and aviator's sunglasses, shake his head and frown. The chopper pilot, I realized, *with* them but not *of* them, exactly. Interesting.

"What are you waiting for, kid?" Farrell asked Richard, drawing herself up to her full height, grinning down at his irritation. "Aren't you going to bring some balls out and juggle, or pull a chicken out of your ass or *something*?"

Those around our two groups had stopped to watch. Several people laughed. The Saints likely weren't popular locally. The pilot shook his head again, looking disgusted.

Gregorson clearly had never experienced anything like this in his life. His eyes narrowed in anger, and the skin around his nose tightened and blanched. The tendons in his neck looked ready to pop. He made a small hissing noise.

Farrell held out her hands, palms up, making come-on motions. "*Sing* or whatever, okay? How about 'When the Saints Go Marching In?' That's a good one, huh?"

The crowd surrounding us had quickly packed up to four deep, jostling for better vantage points, smiling and laughing, enjoying the Saints' discomforture. I couldn't see the pilot any longer, and I guessed that it wouldn't take more than a few minutes before the police became aware of the commotion and took an interest.

"Farrell, please," Beckin said, placing her left hand on Farrell's shoulder while she smiled at Gregorson. "Can you not see these boys are troubled over something? Let us hear what they have to say."

Gregorson blinked for a couple of seconds, unsure of his response now that the situation had suddenly moved away from an angry confrontation. "Several of our friends were murdered east of here in the forest," he began.

"And you think *we* might have had something to do with it?" Beckin asked, her tone incredulous. "Three *women*? How many of your friends died?"

"Nine," one of the guards said.

"Ah," Beckin replied, "and did they possess weapons, or were they innocent pilgrims or somesuch? Attacked without warning or provocation, perhaps?"

None of the Saints had anticipated a question-and-answer session in front of a growing number of witnesses. Richard looked around at the crowd before answering, and the two bodyguards unbuttoned their light jackets. Packing, I thought. "They had rifles," he admitted.

"Do you wish to join them?" Beckin asked quietly. She removed her sunglasses, stuck them in her belt pack, and fixed her steady green gaze on Gregorson.

We all have internal monsters, mind-creatures which occasionally knock on the windows of our ids and leer in at us, letting us know they're still there, demons preying on our uncertainties and weaknesses. External monsters are much rarer. To a man, though, the Saints paled when they saw Beckin's eyes. *She* was their monster, their demon.

Even the crowd went silent at the five Mormons' reaction.

"She's giving you a choice, you know," a cheerful baritone voice said from behind the biggest Saint.

52

Brone, wearing a new cowboy hat that put him well over seven feet tall, stepped up next to the kid and draped his right arm over the kid's shoulder, smiling down at him. Brone held a well-licked triple-dip chocolate cone in his left hand. His facial expression was completely benign. He raised an eyebrow at the big Saint. "My name is Brone, and you are..?"

"Bob," the kid answered, sputtering a bit, trying to look up at Brone and down at Richard at the same time, seeking some guidance from his leader.

"A pleasure, Bob," Brone said, still smiling. He took another lick of his cone. "They have very good ice cream here," he said in conversational tones. The crowd, which had been struck silent, began to laugh again. For them, this was clearly a special moment. We were surrounded by a sea of bib overalls and hemp-based gingham, and Brone had just kicked the interest level up a few notches.

"As I was saying," Brone continued, "Miz Gilmer has offered you a choice, young sirs. Were I you, I should consider it very carefully. Will it be life or death?"

Irritated anew, Gregorson snapped the fingers of his left hand in front of Bob's nose, a signal. Bob gave a short growl, spun, and swung a big right fist straight up from the ground at Brone's face.

Brone leaned casually away from the blow, letting it whistle by his head. He caught Bob's elbow and pulled him down, simultaneously driving his right knee up into Bob's solar plexis. The sound of air abruptly leaving Bob's lungs could be heard a block away. He fell to his hands and knees, choking and retching. Brone reached down, patted Bob on the head, and took another lick of his cone.

"There's an example of what I meant," Brone continued, as though nothing had happened. "Bob made a *bad* choice, and we all see that it didn't work out well for him." He regarded the astounded Saints earnestly. "I suggest you don't buy Bob any of this wonderful ice cream. But you still have to make a choice. You have a minute or two to decide, though, I think, before Bob will be able to walk."

Gregorson and his buddies didn't wait that long. They got Bob to his feet and half-led, half-carried him away, still groaning. The crowd parted for them. Richard shot us a final look of pure hatred, and they vanished in the throng.

"Unfriendly fellows," Brone observed, shaking his head as he watched the five Saints leave. Then he turned back to us, waving his depleted cone. "You really should try some of this. It's delicious."

Someone in the crowd around us began to clap. Others took it up, and Brone blushed and looked modest. Farrell and I joined in the applause. Beckin hid her smile behind her hand as she replaced her sunglasses over her eyes. She had noticed, as had I, that a few people in the crowd -- not just the five Saints -- had known what they saw when she exposed her eyes. I hadn't seen any obvious shock, only 'I thought so' expressions. That recognition probably wasn't important, and might even be expected, after so many years of *Siog* visits. But the Empire of the Saints being aware at some level of *Siog* abilities -- *that* was dangerous.

Beckin shook her bag of groceries. "Let us try Brone's ice cream, then leave quickly." She linked her right arm in Brone's left and smiled up at him. He blushed again.

"Where's the booth?" I asked Brone. He gestured toward the grandstands with the last remnants of his cone. "I'll catch up with you," I said. "There's someone I need to talk to."

I walked rapidly away in the direction the Saints had gone, and got them in sight within a minute, struggling with the still-suffering Bob. The pilot strolled along fifty feet behind them, wearing a well-patched and likely much-loved flight jacket over normal clothes and aged zipper-sided jump boots.

54

"Nice piece of flying this morning," I said, coming up alongside him.

He looked up at me and grinned, his blunt narrow face lined by years of squinting through concave plexiglass. "Oh, yeah? You damned near shot my left foot off." He shook his head and ran the ball of his right thumb along his jawline. "Kids are gettin' too quick for me. Might be about time to hang it up."

"Might be time to consider who you're baby-sitting," I replied. "I assume your little fly-by was Crown Prince Gregorson's idea?"

"Sure was." The pilot's grin turned sardonic. "He ain't exactly the Crown Prince, though. There are two older brothers. Richard's more like The Prince Who Wants To Make His Mark. He thinks your friend might be his ticket. Got some bonehead idea that people like her can travel from one place to another without benefit of conventional transport. 'Teleportation,' he calls it, and he's got the others half-believing him."

"Crazy idea," I agreed. Up ahead, Bob seemed to be recovering a little more, getting his feet under him.

The pilot laughed, a cynical sound on such a sunny day. "A crazy idea would be me flyin' these kids around because I know Richard's dad and owed him some."

"*Owed?*"

"Yeah. From 'Nam. Nothin' too big, but important to me. This pretty well evens our account, though. I think I'll be heading down to Portland in another week or so, when this's over." He looked at me more intently. "The government still need good chopper pilots?"

"You think *I'd* know?"

"I know a improved model M-16 when I see one. You work for New Uncle, you and your dark buddy."

I couldn't think of a good reason to tell him any different. Everybody seemed to know we were military. "Right you are," I replied.

"And the green-eyed girl and the big guy?"

"No, they're just along for the ride. We're not here on official business, and we're gonna be heading out in a few minutes. Frankly, we don't need any hassles."

"Which direction? Not east, I'd imagine, and I don't figure you're from around here." The man seemed totally relaxed, but he kept careful track of Richard and the four others.

"The Valley."

The pilot whistled. "Compliance country. *Real* brave."

"Compliance?" I asked. "What's that?"

"You're going to the Willamette Valley, and you don't know all about the fucking *Compliance*? Jesus. If the Saints seem like religious yahoos to some people, the Compliance trumps 'em several times over. Real nutcases." He touched his glasses in a mock salute. "Good luck, lady."

"We'll be okay. I hope." I stuck out my hand. "I'm Megan Connolly, by the way."

"Tom Garris." We shook briefly.

"I won't tell the boys you're military," Garris said, "but I don't mind tellin' you that Richard has his cap set for your green-eyed friend. He'll want to take her back to Salt Lake and wring her dry. He's not stupid, but once he gets his mind in a track, he's stubborn and determined to the point of idiocy. Plus, there's those bodies piled up in the woods. His people, armed to the teeth, four slit to pieces, five with their skulls crushed. For Richard, that's both a score to settle and a mystery to solve. He's pissed and obsessed, not necessarily in that order."

"Yeah, well, that's fine," I replied, "but my green-eyed friend will kill him if he gets in her way again without a crowd watching."

"She that good, huh?" Garris seemed doubtful.

"Believe me, she could have killed them all in the time it takes you or me to draw a deep breath." I looked off in the direction taken by the five Saints. They'd

56

rounded a copse of young ash and disappeared. "What kind of firepower's that Huey got?"

"Not much. An M-60 out the cargo door. These little Recon ships never carry anything significant. Pasco scares the piss out of Salt Lake brass. They can't afford to antagonize the remnants of the U.S. Air Force. They haven't got the planes to lose. The Saints have every bit of firepower they're ever going to have, and about a month's worth of fuel for all their hardware."

I smiled at the thought of that level of desperation and frustration. "All dressed up and no place to go. But on a purely local level, that M-60's more than enough to clean our clock."

Garris shrugged. "Not if we can't find you. If Richard insists on going after you -- and he will -- I'll tell them I overheard you folks say you were going to John Day. Provided you're not, that is."

"We're not," I said, then had a thought. "Where are you going to get fuel for that amount of air time?"

"All the Saints aren't back in Utah and Idaho. There are fuel drops scattered around on a few isolated ranches here and there. We'll manage." Garris took off his glasses, revealing hazel-brown eyes the same color as Quinn and Maren's. I gulped inside. "What's your rank?" he asked.

His words seemed to fade out. For a long moment, I just stood there and wanted to be with the girls. "We're both Majors," I said finally, a catch in my voice.

Garris pretended not to notice the catch. "I'll be damned," he said. "I was only a Captain when I got out in '69." He began to clean his glasses with a handkerchief he pulled from a hip pocket. I recognized the troubled look in his eyes. The years had fled. He felt both his lost youth and opportunities untaken. "Buy you a beer in Portland, Sir?" he asked at last. "If both of us get there?"

I nodded, and we shook hands again. "I wish you bad hunting, Captain Garris," I said.

"And good hiding to you, Major Connolly." He slipped on his sunglasses, sketched a salute, and we both hurried away in opposite directions.

Time to find the others, tell them what I'd found out, get my ice cream cone, and hit the road hard.

Two hundred very exposed miles of wheat fields and sun-baked semi-desert lay ahead of us over the next two days. Only good luck or a very disinformative Tom Garris could keep us from being found. Maybe both.

But his *eyes*. The *girls*. Oh, damn.

CHAPTER TWELVE

CONDON AND BEYOND

We bolted out of the south end of Pendleton on the so-called Pendleton-John Day Highway, number 395, which was in surprisingly good repair. Things got a tad rougher on Highway 74 west to Heppner, which made me glad I'd finished my cone by that point. The road had been resurfaced since the war, just not recently. Those heavy grain trucks must pound the asphalt pretty relentlessly.

Beckin and I still sat in the rear of the truck, in the shade, with the canvas top rolled back halfway over the bed. This gave us both an unobstructed view behind to the east, and let us keep our rifles up on our laps. Other than getting tired of staring off at the horizon, it wasn't too bad, just boring.

The little army truck motored on through the rolling wheatfields. Not rapidly, top speed being only about sixty, but plenty adequate for road conditions. We came down into Heppner, where my great-grandparents from Ireland arrived in Oregon in 1915, where John Tierney had been their sponsor, before he Changed. I got my first view of the big earthen dam which provided water for the area. The new dam, I remembered. The old one had given way during the early part of the century, and wiped Heppner right off the map for a while, sparing only a few buildings on higher ground.

Still without any sign of the Saints or their chopper, we hauled up out of Heppner and headed for Condon, and it wasn't one o'clock yet.

"We are doing better than I hoped," Beckin said, watching Heppner fall away into the distance, a light summer haze blurring the outlines of the buildings as the town receded into the prairie.

"The *roads* are better than I figured," I said, pointing to a sign, "only forty-one miles to Condon."

Without turning, Farrell said, "I vote we try for the mountains. Just keep going and get the hell out of this flat stuff. I can practically feel that Huey on the back of my neck."

Brone, who'd been dozing happily for the past half-hour, only stirring a little as we drove through Heppner, twisted in his seat and bent to look at Farrell's neck. "You needn't worry. It's not there."

"Quiet, ice cream breath," Farrell laughed, as the truck reached the half-way point of a three-mile straight stretch. It almost seemed as though we could see Condon off to the west, if we looked hard enough. "I just wanta get out from behind this wheel and see our kids," Farrell continued. "Not that I don't enjoy present company, and not that I didn't get off on you teaching those little pukes a lesson back in Pendleton, you understand."

"You *could* let someone else drive," I said, reaching over with my right hand and tugging on her hair.

"And you *could* have the fun of listening to my driving advice" Farrell replied, leaning back into my hand, and rubbing against it, moving her head side-to-side.

"I believe we have stress enough already," Beckin said, briefly turning from her ceaseless scrutiny of the seemingly unending green and golden fields surrounding us.

Neither the stress nor the undulating landscape changed much over the next two hours. The truck droned on, Brone went back to sleep, Farrell drove, and Beckin and I scanned the limitless blue sky.

Occasional small canyons or dry washes would appear, rimmed with cottonwood and juniper. Some of the deeper ones would have pine growing along sluggish streams snaking through bottomlands thick with spring grass. And, increasingly, as we moved west, pine, at first solitary and then in greater numbers, cloaked the ridgecrests of the rising terrain.

After Condon, a collection of homes and businesses clustered around grain elevators, we passed through little towns with names like Mayville, Fossil, Clarno, Antelope, and finally Shaniko, a ghost town near the crossroads with Highway 97. We stopped once to top off the gas tanks and pee, but that was all. Beckin's sacks of food grew steadily lighter as the afternoon progressed.

I began to breathe easier after eerie little Shaniko, with its abandoned storefronts and dustdevils skittering through the empty streets. Even Beckin relaxed her vigilance some. Her maps showed we were well over a hundred miles west-northwest of John Day. A little more than twenty miles ahead lay Maupin, then about the same distance to Pine Grove, and we'd be safely back into timberland, where we could go to ground and not be seen. We'd decided to spend the night in Pine Grove, tucked away in some little gulley or dry wash, and go on to North Cedar in the morning.

The gods are not fair, of course. The Huey sped out of the southwest no more than five minutes later, caught us in open country, and this time they had the M-60 out in plain sight, on the left side of the cargo bay.

The threatening voice that come down from the sky wasn't Tom Garris or Richard, but the meaning was still abundantly clear. "If you don't stop and surrender, we'll kill you."

"Are they within range?" Farrell asked, not slowing.

"Soon," I said. "They don't seem to understand that we have the ability to fill the cargo bay with lead."

"Fools," Beckin said in her dead calm voice, as she eyed the gunship, caluculating the distance. The Huey slid smoothly closer, a tribute to Garris' flying skills.

"*Now!*" the voice said. The kid on the machine gun crouched lower, sighting, preparing to fire. The chopper hovered, two hundred yards away.

Close enough. "Now," I said, and Beckin and I raised our rifles simultaneously, and put twin three-bursts into the gunner. His head exploded. His body jumped, sagged. Garris jinked away in an eye-blink, and the gunner's limp corpse slid around the base of the gun. He cart-wheeled down out of the sky to land on the edge of the dusty road, a quarter-mile behind us. I rather enjoyed the sodden thump it made.

Someone screamed shrilly, up in the Huey.

"One," Beckin said, smiling, "and perhaps more."

I knew Garris had deliberately put them within range of our weapons, and I doubted they realized it. The helicopter floated well out of range now.

"They're having a conference," I said, watching the little gunship.

"Stay or go," Beckin nodded.

"They can still nail us easily," I said, turning to Beckin, "but that would deprive them of you."

"I am such a treasure," Beckin replied, eyeing the Huey. Hunger akin to our Need filled her features. Her inhumanity had never been more apparent to me. "Come back and die, little ones," she entreated in a soft, deadly voice.

"That asshole won't give up this easily," Farrell added from behind the wheel, and I agreed with her.

Twenty seconds later, however, the Huey turned away from us and streaked toward the east.

"Gone," I said, as it disappeared over the horizon.

"That was much too abrupt," Beckin said, her gaze to the east, her expression suspicious.

"Richard might be sharper than we think," I replied, sitting back down.

"Not a chance," Brone said, speaking for the first time since the Huey appeared.

"Another hour," Farrell put in, "and we'll be in heavier timber, be able to flat fucking disappear from those little pricks."

"Had to be low on fuel," I said, sighing.

"No," Beckin said, shaking her head. "It's something more."

Forty minutes passed, with Beckin and I straining to see or hear anything, when a faint -- but dramatically deeper -- helicopter trace came from the southeast. I couldn't see it, not right away, but I knew that sound.

Something bigger headed toward us. Something potentially far more nasty than Garris' Huey.

A Boeing AH-47 Chinook, the Vietnam-era flying truck, the all-purpose lift ship.

Big enough, if it was armed, to sent us straight to hell in about two seconds.

Shit.

CHAPTER THIRTEEN

GUNS-A-GO-GO

"What *is* that?" Beckin asked, as the heavy sound drew nearer. "It's not the Huey."

"A Chinook," Farrell said. "A *big* mother." She didn't let off the gas.

Along with the Chinook, I could now pick up the lesser warble of Garris' craft. "They carry stuff, actually have a cargo bay," Farrell added.

"Twin rotors?" Beckin asked. "Quite large?"

"Yeah," I replied. "They used 'em in 'Nam to haul artillery firebases from hilltop to hilltop. Still do the same sort of stuff, and there's quite a lot of private commercial work, oil prospecting and that kind of stuff."

"The rotor paths overlap?" Already Beckin looked for an edge.

"Yeah," Farrell answered, "and a single gearbox that keeps the shafts in sync. That and rotor shaft vibration are pretty much the only things that ever go wrong with 'em. And there *were* a few Chinook gunships around in the late sixties. Probably not one of those we're hearing, but an ordinary Chinook could have enough troops on board to set a pretty good perimeter in front of us."

"They'll find us quick," I said, searching the sky between the sparse tree cover.

"'Fraid so," Farrell agreed.

"Fine," Beckin said, wheels turning in her sly little mind. "We shall let them capture us, then kill them all at the first good opportunity."

I just looked at her. "Oh, it's that simple?"

Beckin nodded. "They will concentrate on Brone, who they've seen in action. They will handle me very carefully. They won't know what to do with you two. At some point, they will have us inside their group. Nothing will let them guess that you and Farrell can easily break any restraints they may have. We can slaughter them all."

64

"They'll see our Army ID," I said. "Either they'll want to take us back to Salt Lake, or they'll try to kill us outright."

Beckin thought for a moment, stroking her chin. "I hadn't considered that. They will think you spies for the US government, or some sort of forward element for the invasion of the Empire."

Meanwhile, the Chinook came closer, and a few seconds later, I could glimpse both it and the Huey through the trees, about a half-mile behind. Machine gun snouts and rocket pods were all too obvious. "The bastard's armed," I said. I poked Farrell. "That's your cue, Ms. Military Historian."

"Is there a grenade launcher?"

I squinted up into the sky. The Chinook was over-hauling us fast, with the Huey above it, out of the line of fire. I spotted the tell-tale bulge of an M-5 grenade launcher. "Yeah, right on the nose. Rocket pod and a minigun on the side pylons."

"Then we're *really* fucked," Farrell replied, slamming the steering wheel with her right hand. "It's probably one of the original gunships, salvaged from California. I'll pick a wide spot, and we'll stop. Try to look hangdog. Let 'em think we're giving up without a fight."

Brone looked at Beckin, as if awaiting instructions, and, for once, he seemed deadly serious. He'd die to protect her, I was certain. "How do you want me to play it?" he asked her, his voice very steady. The Chinook was almost directly overhead, slightly behind, the grenade launcher tracking us. The noise level made conversation difficult, and the dust it kicked up whipped around us.

"Be friendly," Beckin answered, her eager smile briefly appearing. "*I'll* make the threats."

Her statement worried me. How big a role would the *Siog* deathwish play in what was going down? Beckin was twenty-five, well past the age when *Siogi* youth threw their lives away needlessly. I hoped. I reached over to Farrell and gripped her right arm, willed her to feel my concern.

She laughed, and patted my hand as she let the truck slow, steering over to the side of the road. "Don't worry, Megs," she said. "If we have to wade through the entire Saint Empire to get to the girls, we will."

That made me feel better. The truck ground to a halt, and we climbed out. The Chinook settled slowly and ponderously onto the pavement in front of our truck, its rear ramp down, M-60 pointed directly at us. Garris' Huey floated softly down behind us, and we were neatly bracketed.

Here we go, I thought, trying to think like Beckin.

They're on the ground. They're vulnerable. Almost supper time.

CHAPTER FOURTEEN

BAD CHOICES

Surrounded by his surviving homies, under the tail of the big olive drab Chinook -- no white paint on this helicopter -- Richard Gregorson was, by turns, jubilant, angry, and puzzled. He knew he had us. He just didn't know what he had. When he spread the contents of our belt packs out on the Chinook's rear ramp -- next to the ramp-mounted M-60 -- he only got more confused. He looked up at Farrell and me, his brow furrowed at our non-*Siog* eyes, and his puzzlement gave way to frustrated anger. Somehow that seemed very Richard.

"You're US Army Majors?"

"Yes," we admitted, in unison.

"Whose children are these?" He held identical pictures of Quinn and Maren, one from each of our wallets.

"Ours," we said.

"One of you gave birth to these children?" Regardless of the timeline, Mormon society must be procreation-oriented.

"We both did," I replied, "one apiece."

"That's impossible," Richard scoffed. "They're *twins*."

"We've got science you can only dream of, kid," Farrell said. "Our world is *real* different from yours. We have a thing called Haploid Combination that lets women achieve pregnancy without a man being involved. How's *that* sound?"

For perhaps half a second, Richard's eyes reflected that internal paranoid twist typical of members of a truly closed society. *What don't I know?* his gaze seemed to ask, filled with an inborn xenophobia. And women -- probably lesbian women -- reproducing without men? That had to kick his head sideways. His three companions shuffled uneasily, seeing his reaction, feeling it themselves at some level. Bob scowled, cracked his knuckles, and tried to look foreboding. This was probably his reaction to anything which upset him, but I noticed he'd kept well away from Brone, which made him smarter than I'd initially thought.

Turning abruptly away without responding to Farrell's taunt, Richard went through Beckin's things. There weren't many. Siogi travel light, in Beckin's case only a few dwarven tools of a vaguely-Leatherman type, a slim folding knife, and her remaining local currency. I knew that her kit was a graduation gift from her family, that it was one of her proudest possessions, but from the disinterested expression on her face, you would have thought she'd found it in the dirt five minutes earlier.

In handling it without permission, however, Richard had insured his own death several times over. He would be told about it, too, at the end. I knew that. Good, bad, or indifferent, Beckin always kept score. Only the presence of the crew of the Chinook, standing just inside the ship's bay, armed and ready, kept Richard's payback from being right now. The aura of scorn radiating off her was nearly palpable. The Saints didn't seem to notice, which was just as well. They wouldn't like being the scornees.

Finished with Beckin's gear, Gregorson appeared disappointed, like he'd expected to find the hoped-for teleportation device, the Jewel of Instant Transit or whatever. It was clear that he wanted to question her at length, but understood that this couldn't be the time or place. He might be fixated, but he wasn't a complete fool.

Brone interrupted Richard's mulling. "Again, Mister Gregorson," he said, in his laconic manner, "you must make a choice. The same choice as this morning. Live or die. Release us and live. Retain us and die."

"What do you take me for?" Gregorson asked, looking sharply up to his left at Brone. He held up a fist. "We *have* you. We can do as we wish." He indicated Beckin. "I *will* have her knowledge."

68

Brone regarded him levelly for a few heartbeats. "Then you will never see the spires of your Temple again," he said quietly. His words vanished quickly into the surrounding wind-washed vastness, making no impact on any of them.

"*Enough*," Richard replied. He pointed to Farrell and me, raising his imperious voice still more. "Garris, you will take these two." Garris, a hundred feet away, seated on the edge of the Huey's cargo bay, gave a curt nod. Gregorson turned to his two gunboys. "Go with them. When you reach cruising altitude, put a bullet in each of their heads and drop them in a canyon. We do not fear the US Army."

The corners of Beckin's mouth tugged upward maybe one millimeter, and Farrell grinned outright. Richard, caught in his own ego-trip and still watching Garris, missed it, and none of the rest of them reacted, either.

Stupid little fuck, I thought, separating us, giving Beckin her wish.

After pulling the truck around a handy knoll, to be picked up later by some local Saints, all our gear went in the Chinook, whose crew examined the two LaFrances with a certain level of amazement. Too used to having antique ordnance, I figured.

Then, with enough guns pointed at us to finish off ten people, they manacled us with heavy steel cuffs, and we were led to our respective ships. Before we parted, from my left, way too soft for the Saints to hear, Beckin said, "you have the first move, Megan. Brone and I will wait thirty minutes before we do anything."

Most of the late gunner's blood had been wiped away from the interior surfaces of the Huey, but it was still fresh enough for the Need to stir inside me. That and my rising level of readiness would insure that my blood-lust kept alert. And irritating, of course. I prefer to ride the Need, not the other way 'round, and now it would continue nibbling at the edge of my mind until sated.

We climbed into the little gunship and settled in for what was intended to be a short ride with an abrupt ending. The two Saints made sure we sat with our backs firmly against the door opposite the M-60, our hands between our knees. One of them covered us with a .45, while the other went up to sit next to Garris. Even with the cuffs, they weren't taking any chances. They'd seen how quickly and accurately we functioned.

Garris tipped his cap in welcome before powering up the turboshaft engine, and shot me a grim smile. His left eyebrow lifted just enough to be visible over the top of his sunglasses. "You Majors comfy back there?" he asked, above the thunder of the engine, after putting on his well-used flight helmet. We nodded and grinned.

The Saints didn't like that exchange one bit. The one seated next to Garris spoke sharply to him, and our guy made a feeble threatening gesture with his pistol.

Garris, more of a smart-ass than I'd thought, stuck his middle finger under his co-pilot's nose, but smiled as he did it. The kid looked severely put out, apparently having had his humor gland removed along with taking his job very seriously. I would guess there are probably no Mormon stand-up comedians. After another minute or two sitting on the pavement, with Garris talking intermittently with the Chinook, we lifted off. The ship swung smoothly toward the east, and fell in behind the bigger gunship, keeping low, under Pasco's radar. In my view, the Huey should have been in front, but Garris didn't seem to mind. He found a nearly debris-free pocket in the turbulence behind the bigger craft, and kept that position.

Five minutes into the air, the gunship slicking along nicely, the Saint next to Garris said something, removed his belt, and stood up.

Our turn, looked like. I brought my wrists together, preparing to snap the cuffs, and saw Farrell do the same.

As the co-pilot stepped around his seat, Garris pulled a silenced .22 from under his jacket and shot the kid in the head twice. Then he spun in his seat, leaning over the back, and emptied the pistol into the guy guarding us.

70

The first Saint was dead, though he might not know it yet, sprawling bonelessly down to the deck. Our guy, even with a half-dozen holes in him, was still pretty lively. He staggered toward Garris, raising his pistol.

Fool. He should have shot us first.

I kicked his legs out from under him, simultaneously snapping my cuffs. Farrell broke hers, ripped the Saint's .45 away from him, and tore his throat out.

Stepping over the top of the twitching head-popped Saint, and up behind Garris, who was back on his stick, I put my right hand on his left shoulder. "Thanks, Captain," I said. "That was a nice surprise."

Garris shrugged, not taking his eyes off the Chinook or his hand off the stick. "Even for Richard's dad," he replied, "I have my limits. Richard went over the line."

I nodded. "Made our job easier. Look, we'll throw them out in a minute or so. If you would, don't look behind you until I tell you. Okay?"

"No problem."

I squeezed his shoulder. "Thanks." Then I turned back to the dying Saints. Farrell was well into the program, her guy stretched out on his back, close to bled-out. I hauled the other one over by her, bent down to his throat.

And fed.

CHAPTER FIFTEEN

IN THE AIR

After we drained our victims down to heart-stop, only fifteen minutes remained of Beckin's thirty. We dumped the dead Saints over a tree-lined gully, and tried to decide how to get into the Chinook while both ships were airborne.

After introducing Farrell to Garris, I sat in the co-pilot's seat and said, "Those two were not Saints of the flying variety."

"I dunno," Farrell added. "The one with the big adam's apple did a kind of cute spiral just before he hit the ground."

"How did you break the cuffs?" Garris asked, laughing, still cool, but concerned and curious.

"Special diet," Farrell replied. I pinched her arm.

"I don't want to know," Garris said, shaking his head. "I heard the sounds you two were making back there. And I should let the Chinook know you're dead and gone, and then hope Richard doesn't want to talk to Glenn or Roy."

Glenn and Roy. Good Saint names if I ever heard any, and all that clean living sure does affect the blood. Yesiree.

"Any ideas how we get inside the Chinook, Captain?" I asked Garris. "We've got about twelve minutes before our companions act on their own."

"Can the girl break her cuffs as easy as you two?" he asked. His expression didn't change, but he began to chew on his lower lip. He didn't mention Brone.

"Yeah," I answered.

"Two against ten...well, two against eight, since the pilot and co-pilot aren't gonna be available, and all in a confined space. 'Course, they'd only be able to get at the big guy maybe two at a time, and weapons won't be a factor, unless Richard or Bob get careless. The Chinook's crew's sharp. They aren't wet-behind-the-ears

72

brats like Richard and his friends. Flew a bunch of missions during the Battle of Boise."

"So how do I get on the Chinook?" I asked, keeping my gaze on the big olive drab gunship. 'U.S. Army 413149' in yellow was lettered prominently on the broad tail. Why had they left the original color scheme, I wondered? Who knew. Maybe only the Saint elite got white.

"Easy," Garris replied. "I pull even with 'em, and slightly higher. You empty one of those .45s into the transmission, which is right below the leading edge of the tail section in the shaft tunnel. The rotors lose power, they crash, you hope your friends survive."

"No, I mean while they're in the _air_."

"Kee-rist, Major! There's no frigging way!"

"You got a grapple hook and line somewhere on this thing?" Farrell asked.

Garris nodded. "Behind you, in that storage box against the aft wall. There's a winch in there, too, and a seat." He looked skeptically at me, almost but not quite sneering. "What are you gonna do? Loop it around the M-60 on the ramp? No can do at eighty miles an hour, with the downdraft from the rotors. Nobody can throw that hard and accurately. And even if you could, the gunner's right inside the ramp opening, in a little jump seat. Unless he's asleep -- and he won't be -- he'll see the hook, unless you're real lucky. Blow your ass away with his pistol, even if you could hand- over-hand up into the Chinook."

"No, Captain Garris," Farrell said, "that won't happen, because _I'll_ shoot anybody who comes onto the ramp."

"Then one of the side gunners will blow _us_ out of the sky," Garris replied, shaking his head.

"Get the grapple, Farrell," I said, resigned, and not seeing any other way. "I'll give it a try."

"You guys are frigging nuts," Garris said, still shaking his head, but with a note of quasi-admiration in his voice. "It won't work, and the moment I see one of those M-60 barrels move, I'm going straight up. Over the top of the Chinook, where they won't be able to get at us." He grinned at me. "You can hang on the skids. Okay?"

"Fair enough," I replied, wishing I didn't see Quinn and Maren's anxious little faces on the backs of my eyelids every time I blinked.

"I'll drop slightly back and down, tilt a little, and move in a skoosh. Should be able to get you within forty feet. You oughta be just out of sight of the Chinook crew."

With the hundred-foot grapple line coiled next to the base of the M-60, Farrell taped one of the dead Saints' .45s to the grapple for added weight. "Jeez, this duct tape is *old*," she said, frowning as she stripped the stuff off its roll.

"Use it quick," Garris put in, gradually slipping the Huey rearward in relation to the bigger gunship. "It's probably out of California, radioactive as hell."

Farrell finished her wrapping and tossed the roll of tape back in the grapple container. "Here, Megs," she said, "go for it."

"Yeah, sure," I replied, hefting the grapple while Farrell checked the coiled line. Then she positioned herself right behind the machine gun with the remaining .45 centered on the Chinook's ramp opening.

My idea was to take two steps from the far side of the deck and side-arm the grapple at the Chinook with about eighty percent of my power. I slanted the throw up a bit to try and compensate for the downthrust from the Chinook's rear rotor.

It almost worked on the first try, a tribute to vampire strength. Five feet short, and then the downthrust pounded the grapple and line back under the Huey in a long arc.

"Try to keep it out of our rotor," Garris said dryly, holding up his left hand.

Farrell recoiled the line, and I tried again with everything I had, a little harder and a little higher.

The grapple dropped almost into the ramp opening, then hooked two tines around the hydraulic shaft on our side of the ramp. The line snapped out behind the two ships in a shallow curve. I winked at Farrell and took a tight grip on the line as it yanked me out of the Huey.

Into a windstream that whipped me around like a crippled kite. My eyes instantly streamed. Goggles. Shit, I should have thought of goggles!

Blinking away the tears, buffeted first one way then the other, I started up the line, hand-over-hand. Above and well in front of me, I could see the bottom of the Chinook's ramp.

The Lodgepole pine in my path I didn't see, until I hit it.

CHAPTER SIXTEEN

SAINTS DEAD

I ripped up through the top of the pine and tumbled free in a cloud of small branches and needles, upside down. Only one hand still clutched the line. My other flailed wildly, trying to dislodge the debris clinging to my face and upper body and get a grip on the rope.

My legs went through the last three feet of another tree, but with both hands back on the line and climbing, I cleared the next few. Then those trees were past. I kept going as rapidly as I could, squinting against the air hammering at me.

Seventy feet of nylon rope dangled below me, though, and the possibility of getting it tangled in the next clump of pine -- or the one after that -- was very real. The big Chinook flew as low as it could. A potentially large radar signature had to, so the rope was a snag waiting to happen.

The collision with the first tree must've jarred the ramp enough to be noticeable, or maybe the grapple was more visible than I thought. Someone got curious. Just as I stuck my head over the edge of the ramp, a booted foot appeared in front of my nose.

I grabbed the ankle above the boot, and went straight up his front. A brief glimpse of blond hair, blue eyes, a startled expression, and he was gone. He was trying to draw his pistol when I seized the back of his neck and pitched him off the ramp. Perhaps he got the weapon out before he hit the ground. Or not.

Brone and Beckin sat against the right wall of the big helicopter, on a small bench situated between that side's M-60s. Richard Gregorson and the faithful Bob faced them on a similar bench between the other pair of machine guns.

Somehow, without seeming to look, Brone and Beckin knew I was there. Very casually, Brone flexed his wrists and snapped the manacles. He took one step forward and put his right fist into Bob's face. Quite a ways in. As Bob fell to the deck, Brone pivoted to his right, grabbed the two front machinegunners in his big hands, and smashed them together.

Beckin broke her own cuffs, hit Richard once alongside his head, and tossed him past Brone toward the front of the cabin.

The M-60 gunner nearest me had just realized that his fellow crew member's position on the ramp had been taken, and swiveled in his seat, drawing his automatic. I seized his wrist, kept the .45 extended in his hand, and put two rounds into his opposite number on the other side of the cabin.

As the other gunner dropped away from his M-60, Beckin caught him and frog-marched him off the ramp. Then, without pausing, she spun and headed back to Richard.

I heaved my guy, still struggling, over the side. He windmilled all the way down, screaming. Brone appeared beside me, dragging the limp bodies of Bob and the two forward gunners. Easily. One at a time, he pitched them out. Also easily.

By the time Brone and I got to Beckin, she had the groggy Richard jammed into the cockpit doorway where the pilot and co-pilot could see him. "I have your sacred Prince," she rasped. "Should you wish him to live longer than now, return us to our vehicle and land the ship. Do not attempt to utilize the radio."

Hard to resist that compelling argument. After the two startled crewmen exchanged looks, they turned the gunship, and back we went.

CHAPTER SEVENTEEN

MOVING ON

On the return to the truck, I crouched beside the Chinook's khaki-clad pilot and co-pilot, a liberated .45 in my right hand, resting between my knees. It would have been more comfortable to have my familiar Beretta, but our ordnance bags could wait to be checked thoroughly until we were on the ground. I had recovered my beltpack and that was enough. The girls' pictures were back where they belonged, a few inches below my heart.

Now, after a brief conversation with Garris and Farrell, we maintained radio silence. My job was to assure that silence. We had all the weapons, but the co-pilot's right hand had been inching in the general direction of the radio switch for the past five minutes, and it was just a matter of time before fingers would have to be broken.

Beckin had Richard back in the main cabin. Pretty subdued, our Richard, after being knocked silly and dragged around by the scruff of his neck. He was alone, his buddies were dead, and he realized he was in shit up to his neck. Brone sat wedged in the ramp M-60 seat, his hands folded behind his head, relaxing. He'd just killed three people in about as many seconds, and now he was taking it easy. In my estimation, the world needs more Brones, your basic non-fretters. Of course, with his sperm program, more Brones seemed a fair likelihood.

Weird to think of that. And weirder to think of Eireann Mor, with its stratified static society, the immortal Siogi on top. Technically, Farrell and I had far more in common with the Saints' radioactively-polluted reality than we ever would with Beckin's people. And yet, I felt totally comfortable in Eireann Mor. The rasor-edged Siogi, stolid Berzerks, and proficient Dwarfs had created a simple, functional, and low-impact civilization.

A true ecotopia, underpinned by death, techno-theft, and carnage-for-hire. My kind of folks.

In the meantime, the co-pilot still looked as though he was searching for something to distract me long enough so that he could flick on the radio, opening a line to some Saint listening post in Idaho.

I decided to nip that. "You guys use ranks?" I asked.

The co-pilot started, confirming my thought about him distracting me.

"I'm a captain," the pilot said, without looking at me, biting the words off, at the moment not a happy man.

"And you?" I asked the co-pilot.

"First Lieutenant."

"Well, Lieutenant," I said, "if you keep thinking about turning on your comm-unit, figuring someone out there will come rescue your leader's son, I'll cheerfully break every naughty little finger on that hand. Understand?"

"Big talk from a woman," the pilot growled, "even one with a gun."

Moving faster than they could register, I grabbed the Lieutenant's left wrist and simultaneously put the muzzle of the .45 against the Captain's right temple. This time, they both jumped, and the gunship wobbled a bit. The Chinook's cabin filled with the sound of shallow, rapid breathing. "Gentlemen," I said, in resigned tones, "there are some things you need to understand. The pistol is to intimidate you in a way familiar to you. That's all. I don't need it. I could just as easily hurt you enough so that you'd think of me every day for the rest of your lives, but I don't want to do that. Fifteen minutes ago, I was in the Huey, with an automatic pointed at me. Now I'm here. You need to reflect on what sort of physical skills allowed me to do that." I gripped the Lieutenant's wrist a little harder. "*And* you need to remember that you want Little Boy Blue back there to stay alive."

"If that green-eyed witch was going to kill him, she would've done it by now," the captain grated.

"Good thinking," I replied, admiring a mind that could still function with the barrel of an automatic resting a half-inch away. "I just hope you're right."

As I'd intended, that got him to thinking even more.

The lieutenant's hands were trying to get back in his lap, and he stared at my hand as though I were going to suddenly pinch off his wrist. I let him go. He rubbed feeling into his wrist and hand, unwilling to look at me for a minute, but he finally spoke. "Do you really have children?"

"Sure," I said, fishing out the kids' picture and handing it to him.

Longing showed in his eyes as he examined our daughters. "They're really cute," he said softly, and his mouth curved up in a truly sweet smile.

"Appearances are deceiving," I said, chuckling. "You got any kids?"

"No," he replied, still looking at the girls. "I was in one of the last recovery runs into California. Caught enough radiation to bar me from parenthood."

"It's the Angels for most of us," the captain added, his expression grim.

"'Angels?'" I asked.

"Sterilized women. Those who survived the fallout in southern Utah as children. They minister to the needs of their male counterparts, like us." He shrugged. "It's a two-way street, I suppose, just not what the Lord intended."

He didn't sound horribly bitter, and my heart went out to him for that. A Mormon without children must be a kind of outcast. A terrible void in their lives.

My life has been so full. Farrell and I have been together since we began college at the University of Oregon in the fall of 1984. We've been lovers since '92, when I gave her the Change. The girls were born in the spring of '95. We are a family in every sense of the word, accepted and cherished by our parents and siblings. Farrell's brother and sisters dote on their little nieces, and Desmond and Mairead -- my sibs -- are equally devoted. Even if none of them -- except Mairead, who is also a Changeling -- can figure out why Quinn and Maren are so precocious.

"You're very fortunate," the co-pilot said, briefly holding the girls' picture in front of the pilot's face before handing it back to me. The pilot grunted his approval.

"How bad was the fallout?" I asked, tucking the photograph away.

"South of Salt Lake," the pilot answered, "progressively worse all the way into Arizona almost to Mexico. Would've been more, but the bombing came late enough in the spring so a lot of the storms in from the west had already gone through."

I thought about Mormon families sickening and dying all across southern Utah. My mind conjured up a vision of a young woman standing beside a pair of small graves, her teeth loosened and her hair falling out, grieving for her lost children even as she herself died slowly. Dust blew out of crevices in the parched soil, flowing like water over her bare feet and around her bony ankles, disappearing into the withered dying grass of a small churchyard with too many fresh graves.

What an image. Sometimes I am one morbid little bloodsucker.

Unfortunately, that image was probably a lot more true than I wanted it to be. "It must have been horrible," was all I could say.

The pilot nodded. "It was. Most of us lost family. Some lost everything but their lives. Some of those lives weren't hardly worth living. Suicides went up alarmingly."

"Our faith sustains us," the co-pilot said, and sounded like he believed it.

"And President Gregorson," I added, and saw cynicism appear momentarily in their expressions. Maybe Richard took after his daddy. "Does Richard have kids?" I asked.

81

"A boy and a girl," the co-pilot replied, and, in response to my unasked question, "his parents were in Salt Lake when the war started. Richard's older brothers were almost school age. The Gregorsons were lucky to be there. Manti was well inside the fallout zone. Their families were wiped out with the rest of the town."

"Where were you two?" I asked.

"Hill Air Force Base, by Ogden," the pilot said, "both of us. Just kids ourselves." That must have been interesting, I thought, wondering how easy the Saint takeover of the base had been. That question would go unasked.

"Just about back to your truck," the co-pilot said, peering out the front windscreen.

What I could see of the terrain below looked familiar. "Put down facing east," I said, "on the north side of the road."

"Don't trust us, uh?" the pilot answered, with a grim smile, starting to bring the big gunship around and lower.

"Would you?" I asked. "We didn't ask to be confronted in Pendleton, and we don't like being kidnapped and threatened with death. All we want is to be left alone and get back together with our daughters."

"Can't argue with that," the captain said, dropping the Chinook slowly onto a wide flat spot alongside the road, not more than a hundred feet from where it'd been before. Dust and small bits of pumice billowed up around the long gunship as it settled solidly onto its wheels.

I stayed right with the pilot and co-pilot as they shut down the Chinook and exited the ship. Beckin and Richard stood beside Brone on the ramp, Beckin very close to Richard. He looked subdued, but no longer like his chimes were still ringing. The Chinook's two surviving crew members hopped off the ramp and stood beside it. They looked relieved to be out of the confining ship. They didn't take their eyes off Beckin, however.

When I reached Beckin, she gave me a little smile. "Can you disable the craft enough to render it inoperable but repaired easily, yet parts will still have to be brought here?"

"Sure," I replied, looking over her head, watching Garris set the Huey down a couple hundred feet to the west, in a cloud of dust far smaller than the Chinook had kicked up. The rotor thupped slowly to a halt, and Farrell jumped out, with Garris following. When she saw me watching Farrell, Beckin smiled again. She may not be exactly human, but Beckin has learned, and she doesn't miss much.

Garris stood quietly by the Huey for a few moments, while Farrell hiked off to fetch the truck after blowing me a kiss. When she was out of sight, Garris walked slowly toward us, hands in his pockets.

I lugged our ordnance bags out of the Chinook, then went back in and pulled a fire ax off the wall. After Garris' remark about bringing down a Chinook, I knew just what to do.

On the right rear third of the Chinook airframe, a series of steps ascends up the side to the front of the tail section. Each step is inset, with a cover that folds back when you push your foot in. I could have merely jumped up to the roof of the gunship, but instead I dutifully climbed to the front of the tail, holding the fire ax in one hand. Undoing the two snap-hasps securing the clamshell covers over the transmission, I exposed the tunnel that houses the big shafts that drive the rotors. The transmission, built to handle the two engines' combined six thousand-plus horsepower, seemed surprisingly small. I spit on my palms and went after it with the fire ax, vampire muscles cracking open the housing and trashing the internals in only a few blows. No more air time until a new transmission arrived.

I buttoned up the covers and leapt back down to the ground.

"You knew to do that," the Chinook's pilot said.

I nodded. "Sure. The U.S. Army still has plenty of Chinooks, even though Boeing Vertol doesn't make 'em anymore." No need to mention that I'd gotten the info on the transmission from Garris -- who grinned at me from over the two Saints' shoulders -- or that *my* Army wasn't in this timeline. "You can get a replacement unit in here, can't you?"

"Yeah, by tomorrow, probably, from Boise."

"No problem, then." As I spoke, Farrell and the truck appeared around the little knoll. She pulled slowly onto the pavement between the two helicopters and stopped. I ran to her, took her face in my hands, and gave her a long, deep kiss.

She responded appropriately for twenty seconds or so, then -- typical Gray -- said, "You look like shit, and I nearly popped you in the back when you ran up the front of that guy on the ramp. I had him all sighted in."

"And I love you, too, asshole," I said, smiling in spite of myself. I may disagree with Farrell on a regular basis, but staying mad at her for any length of time is something I've never been able to do.

"Yeah," she replied, and her copper eyes grew very soft, "there is that." She kissed me again. While there are all sorts of things vampires do well, kissing is right near the top, and Farrell's mouth is one of her best features -- except maybe when words come out. "So," she asked, glancing toward the Chinook, "is Beckin gonna whack Richard now?"

I followed her gaze and shrugged. "Dunno. She only roughed him up pretty good, when I thought she'd throw him over the side. Sometimes she's hard to figure."

"Yeah, but judging from the number of frequent flyers in about a one-mile stretch back there, Beckin hasn't altered her basic approach to life."

"No, and Brone is real scary when he gets moving."

Farrell laughed as she got out of the truck. "Sorta like Popeye in the old cartoons, after he gets his spinach, only without the hornpipe tune."

"And Bluto doesn't jump back up, like in the cartoons."

"No kiddin.' At the Shift Point, the guy was a juggernaut."

At the moment, the juggernaut sat nonchalantly on his butt on the Chinook's ramp, his hands clasped in his lap, watching the Mormons the way a well-trained guard dog watches captives. Shaking her head at Brone's ability to completely relax, Farrell slung her left arm around my shoulders, I put my right around her waist, and we walked slowly back to the Chinook. Once again, alive was good.

The expressions on the faces of the three Mormons as we approached were a pure delight, a blend of mild horror and incredulity. Not one of them appeared to be concerned about our immortal souls, either, though I thought the Chinook's co-pilot showed some interest in our immortal bodies. The old male 'hero sandwich' fantasy, maybe, with him between the two pieces of lesbian bread.

Richard's reaction to our obvious togetherness was brief and muted. Understandable. Priorities change when you're literally looking death in the face. He didn't beg or bluster, though, and he didn't flinch away from Beckin's ice-green gaze. He stood straight, ready to take whatever she dished out.

That probably saved his life.

"Your foolish pursuit of a false dream," Beckin began, addressing only Richard, "has caused the deaths of ten people today. I should send you to join them in whatever passes for your eternity. Instead, against my training, life experience, and better judgement, I give you your life, such as you make it from this point on." Her right hand flashed up from her waist, holding a silver ovoid from which snicked a thin, nastily-gleaming blade. A cunt-knife! The little shit. She'd had it the entire time.

"Do not disappoint me," Beckin continued, keeping the blade's end a few inches from Richard's nose. Her

85

next words included them all. "Repair your ship, return to your homeland, and consider the gift I have given you this day."

Richard's features were death-pale, but his eyes didn't waver. "We will," he replied, and his voice was very controlled and determined. I suspected he'd grown up a bit in the back of the Chinook, or at least been jarred into some heavy self-realization. Imminent death'll do that.

Farrell leaned around Beckin and rested a hand on Richard's shoulder. If possible, he grew even paler. "One more thing, kid," she said, grinning predatorily. "When you want somebody killed, always do it yourself. It saves time and prevents an uneasy conscience."

"Was that last sentence a Mark Twain quote?" I asked quietly, as she stepped back to my side.

"Almost sounded that way, didn't it?" she replied, snorting. "And there's one more thing we need to do, just in case these guys suffer an abrupt loss of intimidation." She turned toward the M-60 on the Chinook's rear ramp, stepped around Brone up beside it and braced her right hip against the barrel. Gripping it firmly with both hands, she bent it ninety degrees to her left, then released it and nodded to the watching Saints. "Don't try this at home, kids," she said, and dropped to the ground.

The milli-second look Beckin gave her would have taken the paint off a Bradley Fighting Vehicle, right down to the second layer of armor. Like us, Beckin doesn't like to put her talents on display -- except in suddenly lethal ways which leave no witnesses.

Beckin never missed a beat, though. "We will leave your weapons a half-mile down the road," she said to the Mormons. "By the time your ship is repaired, we will be well into the Valley."

"And the Compliance will have you," Richard said, with what looked and sounded like genuine concern. His earlier fear had washed away. He might still want what Beckin knew -- or our secrets -- but his scent bore no trace of anger, greed, or harbored revenge. Maybe Beckin should go into the forced maturation business.

"They will have no more inkling of us than is necessary," Beckin replied. "We need only to touch the eastern borders of the Valley, not penetrate deeply into its heart."

"Pray you don't end up in Salem," the Chinook pilot said. From his facial expression, if he'd been Catholic, he'd have crossed himself. Richard and the co-pilot looked the same.

"I appreciate your concern," Beckin said, "and I wish you good speed back to your lands. Do not spend my gift of life foolishly." Those final words were aimed more at Richard, I thought.

Brone got to his feet, and the four of us walked away, boots crunching in the pumice, Farrell carrying three .45s and a pair of old M-16s. Surprisingly, Garris followed us. "Got a minute, Major?" he asked, coming alongside me.

"Beckin, give me five minutes?" I asked, and she nodded curt assent.

Garris and I sauntered off to the north. "First," I said, "thanks for making our job easier in your ship." When he didn't respond right away, I looked slyly at him. "Richard seems to be shaping up some. You still heading for Portland, then, Captain Garris?"

"Yes, M'am," he replied, smiling, "but I think I might have underestimated the influence Richard's late close associates had on him. And your friend jerked loose a lot of comfortable assumptions he'd acquired over the years."

I nodded. "He's more adaptable than I thought."

"Oh, Richard's a smart boy. When he was a little kid, I always figured he'd be the one to sort of leaven the mix if his dad stayed in the Presidency. Richard's older brothers are the kind of people who get their throats cut in alleys, or shot in smoke-filled rooms -- well, *non*-smoke-filled rooms in this case -- but you get my drift. Anyway, punching all those tickets today might have got him back on track." Garris' smile turned sardonic. "Not that it matters to me. I'll be back in the real world again."

"Good luck," I said, "and thanks again."

"No problem. And, Major, if you would, could you show me that picture of your kids?"

Even in absentia, the girls were proving popular. Thinking about them, I felt a painful twist in my chest. Surviving getting dragged through trees hanging below a giant gunship had made me forget for a few minutes. "Sure," I said, getting out my wallet again, and sliding their photograph from its holder. "You'll notice their eyes are the same color as yours."

Garris looked up sharply before taking the picture from me. He held it in the palm of his left hand, and, as he examined Quinn and Maren's little smiling faces, his hand began to shake very slightly. His eyes misted.

"I should have known better than to do this," he said, his voice barely audible. He brushed away a tear.

"What's the matter?" I asked, puzzled, touching his arm.

"My wife and daughters were visiting her folks in San Diego..." He paused, gulped. "...when the bombs hit. I was in Portland. Don't know to this day whether they lived or died." He shook his head. His right fist clenched. "Nothing I could have done, but I'll never know, only hope it was quick." He gulped again, tapped the girls' picture.

"The oldest, Jenny, was about this age. Bree was two..." His voice trailed off.

"I'm so sorry," I said, ready to cry for his lost children, the earlier pain in my chest returning, intensified. Christ. Mormon kids, Garris' kids. Fucking Nixon. If the girls had been here now, I would've hugged them till they squealed.

Garris took a deep breath, composing himself. He handed the photo back to me, his eyes still wet. "Sorry," he said, sighing deeply, "it catches up with me sometimes."

"I understand," I mumbled, blinking back a tear myself as I put the girls' picture away again.

Then Garris said something that took me by surprise. "Who's the President now?"

"William Jefferson Clinton," I answered.

"Where's the Capital?"

I regarded him steadily, trying to decide whether or not to lie. But I found I couldn't lie to a man who'd lost his family under such horrible circumstances. "Washington, D.C.," I said.

A knowing light came into his eyes. "So Richard isn't right, but he's thinking in the right direction?"

"About what?"

"Don't play dumb, Major," Garris laughed. "Your buddy can't travel instantly from one place to another, but she can do something *like* that, can't she?"

"Something," I admitted.

"Tell me."

"What she does is go from one place to the *same* location in another, slightly-different history. *Our* Nixon didn't bomb Hanoi. There was no nuclear war. In the Seventies, we basically said the war was over, and pulled out of Vietnam."

"So my family..?"

"...didn't die, at least not that way, provided you married the same person and had the same children. And weren't killed in Vietnam yourself."

"Jesus. It gets complicated."

"Quickly," I replied, nodding.

"I won't tell anyone," he said, as we started back toward the helicopters and the truck.

"I'd appreciate that, Captain, but I wouldn't have told you if I'd thought you would. Beckin's people take a dim view of that information getting around. And you should understand that if they'd been in charge of things in Vietnam, the war would have lasted maybe a month, and they would've scorched Laos for even thinking about provisioning the Viet Cong. They can out-fight anything you or I have ever seen, and their ordnance matches their skills."

"Really?"

"Actually, I'm understating the reality. They almost come out of the womb with weaponry."

By then, we were within a hundred feet of the truck. Garris stopped, and we shook hands. "I meant that part about buying you a beer in Portland, Major," he said.

"I should buy, Captain. You made our job easier."

"Tell you what," he replied, grinning. "I'll flip you for it." Then his eyes turned serious, and his voice softer. "Take care of those little girls."

I could only nod around the lump in my throat, and I'm not sure I've ever felt sadder than I did watching Garris walk to his Huey, fire it up -- already warm -- and ascend into the blue sky. Everything that ever mattered to him had been lost. Only his honor and integrity remained. I wondered how in hell he'd managed to hold himself together this well, this long.

Now I'd never know. The four of us and the three Mormons stood alongside the road and watched the little gunship disappear. Even at a distance, I saw dismay on Richard's face, and I didn't think it involved just the disappearance of one of his father's helicopters. Garris must have been a family friend, and perhaps Richard's newly-minted conscience yanked on some mental chain at the off-hand way he'd treated his dad's buddy. Another thing I'd never know.

By the time we drove away, only Richard remained outside the Chinook. The pilot and co-pilot were doubtless on the radio with their parts order.

Beckin waved good-bye, which surprised me. When she saw my raised eyebrow, she said, "I feel sorry for him, in a way. He has a valuable trait -- ruthlessness -- without the wisdom to exercise it properly. In essence, he was willing to sacrifice the two of you to prove a point to himself. 'Showing off,' you would call it."

The *Siogi* are not herd creatures like us. Beckin seemed to be attempting to align her own intensely individual concept of inner honor and responsibility with our society's more group-oriented sense of ethical and moral behavior. "You're starting to act human, Beckin," I said, and Brone snorted from the front seat.

"'Beckin's got a boyfriend,'" Farrell sang.

Quick as thought, Beckin grabbed Farrell's right shoulder. "Speaking of showing off, *I* would not let normal folk see *my* power, as *you* did."

"Yeah, yeah, yeah," Farrell replied blithely, "and now I know where that metallic taste last night came from."

At Farrell's reference to the cunt-knife, Brone looked away. I couldn't decide if he was embarrassed or fighting laughter.

Beckin couldn't, either. She glanced at him for an instant, her features troubled, then turned back to Farrell, eyes narrowed. "I can only hope that your daughters are *ruined* by Morag."

That, I thought, would be an easy reach. The girls adored Morag, who was a powerful legend even among her own kind. Quinn and Maren would hang on her every word and deed.

And I missed them so.

CHAPTER EIGHTEEN

BUSTED

Pine Grove proved to be a small collection of well-cared-for buildings of indeterminate vintage, set in -- surprise -- a stand of mature Ponderosa pine. There was quite a lot of cinder block, mostly painted white. The mom-and-pop combination gas station, grocery, and bait shop looked as though it'd been there forever. As we climbed out of the truck onto the gravel parking lot, I saw that many of the signs on the building and in the windows pre-dated not just Nixon's nukes, but also World War II.

Once inside, the scents of decades of commerce permeated the interior of the store. Tobacco, coffee, licorice, buckwheat, and gunpowder all combined in a comfortable, homey blend of bygone Americana. Well, not so bygone in this rural outpost, maybe. I inhaled deeply, and felt about twenty years younger, the smell taking me back to
the little neighborhood groceries in Molalla, where I grew up, in the Willamette Valley.

Two small, dark kids watched us over the top of the counter, near the west wall of the store. Their interest, naturally enough, centered on Brone, and the closer he came, the bigger their eyes got. A slight, sinewy woman as dark as the kids, probably their mother, looked up and smiled at us as we came toward the counter. She scooped dried pine nuts from a jar into small bags, then folded small white labels over the ends of the bags before stapling them shut.

"Good day, travellers," she said in a friendly lilting voice, putting down the bags and screwing the lid back on the nuts. "How may I help you?" Her words lacked any of the displaced New Englander flatness of my valley speech. She'd spent her life here in this high country, where the influence of Irish and Basque

92

sheepherders had given the local spoken English a bit of flavor.

"Just some food and something to drink," I replied, removing my sunglasses. "I'm Megan Connolly." I held out my right hand.

"Louise Garmindia," she said, shaking my hand, her teeth flashing as brightly as her sea-green eyes, eyes a much darker green than Beckin's. "These are my children, Paul and Monette."

Brone reached down and shook hands with Paul and Monette, whose eyes stayed big as they looked at the size of the offered hand. Louise smiled over at Brone, seeing him for what he was, a big, friendly guy. She shook hands with Beckin and Farrell, and seemed unintimidated by the fact that even Beckin towered over her.

"Are you going on tonight?" Louise asked. It was pushing six o'clock by then.

"No," I answered, shaking my head, "we'll just pull off the road and doss down somewhere convenient."

"Oh, I see," she said, nodding, her gaze thoughtful. "Well, have a look 'round the store and see what you favor. Any questions, myself or the children will be glad to
answer." By then, Paul and Monette, putting their hands around Brone's right biceps, had discovered that four small hands couldn't reach the full distance. Kids always seem drawn to large men, and Brone's obvious approachability made him fair game. We all smiled at him, and I thought it just as well that the nice Garmindias hadn't seen him pitching Mormon bodies out of the Chinook.

"No complaints about selection, big guy," Farrell said, "since you're too busy making friends to help."

"It makes no difference," Brone replied, laughing as he lifted the kids up to sit one on each shoulder. Monette giggled, Paul tried to look unfrightened at the height, and I remembered the times Brone'd done the

93

same with Quinn and Maren. One more day, I reminded myself.

When I looked back at Louise, I saw speculation and concern in her eyes. Somehow she'd seen that brief thought of the girls flicker over my face, had known something wasn't quite right. She smiled reassuringly at me.

"We're going to meet our daughters tomorrow," I said in explanation. "They're about the same size as your children." Monette and Paul were now occupied with touching goods hanging from the ceiling, something they couldn't ordinarily do without a ladder, which probably wasn't allowed.

"I see," Louise replied, and her warm smile at Brone and her children seemed to fill the store. "Children are our greatest treasure."

Farrell and Beckin roamed around the place, examining the stock. I stayed by the cash register, talking with Louise. The federal government had the Mints up and running again, and she proudly showed me the new coins and bills that had been brought out from the Bank of Madras only a few days previously. Plates and dies must have been salvaged from somewhere. The bills and coinage were the same as ours, though the coins all had '1999' stamped on them.

"Where's the federal government headquartered?" I asked, willing to show my ignorance in this out-of-the-way spot.

"St. Louis," Louise said, grinning at the similarity to her own name. I saw the question in her eyes, though, wondering why I wouldn't know where the Capital was, but she was too polite to ask.

After we'd paid for our collection of nuts, dried fruit, jerky, and coarse bread, Louise handed us our change and said, "You may stay the night in our barn, and for supper with us, if you wish. Michael and the crew will be in with the flocks shortly, and I know they would love to talk with people from the outside world." As she spoke, she smiled again at Brone and the children, who were now seeing how long Monette and Paul could hang from Brone's outstretched arms. He pretended to grunt from the effort, the big faker.

"That's very kind, Louise. We'd love to," I said, accepting for all of us.

The words were scarcely out of my mouth when an older woman, resembling Louise but slightly taller, stepped almost silently through the curtain covering the door from the living quarters at the rear of the store. Had I not seen her enter, I wouldn't have known she was there.

Standing stock still, she slowly let her gaze travel around the room, from her left to her right. It lingered on Farrell, and she smiled with cold satisfaction. Then, still with the barest of sounds, almost without appearing to take steps, she glided to Louise's side. Louise regarded her with mild concern. "Mother..?" she began to ask.

"My nose did not betray me," the older woman said, clutching Louise's left arm with slim, lovely hands. Her voice was even more melodious than her daughter's. Her cold gaze shifted to me. "Vampyrs," she said, smiling, displaying perfectly white, perfectly even, and rather sharp teeth.

I smiled back. Not much else I could do. We were busted.

Werewolves got the best noses.

CHAPTER NINETEEN

PACKED

We'd had the advantage of Louise. Farrell and I had met werewolves previously, so we knew. And they were *all* werewolves, of course. Both the kids, too. Whatever little genetic bit creates lycanthropy, it's a dominant. Louise had realized that Beckin, Farrell and I were something odd the moment we entered the store. She just hadn't known *what*. Her mother, Marie, over a hundred years old, *had* known. She'd met our kind before, if not Beckin's.

She'd met John Tierney, our boss.

"The year was 1914," Marie said, brushing wings of lustrous grey-shot black hair back from her face. She smiled at the memory. "I was only twenty, had just arrived in the United States from Spain a year earlier, and was working in a bordello in Pendleton..."

"*Mother*!" Louise said, practically slamming a hand over Marie's mouth. Monette and Paul, seated on the counter next to Brone, leaned in a little closer, recognizing the 'not for little ears' signals.

Marie shot her daughter a glance of pitying disdain. "Louise, your children cannot be what we are and remain innocent much longer." She patted Monette and Paul on their heads. "I will explain later, my darlings, and your mother can listen so she may approve my words."

No one noticed that Farrell and I were leaning in closer, too, hoping to get teasing rights on John. Our John Tierney would have a common history with Marie's John Tierney until 1970, quite probably.

A bordello, huh?

Unfortunately, they'd met in a drygoods store, not the bordello, and John had been reserved and proper, the Victorian gentleman he still mostly is. He'd bought Marie lunch, and she still had the impression she'd talked much more about herself than John had about himself. Farrell and I assured her that hadn't changed, either. He's still tight-lipped. "Did he ever find his great love, the one who gave him...whatever it is you call it?" Marie asked.

"The Change," Farrell replied.

"Deirdre," I added.

Marie shook her head. "He was so very sad, my heart went out to him." She continued shaking her head, her lips pursed and her eyes cast down. "Such a handsome man, too."

"They are together now," Beckin said, all serious. She considers Deirdre and John the perfect lovers, despite the nineteen hundred year age difference. The absolute hellishness of Deirdre's first twenty-five years give her a sort of elvish appeal, I'm sure, and Beckin's read all the plays and legends of Deirdre of the Sorrows. The present reality of Deirdre, her cold regal beauty alloyed with equal parts ambition and ruthlessness, readily cross-references with *Siog* mind-sets, too. It's still pretty sappy for Beckin, even though she doesn't exactly wear her heart on her sleeve.

The news about John and Deirdre perked Marie right up. "Good. Almost I could see myself with him. He was so handsome!"

Monette and Paul were nearly ready to topple off the counter by now, stretching as close as they could so as not to miss a single word. Louise looked from them to her mother, exasperation on her features.

But Marie wouldn't be quelled, holding court with a new audience, her gestures fluid, graceful, and very Latin. We were captivated, even Beckin, whose experience with cultures other than ours and hers was pretty much limited to stalking and killing.

After spending far more time on John than I felt necessary, with Farrell and that damned Beckin giving me knowing looks -- for having slept with him before he re-found Deirdre -- finally Marie ran down on the subject. She turned to Beckin and said, "I know what *they* are, but you do not smell the same. What sort of person are you, if I may be so presumptuous?"

"I am one of the *Siogi*," Beckin replied. "In your mythology, we are the Fallen Angels, who rebelled against Heaven's rule, and fled to another place in the corridors of time, where we could be safe and lead the lives we choose."

"You were not cast down?" Marie asked, twinkling at Beckin, delighted with this new thing.

Beckin shook her head. "No. As I understand the process, it was more like sideways. It all happened thousands of years ago, well before my birth, though some who lived then live still."

I remembered one of those, Desleen the Eternal, who'd been visiting the School of Death when we were first there, before the girls were born. Desleen, decanted in a laboratory on the far side of the Moon, without benefit of mother or father, one of several hundred identical others. I recalled a tall, slender form of infinite grace, and green eyes in whose depths shone something colder than Hell and older than dirt.

Marie considered Beckin's words for a few long moments, nodding and smiling to herself. Then it was Brone's turn. "And you, sir, whose heart matches his size. You appear to be merely a large human, but the company which you keep suggests otherwise."

Brone was ready. "I am but a simple warrior of rural background, my dear lady, sworn to protect these young women from those evildoers who would place obstacles on the road of their lives."

"Oh, *brother*!" Farrell and I said in unison.

Marie accepted Brone's explanation without question, saying only that it was good to see such a helpful attitude on the part of one so young. This was said with her tongue lodged firmly in her cheek, and with a pointed glance at her small grandchildren. Brone the good example.

By then it was closing time. Louise locked the front door and flipped the Open/Closed sign around, mentioning that if anyone needed something bad enough, they would know where to find the Garmindias.

"Is there something we may do to earn our meals and lodging, Louise?" Beckin asked, as we walked through a small storage area between the store and the large Garmindia kitchen.

"There's wood to be split and stacked," Marie said, shutting the door to the store, chuckling as she spoke.

"*Mother*," Louise said again, in a more ominous tone.

"That sounds fine," Beckin said, resting her fingertips on Louise's arm in reassurance. "It's settled, then."

Farrell and I exchanged knowing glances. Marie reminded me entirely too much of my own grandmother, Rose Connolly, who would rule the world if she could muster the votes or the firepower. Plus, she treats me as though Farrell and I were switched at birth, and Farrell is the real granddaughter. Farrell, of course, thinks this is hilarious, but it just pisses me off. Rose is wonderful to the girls, though, so I bite my tongue and smile till it hurts for their sakes.

The Garmindia kitchen proved to be an Old World delight, high-ceilinged, with big windows facing east into the sunrise. Heavy carved wooden shelves were laden with colorful crockery, bowls, and vases that had to have come from Spain, and drying herbs and vegetables hung from pegs set in the wall-beam above the windows. On the left, a french door, its upper half open, revealed an arbor-shaded brick patio, cool and inviting. Thick knotted grape vines twined up the support posts before spreading across the arbor itself, and rectangular terra cota planters filled with bright spring flowers were scattered around the periphery in the more sunlit areas.

"That looks like a nice retreat on a warm day," I said to Louise, nodding toward the patio.

"Warm nights, also," she replied. "The brick is very cool on one's belly after a run."

Her easy reference to her wolf-form jarred me momentarily. A gut-level reaction. Our condition has

99

such a matter-of-fact scientific explanation that it seems somehow easier to accept. Werewolves, harking back to ancient primate campfire fears, are another thing entirely. The deadly creature lurking just outside the circle of firelight, waiting in the darkness, eyes aglow in the light of dying embers.

They probably feel the same way about us. As Farrell would say, it's a point-of-view thing.

None of those things affected the simple beauty and functionality of that charming kitchen, however. After a day featuring more excitement than I cared to think about, a true oasis of calm was good to find. I wished I could take off my hiking boots and wiggle my bare toes on the smooth worn granite flagging of the floor. From the way Farrell's shoulders relaxed when she entered the room, she felt the same. I put my hands on her shoulders, kneaded her neck with my thumbs. "Nice, huh?" I murmured in her right ear, as her gaze traveled over the flower-emblazoned tiles of the countertops and the thick white ceiling beams.

"Better than that," she replied. "This is the most peaceful place I've seen in a while. The only way it could improve would be if the girls walked through the door."

"Tomorrow, my dear," I said, running my right index fingertip down the back of her ear. "Right now, we have wood to split." To my left, I caught Marie's warm chuckle, a more appreciative sound than my grandmother would have made. Rose doesn't approve of public displays of affection unless she's making them.

"You may move your truck around to the rear of the house," Louise said, then asked Beckin, "Do you have luggage?"

Beckin grinned, laughing. "Underwear, a few outer garments, weapons," she paused, grinned even wider at Brone, then continued, "*treats* for Brone."

Brone, who I didn't think could, looked abject and hurt for an eyeblink, but no one was fooled. Farrell shook her head at him, and pulled at my arm. "C'mon,

100

Megs," she said, "we need to move the truck around and unload our stuff."

We walked out through the patio, which felt as inviting as it looked. Birds flitted around in the overhead vines, chirping happily, late-day breezes softly stirred the leaves, and I just wanted to plop down in a chair and veg out. An afternoon of getting dragged through treetops and pitching people out of helicopters always does that to me.

Plopping wasn't going to happen anytime soon. Farrell had been awfully quiet -- for her -- since we'd been back on terra firma. When Farrell gets quiet, I pay attention. Especially when the smile lines around her mouth get tight.

"So, what's up, Gray?" I asked, when we were fully into the sunlight and heading around the side of the store. "You think you were gonna lose me?"

In the lowering sun, her copper eyes were red-gold, and my breath caught. Even though we're together almost constantly, when she turns the full power of her physical presence in my direction, she just rocks me right down to the soles of my feet. The rest of the world clicked off, leaving only the two of us. "Yeah," she replied, her voice as deep as Brone's, and filled with something akin to pain. She didn't blink, and her serious gaze held steady.

"Oh, *Farrell*!" I said, and pulled her to me, wrapping my arms tightly around her, nearly getting crushed in return.

We stood for a long minute, trying to blend into one another. "I will *never* leave you," I whispered, nibbling on her left earlobe, "at least not without better special effects than a tree."

She gave a loud sniff, and squeezed harder. "Our whole fucking *life* is a special effect."

'Life,' she'd said, not 'lives.' I liked that, the implied togetherness. "I love you so much," I said, pressing her even closer, feeling happier than at any time since this whole mess began, and wishing there weren't any clothes between us.

And that the girls were here.

Always that, just now.

CHAPTER TWENTY

EARNING OUR KEEP

The stack of Ponderosa rounds, each sixteen-inch round about two feet in diameter, looked daunting. "So short," Brone said, picking up a round and examining it, turning it in his big hands. In Eireann Mor, heating is done almost entirely by electricity generated by Starcore units, so fires are decorative and traditional only, and the chunks of wood burned are longer to fit their huge stone fireplaces.

Like ours, *Siog* bodies have the ability to simply adjust heat production to fit the circumstances. A *Siog* can comfortably run nude through a winter storm, as long as their fuel supply holds out. In the home, they tend to wear either shorts or nothing. We stripped down to shorts and sports bras and went to work. Air temperature was still in the eighties, and vampire exertion needs cooling.

Brone elected to use the splitting maul, a ten-pounder with a steel handle. I would throw a round to Beckin, she'd position it, and Brone would split it with a single roundhouse overhead swing. Then Beckin would rotate the halves for another pair of swings, throwing the split pieces to Farrell, who stacked them in tidy cords.

The wood flew. We did the entire pile -- roughly ten cord -- in a little over an hour, moving as rapidly as possible, grabbing water when we could, and sweating like draft horses.

At the end, our clothes were soaked, and my boots squished with sweat, almost as though I'd walked through a creek. I looked over at Farrell, standing by the freshly-stacked wood. She gleamed like oiled mahogany that had somehow been granted life and movement. My libido took a nice little hop up the lust-ladder at the sight of her.

Then my awareness expanded away from Farrell and what we'd been doing, and I saw a group of people standing in a line between us and the back of the house. Four men and one woman wearing loose dark work clothes and heavy boots, with scarfs around their necks and jaunty blue berets perched on their heads. More Basques, all werewolves, with five lanky concerned-looking Aussie sheepdogs among them, crouched low against the dusty ground.

The rest of the pack had come home.

As our two groups exchanged tentative nods and smiles, and Brone wiped his hands on his pants, Marie stepped out of the house and spoke loudly to the assembled Basques. I caught the word "vampyrs," but the rest was completely unintelligible. I have German, Arabic, some Spanish, and more dialects of Gaelic than currently exist, but nothing of whatever these people spoke, apparently Basque.

Even without knowledge, understanding was possible. Marie's meaning left no doubt it was time to quit staring at the guests, get cleaned up, and help with dinner. Five pairs of feet shuffled in the dust, punctuated by soft laughter, shrugs, and gentle smiles. They were on familiar territory -- Marie's.

The oldest of the men, who must be Marie's husband and Louise's father, came forward a few steps and bowed to us. "I am Henri Barinaga. You have doubtless met the truly powerful persons amongst us." Here he indicated Marie with one thick-fingered hand while pulling on his waxed black mustache with the other, grinning wickedly. "Besides myself, these other lesser beings are my son-in-law Michael, his brothers Daniel and Jean, and our younger daughter Corinne."

Michael, Daniel, and Jean Garmindia were all olive-skinned, auburn-haired, and freckled -- though nowhere nearly as freckled as me. Michael was marginally the cutest. Corinne favored her father more than Louise did, but was still recognizable as Louise's sister, with the same deep green eyes, black hair, and skin burned even darker by the high mountain sun.

We introduced ourselves and shook hands all around, the men -- except for Henri -- doing their best not to be overwhelmed by Brone. Corinne lingered a bit with Farrell, but her sensitive nose must have told her how it was with Farrell and me. She gave me a half-inquisitive piercing look when she shook my hand, and I flicked her a private grin. No baby werewolf would be hunting in my preserve.

With introductions complete, Henri examined the rows of neatly-stacked pine, emitting a low whistle as he walked the length of the corded wood, still tugging on his mustache. Turning to us, he spread his arms wide. "If you would care to spend another day here, we have more wood which could easily be brought in from our higher groves." His eyebrows rose as he finished speaking, and he hooked his thumbs expectantly in his belt.

Farrell shook her head, sending a sun-haloed shower of sweat onto the dry needle-strewn ground. "Huh-uh. And if you had to feed us for another day..."

"...it might be cheaper to split the wood yourself," I finished for her.

Brone retrieved his T-shirt from where he'd hung it on a young pine. Displaying a broad expanse of teeth as he slipped it over his massive torso, he said, "Speaking frankly, I am quite hungry just now."

"In all your life," Beckin said, grinning up at Brone, "there has never been a time when you were not hungry." There had never been a point in either of their lives when they hadn't known one another, either. Brone loved Beckin with all his heart. I saw that total devotion in his eyes as he returned her grin. Choosing a mortal lover was something few *Siogi* ever did, and then it was *Siog* males and normal females, with the result of that unhappy pairing either a broken heart or a rare halfling child belonging to neither world. And sometimes, of course, both, though the *Siogi* utilized halflings to serve in other timelines, since they typically lacked the distinctive green eyes.

But a Berzerk and a *Siog* would be an unlikely thing, so Brone and Beckin might never be more than what they were, no matter how much Brone desired it. A pity, I thought, watching them.

Henri took our responses as negative. He shrugged. "Ten cord is quite enough in exchange for a single meal, no matter how gargantuan the appetites, and your swiftness was amazing to behold." The other Basques nodded to emphasize his point.

"Where can we bathe?" Farrell asked. She'd put her T-shirt back on, too, to the disappointment of the Garmindia brothers and Corinne, who'd probably never seen muscles like hers under skin that perfect.

"Ahhh," Henri said, pursing his lips and looking thoughtful. He cradled his chin in one hand, gazing up into the Ponderosa limbs.

"We could all go to the stream, Father," Corinne said sweetly, with a quick glance at Farrell, "the deep hole below the smaller falls." The expression of innocence on her brown features was so patently obvious that even Beckin looked amused, and her father snorted as he saw it.

"Yes, of course," he said, shaking his head, his eyes twinkling. "I should have thought of that. I must be growing old." Yeah, sure. Henri appeared about fifty, only
his salt-and-pepper chin beard displaying any grey, but he could easily be twice that. I knew werewolves commonly lived in excess of a hundred-fifty years.

With that settled, the four of us rummaged through our bags for soap and some clean clothes, while the Basques went to their living quarters and collected their own things. I heard the children run to meet Michael with happy laughter.

"Good thing we brought so much stuff," Farrell remarked as she pulled out her toiletries kit.

I jerked a thumb toward Beckin, who already had her own things and stood impatiently waiting for us.

"Beckin insisted. 'Something might happen,' you'll remember her saying."

"Something sure as hell did," Farrell replied, snorting. "Those kids had better be all right." The last muttered under her breath.

A tiny frown creased Beckin's brows. I knew it wasn't because she was uncertain about Quinn and Maren. No, it was Farrell's concern and irritation. Guilt is not a big factor in *Siogi* lifestyles, but Beckin had spent enough time around -- and in -- us, so that she understood how worried we were about the girls. No *Siog* would be. They were with Morag; there wasn't any problem. We would be reunited tomorrow in North Cedar. End of story. We need to get clean and eat now.

"Hurry," Beckin said, as if reading my thoughts, "or I shall starve before we reach the bathing pool."

From the other side of the truck, I heard Brone's deep laugh. "It's *patience* that's the virtue," he said, "*not* impatience." He tucked his toothbrush behind his right ear, tossed his soap in the air, then his shampoo, and began juggling the two, grinning over the truck bed at Beckin.

Watching them, Farrell and I laughed.

Beckin glared at him and then us. "I do hope I am projecting an aura of resignation and exasperation," she said tersely.

"We're ready now," I said, fishing my shower stuff from the farthest corner of my bag.

"Big and slow, the lot of you," Beckin replied, stomping off to the patio, where she flopped down in a chair to wait for the Basques, sticking her tongue out at us as we sauntered toward her. Then her head snapped in the direction of the french door, and I saw her nostrils widen. An instant later, I smelled it, too. *Lamb*, and some spices I didn't recognize, which didn't keep my mouth from watering. At my side, Farrell gave a little groan of pleasure as the rich scent reached her, and Brone's pace sped up noticeably.

All four of us probably would have hit the kitchen door together, if Marie hadn't suddenly appeared in the opening. She menacingly waved a ladle sturdy enough to fracture the average skull, and said, "Nothing is ready except the bread, and you will get not a single bite until you are clean and the tables are set." She called back into the kitchen. "Corinne, our guests are ready for their baths!"

On cue, Corinne came up behind her mother, the smile on her face one I recognized from my little sister, that of the indulgent child humoring the demanding parent. She wore shorts, sandals, and a beige man's shirt which seemed to have lost all but the most strategic buttons. "Well, I'm ready, Mother," Corinne said, all chipper and bubbly.

Who would ever have thought a perky kid werewolf could be irritating? Behind her back, I poked Farrell, and was rewarded with a sullen grunt.

Corinne bounced out the door, soapdish in one hand and rolled-up towel under an arm. As she led us toward the smaller barn, her father and the Garmindia brothers fell in alongside. Nine of us altogether, so it had better be a large pool. And no one seemed to have a swimming suit. Werewolves apparently had no nudity problems.

"The children wanted to come, also," Henri said, double-timing along the well-worn trail between the two barns, "but I refused." He smiled up at Brone. "Hero worship can only go so far. I assured them that helping with setting the table would be more useful." He had on only a pair of shorts, sandals on his feet, and his torso was nearly hairless, just a light down on his chest. The Garmindias looked to be the same, though they all wore shirts. Not at all what I'd expected. Werewolves ought to be hairy even in their human forms, right? They *were* lean and sinewy, although Corinne managed some intriguing concavities and convexities in the correct locations. For a small girl, she was close to perfection, butter-smooth and glowing with health. And, as Farrell

108

would have put it, she smelled needful. I wondered how werewolves keep secrets from one another, and decided that they didn't -- the ultimate open society, where all wants and needs were posted on the olfactory Internet.

We Changed are virtually the same, of course, except that we don't pack up in any numbers, traveling usually in no more than twos or threes. Deirdre, in fact, had been basically alone except for sexual companions for nearly two thousand years, and John had been chaste and solitary for over seventy. Until I came into his life, when we buried that seventy years in one night. As I remember -- and we have no choice on memory -- several *deep* burials.

The trail wound across a broad shaded meadow, down a fenced aisleway with filled sheep pens on either sides. No dogs were in evidence around the bleating hundreds of wooly bodies, and predators -- except perhaps cougars -- would never consider trespassing on werewolf lands. These sheep were likely the safest in the world. There probably wasn't even a coyote within thirty miles.

Seeing us looking at the sheep, Henri said, "In another week, two at the most, the snow will be off, and we will move the flocks up to the high pastures. These four youngsters will spend the summer reading and carving flutes." He made it sound confining and dull.

"We will be *free*!" Corinne said, raising a fist, and, in that moment, walking beside us, her features were as wild as any beast's. For werewolves, the exile of the shepherd, the clean aching loneliness, would never be. The constraints of human society would lie far below the mountain meadows. Open to the sky and the stars, they could lead the life they were meant to, the life they chose. We should all be so lucky.

"Your mother and I shall visit as often as possible," Henri replied, and in his eyes I saw fond memories of his own isolation in the fastness of the high country. And yearning showed there, too, the desire to shrug off humanity and run free as the wind. I wondered how often they took wolf-form, how truly different it must feel.

The only other werewolves Farrell and I had known were a Bell Canada installer and an Irish cardiologist, both of whom we'd met in Saudi Arabia. Louis Bergeron's family owned a Christmas tree farm in Quebec, but Jim Skahan's people lived in house-bound Dublin. Neither of them had talked much about their lycanthropy, though we'd seen them as wolves.

So I didn't ask, figuring that could wait until a better time, and we quick-stepped along the trail, which now began to angle downward. In the distance, I could hear rushing water, both the muted roar of spring run-off sluicing around boulders and hissing descents over ledges of old granite and sandstone. A line of Aspen and puckerbrush showed ahead of us, filling a wide, shallow gully running downslope west to east.

The closer we came to the stream, the more powerful it sounded, and I could clearly hear a series of short falls stair-stepping along its course. The evening air grew more cool and humid, and in that moisture the smell of sulfur and iron stood out. Somewhere in the stream must be natural hot springs.

The trail entered the brush and trees. Grass appeared on its margins, and patches of rich black earth, damp this close to water. In those damp, shaded bare spots were the imprints of large canine paws, far too big to be coyotes. Not a lot of doubt on the origin of those. Corinne smiled at me when she saw me notice the prints, a proud smile that said 'I made some of those, and you can't.'

Shape-shifter brat, I thought, but refrained from giving her an 'I'll never get old' smile. That would be mean, we were guests, and Corinne should be celebrating her supple, youthful beauty. She certainly caught the eye, and I'd bet she was just as arresting in her other form.

Their bathing pool, when it finally appeared, across a short stretch of exposed sandstone, lay below a broad

110

ledge of weathered granite. The stream spread out into a transparent veil of shimmering water that fell smoothly into the twenty-foot-wide pool. The hot springs apparently lay under the edges of the granite, and steaming water slid over yellowed rocks into the pool, mixing evenly with the colder water of the falls.

"Oh, wow," Farrell said, yanking off her boots, and piling her clean clothes on top of them. I followed suit, shucking my T-shirt, bra, and shorts almost as fast as she and Beckin. Quick as we were, the Barinagas and Garmindias were quicker, all of them in the water before us. Brone was slowest, taking his time, laughing at our haste.

Beckin and I walked slowly into the water, maintaining some dignity and grace, but Farrell sprang twenty feet into the air with an exultant whoop, and cannon-balled into the very center of the pool. The resulting wave reached mine and Beckin's knees, and swamped the werewolves completely.

None of it kept Corinne's hungry eyes off Farrell, however. When she'd blinked away the water, still half-submerged, Corinne darted a glance at me. I shrugged and grinned, and her face colored under her tan.

"Naughty little thing, isn't she?" Beckin whispered, but there was speculation in both her green gaze and her thin smile. Farrell had corrupted Beckin far more thoroughly than *Siog* society ever had, even though mature *Siogi* are mostly as horny as dolphins.

"As naughty as you, you think?" I asked quietly, letting my long look slide down her nude slimness.

"Perhaps," Beckin replied, giving me a smug, haughty expression. "Just maybe."

The little elf turd.

"That's enough," Brone said from behind us, with a rumbling laugh, and pushed us both headfirst into the pool.

Without any dignity or grace whatsoever.

CHAPTER TWENTY-ONE

NAUGHTINESS

The warm waters of the pool were so restorative, so peaceful and relaxing, that I even forgot about Quinn and Maren for a while. I lay on my back in the shallows of the big sandstone bowl, one hand touching Farrell, my half-open eyes on the deep blue sky overhead, and went totally boneless. The Need, fed heavily only a few hours ago, nearly disappeared.

Only mild hunger from our wood-splitting session kept me awake. That, and keeping track of Corinne's gradual progress around the edge of the pool in Farrell's direction. We'd all soaped and shampooed when Beckin and I recovered from Brone's unceremonious dunking, and now, except for the cascading water and the chiming of Aspen leaves, total silence reigned.

Corinne was easily as shameless as Farrell, however, and no one in the pool missed her slow approach. So intent was she, however, that she didn't notice Beckin slipping up behind her. Corinne had just begun to trail the fingertips of her right hand along Farrell's left arm -- with every eye, except maybe Brone's, surreptitiously on her -- when Beckin curled both arms around Corinne's middle and pulled her backward into a tight embrace.

The contrast between Corinne's look of utter surprise and the expression of exultant delight on Beckin's face was worth more than the price, whatever that might be. Beckin wrapped her legs and arms around Corinne, pinning her helplessly, and nuzzled Corinne's neck while Corinne struggled in vain to free herself.

"Relax, little one," Beckin murmured in Corinne's ear, letting the tip of her tongue trail over Corinne's jawline as the young werewolf twisted and fought. "You will find me not a bad second choice -- and a kind mistress." She winked at Henri and the Garmindias as she said it, though, then winked her other eye at Brone and us.

"Let me *go*!" Corinne growled, trying to dislodge Beckin's iron grip, but even I could see that her heart wasn't really in it. Few would be at this point, with every long inch of warm, slick Beckin pressed against them, and a sneaky little grin of pleasure began to appear on Corinne's brown features. She quit spluttering, too.

When he saw that, Henri released his held-back amusement in a full-blown bellow of laughter. "A pity you cannot stay longer, Lady Gilmer," he said, climbing from the water and shaking himself. "Your methods of discipline seem far more effective than any tried by her mother or father." He turned to the Garmindias, who looked -- at least Daniel and Jean -- as though they'd be drawing straws to see who'd be next in line for Beckin's discipline. "Don't you agree, lads?"

Nods all around, but Daniel and Jean didn't look up at him. They had better things to occupy their eyes.

And when Farrell rolled to her left, gently gripped Corinne's round chin with her right hand, and kissed Corinne long and thoroughly, the temperature of the pool seemed to rise several degrees.

I looked over at Brone. "Do you think it's something in the water?" I asked.

Pretending to be puzzled, he shook his head. "Maybe. I know it's not something in the stomach." He heaved himself to his feet in a single fluid motion, water sheeting down a body that seemed to have more commonality with the stone under our feet than humanity. It's easy to forget how freakin' *big* he is until he's standing over you while you're lying down. And even half-erect, his cock matched the rest of him.

Brone led the way back to the house after we all dressed, the Basques following him like Lilliputians behind Gulliver. Corinne stayed quiet the whole time, padding along, her head down. A lesson learned, perhaps, though I wasn't willing to bet on that.

"Quite a show back there, lover," I said to Farrell, as we walked along side-by-side, Beckin close in front of us, a ways behind the others.

"I doubt we did much good," she replied, her eyes thoughtful. "The kid's got a nice mouth, though." She paused for a moment, still thinking, then added, "I suppose that would be bestiality."

"Better than that," Beckin snickered.

"I am surrounded by perverts," I said, wishing I weren't too close to flick them with my wet towel.

"As if!" they answered together.

"Worse yet, *Valley* perverts."

From farther up the trail, hearing our laughter, Corinne looked back over her shoulder. Her smile held no element of contrition, only warm invitation.

"We seem to stir up evil wherever we go," Beckin observed, sighing.

"From here," Farrell replied, "evil looks mighty sweet."

I scooped up a broken Aspen branch from beside the trail, and swatted both of them on their butts. "Food, sleep, duty, our children," I reminded them.

"You're no fun," Farrell said, massaging her rear.

"And *you* have a short memory," I retorted.

"*I* do not," Beckin said, reaching up and touching my face, her voice even more throaty than usual.

With these two, this conversation could only go in one direction. I shut the hell up.

CHAPTER TWENTY-TWO

BELLYS AND SOULS

When we arrived back at the house, a dark green Chevy pickup from the mid-fifties sat beside our Army truck. The Chevy hadn't been there long. The engine still pinged and popped as it cooled.

I made out the spindly silhouette of a tall man in a dark suit under the grape arbor, holding a wine glass. The Basques clustered around him, smiling, and Henri was speaking -- in Basque. This wasn't a customer, then, but a friend or acquaintance, perhaps someone invited for dinner. Brone was nowhere to be seen. Probably the kitchen had claimed him.

As we got closer to the group, the man looked politely toward us, his features so extraordinary that my mind barely registered that a Roman collar circled his thin neck. Gaunt and spare, all human frailty had been burned away from that face, distilled down to barest necessity. It held nothing extra, a face from Dachau or Bergen-Belsen, but without fear or deprivation. Anchorite hermits in their desert caves must've looked like this. Brown eyes, glowing with a holy light, seemed to reach out and touch my soul.

I stopped in my tracks, my feet grinding to a halt. Beckin and Farrell moved closer to me. They felt it too.

"Ah!" Henri said cheerfully, his wave encompassing the three of us. "Here are our other guests. Come, ladies, and meet Father Simon Ibarra, our spiritual leader."

Father Ibarra stepped out from under the arbor, his right hand extended, his features blue-jawed despite signs of a recent shave. He smiled, and when he did so, all the humanity life and time had scoured from him flooded back. The world became a safer and more friendly place. At my side, Beckin relaxed almost audibly.

I took his bony hand gingerly, thinking how easily-broken this sticks-and-wire man must be, and found it strong, resilient, and warm, iron under scant flesh. He sensed my surprise; his eyes sparkled with amusement. "A pleasure to meet you," he said, inclining his head, his voice as deep and resonant as that of any tent preacher.

Watching him shake hands with Farrell and Beckin, I imagined Abraham Lincoln had moved and sounded like this, a man immeasurably human yet formed of sharp contrasts: black and white, warm and cool, skeletal and strong. Even Father Ibarra's short coarse hair had greyed uniformly, a perfect blend of white and black. In his tailored clerical garb, any holy Order would have been pleased to use him for a recruiting poster. Provided they regularly recruited werewolves, that is.

For he was. Despite his height, no more than a hundred-sixty pounds clung to his bony frame, roughly what Henri weighed, though Father Ibarra overtopped Henri by more than half a head. Even lycanthropy had limits. Mass was mass, whether wolf or human. Marie, Louise, or Corinne, at perhaps a hundred-twenty max, would still be good-sized wolves, but I suspected the upper size limit couldn't be much over one-fifty. Certainly no one in this bunch weighed much more than that, and Louis Bergeron hadn't, either.

So the attenuated Father Ibarra fell neatly within the physical guidelines, if not the usual job description. Well, he *was* rural, and presumably he *had* a flock, just not the same sort of flock as the Barinagas and Garmindias. Father Ibarra had just discovered that Beckin and Brone's society held no Christians, when Marie and Louise, followed by Brone, wheeled out the evening meal, Monette and Paul tripping alongside, holding onto the edges of the cart Brone alternately pushed and lifted out the door and over the patio bricks.

"Ah!" Marie said, steam from the open pan she held drifting up in front her of face. "I thought I caught the scent of a theological discussion. Remember, Father Simon, you mustn't offend our guests until after the meal, when all the bellies are filled and at least the first three bottles of wine are emptied."

Everyone gravitated to three tables which had been pushed together to make enough room for fourteen people. Three overlapped checkered tablecloths covered the tables. Brone placed everything from the cart on the middle table, a covered salmon dish of some sort in a large Pyrex pan, three long loaves of french bread still warm from the oven, a huge salad, and six bottles of unlabeled red wine. Marie sat her pan beside Brone's, and the combined smells of lamb and salmon drove my tastebuds wild.

"We have no Hake here," Marie said, "so we have Salmon *koxkera* instead, but Salmon is an acceptable substitute, I'm certain you will agree."

We all sat down quickly and eagerly. "I will say a small grace in *Euskera*," Father Simon said, "the native tongue of our people." Everyone bowed their heads, even Beckin and Brone, and Father Simon was mercifully brief. I think I recognized the word 'Jesus,' but the rest of the prayer was a mystery.

We fell to like famished sailors.

"This is delicious," Beckin said, after her first bite of lamb, and Louise and Marie smiled in graceful acknowledgment. *Siogi* cuisine is not heavy on spices, and Beckin had been stunned by the ethnic foods we'd introduced her to when she first arrived in our Oregon.

Brone sat at one end of the table, Father Ibarra at the other. Monette, Paul, Beckin, Louise and Michael were at Brone's end, the kids right next to him, watching his every move and chattering like magpies in between bites. I watched them in silent longing, missing Quinn and Maren even as I enjoyed the two little werewolves.

At our end of the table, Farrell and I sat on either side of Father Ibarra, with Corinne next to Farrell. So close to the priest, Corinne minded her manners, eating daintily and making small talk. Father Ibarra missed nothing, not a word or nuance, and Corinne must be well aware of that. So we ate and chatted, with my

117

Catholicism and Farrell's Episcopalian childhood getting good marks.

"Your daughters are as you are?" Father Ibarra asked, as he sopped up residue from his *koxkera* with a torn-off piece of bread.

"Yes," we answered.

"But you were adults when you acquired this..."

"'Change,'" I said.

"...'Change,'" the priest said, nodding more to himself than us as he mulled over the term. "Your children, however, have been this way since birth?"

Farrell laughed. "You've just put your finger on our most difficult parenting problem, Father."

"They don't appreciate human limitations," I added.

"Ah, I see, but that is not quite correct." Father Ibarra paused and pursed his lips, rubbing his hands together in front of him. He regarded his near-empty plate without truly seeing it. For him, this knowledge quickly entered something of a theological dimension. "They have never *had* human limitations, only their own. They are unique in their state, having no memories of a former life bounded with the physical borders of most of humanity." His thoughtful, musing smile became even more gentle. "A challenge for their mothers," he concluded, looking up from his plate.

"Amen," Farrell said, gnawing on her own piece of bread.

"They surprise us with what they *can* do," I said, "because *our* mindsets for their age group still have our childhood memories."

"Walls of the mind," Father Ibarra said. "We all have those boundries. How do they regard those mere mortals in whose society they dwell? Are your parents still living?"

"They love their aunts and uncles and grandparents," I replied.

"They're actually normal that way," Farrell said, pouring herself some more wine, "and they really like

Megs' Grandmother." She grinned at me mischievously. "But then, *everybody* loves Rose."

I shot her a withering look. Rose had taught the girls to play cards -- cheating shamelessly -- as well as how to make Irish shortbread and potato pancakes, and Quinn and Maren loved to visit her. They understood the value of family and the importance of history, although I did remember nearly clamping hands over their mouths when they saw an old picture of John Tierney standing with my great-grandparents in Heppner in 1915.

"I can see that Rose's granddaughter differs with you on the issue of society's affection for Rose," the priest observed, turning his gentle smile toward me.

Farrell took her first taste of the Salmon *koxkera* before responding. Corinne had thoughtfully put some on Farrell's plate when she'd filled her own. "Megs is too close to the forest to see the trees," she said dismissively.

"Yet she wisely refrains from attacking your estimate of her ancestor," Father Ibarra replied. "Surely this is an aspect of true conscience, of true character, perhaps even a trait inherited from Rose."

"Uh...no, I don't think so," Farrell said, then quickly added, "at least the part about the inheritance. If Rose has the thought, she speaks out."

"Megan is kinder, then," Corinne put in, and, surprised, I looked at her and saw belief in her sea-green eyes. Wiser than I gave her credit for. Farrell might be the enchanting, beautiful flame, but I was the steady fuel that fed that flame, that kept it burning so brightly, and apparently Corinne had seen that.

Father Ibarra nodded approval. "Humanity is infinitely variable in displaying the twin natures of the divine and the created. We all walk a path between those two opposite poles. That path is seldom straight. Those experiences which formed Megan's grandmother's behavior might be the only difference between them. Megan's upbringing, being hopefully more benevolent, would let her inherited traits manifest in a different way."

"With a different life," Farrell said, looking happily at me, "Megs might have been a real bad girl."

"I think *one* bad girl in our relationship is enough, Father," I said.

"One bad girl is enough for *any* relationship," Father Ibarra replied, taking another swallow of wine. "Don't you agree, Corinne?" he asked.

Corinne's eyes widened for an instant. He'd caught her by surprise. "Yes, of course, Father Simon," she answered quickly, and butter would not have melted in her mouth.

"Does the Archdiocese know what you are, Father?" I asked, changing the subject, certain that the Church wasn't aware they had a werewolf shepherding the local faithful.

"No, I think not," he said, laughing quietly, "though I believe the duel nature of my created side presents an additional aspect of my soul. Other men and women, holier than I, may sense this at some level, to my benefit."

"Does it really enhance your spiritual side, Father?" I asked, intrigued.

He put down his glass of wine and looked thoughtfully at me. "Yes, I believe so. I truly do. Henri and I speak of this on occasion. There is a purity and mental clarity to the time we spend in our altered form. That spiritual simplicity lends a clearer perspective of our higher selves. A truer perspective, perhaps. With our senses expanded, the world around us becomes more accessible, and to a greater degree."

"Wouldn't that apply to us, too?" Farrell asked the priest.

"Yes, but your nature remains essentially the same, though greatly enhanced. You certainly have a higher and broader perspective from which to observe yourselves, of course. However, lycanthropy is really a completely different point of view. And because it is not a *constant* state, one is free to meditate on its revelations about oneself and wider creation when one is out of the fur."

'Out of the fur,' huh. What a cool term. *We* don't have anything comparable that doesn't sound like a bad rap song -- with spurting blood.

"*Is* there a God, Father?" Farrell asked. Her plate was empty again.

Father Ibarra regarded her above long fingers steepled over his own empty plate, tapping the tips of his forefingers together. The warmth in his brown gaze intensified. Clearly this was discussion he could relish, with someone besides Henri. He appeared to choose his words carefully. "I believe there is a Creator," he said, "It has a nature, and that nature is benevolent. I am unwilling to believe that minute-by-minute scrutiny takes place, or that our destinies cause much pain or joy in our Maker. Some, perhaps."

"So" Farrell replied, "we're something like a cosmic miniature train set in the corner of a celestial basement?"

I'd seen that one coming. Farrell's natural irreverence expresses itself in interesting ways. But the priest was likely used to careful, considerate, thoughtful words, and Farrell challenged and surprised him. Not as much as she did Corinne. The kid practically blew wine out her nose, her mouth dropping open. Then, of course, her eyes lit up, admiring Farrell's bullshit. Kids. Go figure.

Father Ibarra slapped one spindly thigh and gave a snort of approval. "A fine depiction of our true importance in creation, Major Gray, if darker than I would prefer."

The real truth is as bad, just not as impersonal, though I wasn't about to tell this good and kindly man of god. Two million years ago, a group of interstellar power brokers decided to improve trade possibilities in our corner of the Milky Way Galaxy by upgrading a bunch of chimp-like primates into humanity. Manufacturing markets, our own financial movers and shakers would probably call it. When we achieve some

121

political stabilty and true space capability, they'll be back for the Second Coming -- or maybe the Second Breathing Hard. Depends on your point of view, I guess. I just hope we're around to see it happen.

"Basically, Father," I said, "I think we agree with your assessment, despite what my partner says." And there are really *angels*, Father, living in their teeming millions beneath the surface of the back side of the moon, and they have every science-fiction gimmick known to man, force-fields, gravity drives, disintegrators, you name it.

Kick your butt from here to the Oort Cloud in about a nano-second, but they *are* -- and this is important to point out -- on our side, within limits. They *do* protect us. The biblical job description is basically correct.

With an even more gracious and kind smile, Father Ibarra nodded and said, "Thank you. Sometimes I am so obscure I am almost Jesuitical. Certainly, what we are..." His sweeping gesture took in the other werewolves. "...makes any theosophical discussion rather arcane."

"What can you tell us about the Compliance?" Farrell asked.

"Since we're going to go down into the Valley tomorrow," I added.

"Oh, dear," Father Ibarra replied, a frown of concern settling onto his features. "How to tell you about a group begun with the best of intentions and most moral of missions that is now the most repressive and onerous small-scale religious police state in the Northwest? And one of the few remaining anywhere, since the federal government has become strong enough to start to reunify the United States."

"Are they that bad?" I asked, "the Compliance, I mean."

The priest nodded. "Sadly, yes. Not at first, of course. In the immediate aftermath of the bombs, the central Willamette Valley north of Eugene and east of the Willamette River itself almost literally caught fire.

122

Salem's population, like Portland's, contained enough of a discordant element so that opportunistic rioting and looting began almost immediately. The police and related authorities were able to contain it for a time, but fire is chaos' friend, and fire quickly became the weapon of choice for the rioters. Then they blew the bridge into West Salem, and that significant isolation nearly spelled the end for the capital."

"Is there a guy on a white horse in this story?" Farrell asked, as she filled all the wine glasses on our end of the table.

Father Ibarra let a long drink of wine roll around his tongue and down his throat before replying. "Elrod Macklin returned from Vietnam in 1969, and worked in his father's hardware and feed store in Mount Angel. His service time was as a Military Policeman. When Salem began to come apart and the violence spilled out into farming communities like Mount Angel, Macklin went to the granges and VFW halls and recruited men and women like himself. With weapons and light armor from the myriad of National Guard facilities up and down the eastern valley, they took everything back within six months. A rough order had been restored."

A true violence junkie, Farrell now looked much more interested. She leaned forward. "How long did it take to get things really in order?"

Father's Ibarra's gentle smile sharpened up a notch. "Some years. 1973 or 1974, I believe. Macklin created a position similar to a Circuit Judge, but with additional powers of punishment. The *Executioners*, they were called by the people. I imagine they still exist, still fulfill the same role, and still use the exclusive chrome-plated officer's .45 to carry out their sentences. The pure and inviolate avengers of the Lord God Almighty."

It wasn't difficult to understand what sort of punishment a .45 meted out. "What crimes required an Executioner?" I asked.

"Murder, theft, and so-called 'family crimes.' The latter included spousal and child abuse, or children against their older parents, and theft also meant cheating of employees or the public. 'Gouging,' I believe cheating was called."

"It sounds like a very *moral* society," Farrell said.

The priest nodded. "Oh, yes, but eventually, when the returning influence of the federal government began to spread south from the Seattle-Tacoma area, and Portland settled into the new order, the Compliance became more paranoid. They realized they would be absorbed by the Reunited States. Elrod Macklin might be a good man, but his power had attracted those who were less ethical and more concerned with their own agendas. Then, about five years ago, when word came out of St. Louis that President McPherson intended to forcibly restore the Union, information and commerce from the Compliance dwindled to nearly nothing. Surrounded to the north, east, and west by populations who consider themselves citizens of the United States, the mood in Elrod Macklin's lands must be anything but sanguine. Clearly the handwriting is on the wall, yet the tales of repression and horror which filter out of Salem show no signs of abatement, but rather an increase. They will not peacefully return to McPherson's fold, I fear."

"Oh, swell," Farrell said, looking at me, a sour expression on her face, "and we'll be there tomorrow for the festivities."

"Where exactly are you going?" Father Ibarra asked.

"North Cedar," I replied.

"You may be safe. Small numbers of Compliance troops will be stationed at Flint Dam, west five miles more or less from the town of Flint, but probably no closer. They have little to fear from our side of the mountains. When the time comes, McPherson's reclaiming force will move down the valley from Portland."

"We'll be going right into Flint, then left to North Cedar on Highway 22," Farrell said.

"An important intersection," Father Ibarra said, tapping on his front teeth with a fingernail as he thought. "Still, they must be spread rather thin just now, and it's only a short distance east to North Cedar."

"Guess we'll find out tomorrow," Farrell replied, smiling cheerfully as she scooped up another serving of lamb.

Hard to argue with that.

CHAPTER TWENTY-THREE

NIGHT MOVES

When the meal had ended, Henri and Father Ibarra both lit up pipes -- briefly, since tobacco, they said, came only intermittently over the mountains from Portland. Cigarette smoking, in fact, had virtually died out during the turbulent years after the bombs. A whole generation had matured who'd rolled only marijuana.

By twenty-two hundred hours, it was obvious that the Basques were growing restless. The moon, a little past half, had risen in the east, and shone strongly into the tall Ponderosa where we'd stacked the split wood. Even Father Ibarra glanced frequently in that direction, and Corinne seemed much less interested in Farrell, which I thought was a hoot.

Conversation died down. We helped clear the tables and stack the smaller plates and silverware in what appeared to be a fairly-new Kitchenaid dishwasher. The bigger trays and serving plates went into the sink to soak. Marie put powdered soap in the dishwasher, closed it up and set the timer, then squirted liquid soap in the filled sink. "There," she said, "we can worry about these later."

We went back outside. The tables had been returned to their usual positions, and everyone was standing at the edge of the patio. Glancing over at us, Henri cleared his throat. "Would you consider doing us a favor?"

"After that wonderful meal?" I replied, and Farrell grunted. "Name it," she said.

"Would you watch the children while we run? Only rarely can we all course together, since someone must stay with Paul and Monette."

Beckin and Brone had come over as Henri spoke. "We'd be glad to," Beckin said, laying her right hand on Henri's forearm.

"That's very kind," Marie said, smiling as she stepped out of the kitchen, wiping her hands on a towel. She hung the towel on a convenient peg alongside the door. Behind her, the dishwasher began its cycle. Everything seemed so normal and middle American, as though we were watching the kids for a while so the family could go down to the corner ice cream parlor for late evening sundaes.

Instead, they stripped, laid their clothes on the table tops, walked into the moonlight, and shifted into wolf-form.

Easy to say, but words can't begin to describe the actual process. If words could, the first word would be beautiful, not a word I would've thought. Human flowed into wolf, effortless and smooth and eye-rivitingly lovely. My heart was in my throat by the time they'd ghosted off in among the moon-shadowed Ponderosa, and I had to remind myself to breathe again.

"Migod," Farrell said, and Beckin and Brone were silent.

Though they must've seen it many times before, Monette and Paul's eyes still shone, as much in wonder as in anticipation of their own future, when puberty would let them do this. Almost I envied them, and wished that Quinn and Maren had been here to see. Perhaps we could go to *our* Pine Grove when we were back together, and see who operated this little oasis for travelers.

In the meantime, Monette and Paul needed to bathe, brush their teeth, and be tucked into bed. Even though there was no school this time of year -- assuming they *had* schools -- I seriously doubted little werewolves were ordinarily allowed to stay up this late.

"Did I miss the instructions from the parents?" Beckin asked, a hand on top of each small head. She smiled down at them, tousling their hair, and Brone rumbled approval.

"They came without," Farrell said.

"What time do you guys go to bed?" I asked Monette and Paul, kneeling down in front of them.

127

They hesitated, the hesitation of children who wished they'd thought ahead to decide what they could get away with.

"Now," Monette reluctantly admitted, and Paul nodded slowly.

"Do you take a bath first?"

"Before dinner," Paul said, "while you were at the pool."

"Do you have a story before sleeping?" Beckin asked.

"Yes!" they chorused, instantly excited, presented with an opportunity to put off bed.

"Then go and pick a book, and I will read to you," Beckin said, and they scampered off through the kitchen, small feet pattering on the stairs as they went up to the second floor.

"Wow, Mom," Farrell said, grinning at Beckin, and Brone chuckled.

"They are very sweet children," Beckin said defensively. "If you were in charge, you'd only teach them knife-throwing or somesuch."

"No," Farrell replied, "I'd do exactly what you're doing, and enjoy every minute of it."

Beckin regarded her warily, waiting for the typical Gray punchline. It didn't come, and finally Beckin shook her head. "I have become too used to being set up, and expect it every time. Then you display your maternal and compassionate side and I am confounded. Nearly as bad as being the butt of your vile wit."

"Worse," Brone added, smiling, "because it's so unexpected." He raised one arm, his hand brushing through the grape leaves on the underside of the arbor. "May I read a story, also?" he asked. We all three just looked at him. The physical appeal of Brone to small children was easy to figure; the thought of him reading aloud, holding a kid's book in one of his huge hands was literally a different story.

Our momentary consternation disappeared with the re-appearance of Monette and Paul, each with a book.

128

Monette had the 'Pokey Little Puppy," and Paul clutched a well-worn copy of my childhood favorite, 'Where the Wild Things Are,' the Maurice Sendak classic. I hadn't really expected 'Little Red Riding Hood,' or Disney's version of 'Peter and the Wolf,' but these were nice surprises, particularly the Sendak.

Beckin read first, her voice making the Pokey Puppy seem far more sinister than I remembered. I kept waiting for the puppy to pull a knife on the lizard or something, but the story ended as it always did -- the happy canine ending any werewolf would favor.

We made the Wild Things more of a group effort. Beckin read the story slowly, with great emphasis, Max in his wolf suit terrorized the dog, and Monette and Paul giggled like tiny maniacs. When Max arrived on the island of the Wild Things, Brone did the voice of the Blue Bull, I was the Chicken-thing, and Farrell the creature whose face resembled an animated sunflower.

The kids ate it up, of course, delighted that four adults would make fools of themselves just to entertain them. In fact, we got so carried away that we read it three times, playing, altering our individual parts for dramatic effect.

Eventually little eyes began to close sleepily, and little heads began to nod. We closed the books, Beckin picked up Monette and Brone carried Paul, and all of us went upstairs so the kids could brush their teeth, put on pajamas, and be tucked into bed.

I walked behind Beckin as we climbed the stairs. Monette's sleepy half-lidded gaze regarded me over Beckin's shoulder, a barely-there smile on her small lips. "You look like Nikita," she said softly, reaching out to touch my pale hair.

"Who?" I asked.

"On television," she answered, her voice slightly louder.

Well, I *do* look a lot like Peta Wilson, who plays 'La Femme Nikita' on the Canadian series. I have a bunch more freckles, and I'm bigger, but the resemblance is there. *There* was the operative word, since *here* wouldn't have the show. Frankly, it hadn't even occurred to me that this timeline had *television*. *Radio*, maybe, but not TV.

I mulled Monette's words while the kids shucked their clothes, brushed their teeth, and dressed for bed. By the time they were under the covers, down comforters tucked under their chins, I still had no good answer. Or *any* answer. Maybe I hadn't heard her right. But I had. I knew I had.

"Well," Beckin said, dusting off her hands after pulling up a chair and sitting between the two small beds. She stretched out her hands to each of the children. "You will shortly see the Lord of the Night in all his glory. I will give you a song to speed you on your journey to his lands."

Though she hums under her breath on occasion, and I've heard her sing a line or two in *Siog* Gaelic, Beckin had never really sang around us.

Now she did, a haunting lullaby in Creole French, an old Kingston Trio song I'd heard on one of my Dad's childhood albums, featuring dreamboats drifting slow and a singing crocodile. As she sang, Beckin gently rubbed Monette and Paul's hands with the balls of her thumbs. He voice grew more hushed toward the end, both sets of little eyes had closed when she'd finished, and I had a lump in my throat the size of a tennis ball.

In the silence that followed, Beckin turned off the bedside lamp, placed the chair back by the door, and Brone switched on the night light. We tip-toed into the hallway, leaving the door ajar five or so inches, and went downstairs as quietly as possible.

"That was lovely, Beckin," I said, when we were back out on the patio.

She smiled self-consciously. "My mother sang that song to me when I was small," she replied. "Your own daughters are quite fond of it."

The lump in my throat, which had nearly vanished, returned. I choked down a sob. Tears welled.

130

"Tomorrow," Beckin said, seeing my reaction. She brushed my face as lightly as a feather, her expression caring and compassionate. "Tomorrow, and no longer, Megan. Only another day."

I nodded wordlessly, unable to speak.

Farrell's right arm encircled my waist. She kissed the side of my neck softly, her lips warm. "She's right, you know, my love," she said into my ear. "One more day."

I knew.

That didn't make it easier.

CHAPTER TWENTY-FOUR

NODES

A minute or two under a clear night sky filled with stars restored my emotional equilibrium, particularly after a few deep breaths of mountain air while Farrell massaged my shoulders and neck. The moon, nearing apex, brightened the world, the tree trunks of the Ponderosa grove gleaming golden-tan against the deeper shadows among the trees. To the northwest, an owl hooted, reminding the world whose beak and talons owned the night wind.

"Let's take a walk," I suggested, flexing my loosened shoulder muscles, feeling much better. I started to the north, around the corner of the building. Farrell followed me, leaving Beckin and Brone watching us curiously.

"You going off to sit on a stump and bawl?" Farrell asked, walking behind me with her hands in her pockets, concerned, but not overly. She's used to my sappy nature, which is not to say that she doesn't cloud up at times.

"Actually, I'm looking for a TV antenna."

"Because of what Monette said?"

"Yeah. It doesn't make sense. They might have TV, but I can't believe they have cable or broadcast satellites."

"Not the same programs as us, for sure."

It didn't take long to find the thing, on the roof peak above the kids' bedroom, pointing toward the south-southeast.

"A mini-dish!" I exclaimed. The thing looked exactly like my folks' unit, about the size of a concave pizza pan.

"No shit," Farrell said, eyeing the thing, giving a low whistle.

We looked at the dish for several minutes, from different angles, before rejoining Beckin and Brone. No question that's what it was, but it still made no sense.

Beckin's reaction to our information surprised me even more. "Do you not *feel* anything odd here?" she asked, sprawled in a chair near the door to the kitchen. She had one ear cocked for Monette and Paul, through the open french door.

"No," we replied.

"A sense of calm, perhaps, or just a comfortable feeling?" She looked from one of us to the other.

Farrell sat down in a nearby chair, and I perched on its arm, resting my right hand on her left shoulder. I gestured at the patio around us. "Well, this is a very peaceful spot, so, yeah, the tranquility is nice."

"What you feel," Beckin said, "is a tremendously powerful transfer node. A number of parallel ley lines from different directions intersect and converge here. I am no Sensitive, to know which directions the power flows, to which timelines, but I *can* sense its strength. It is at least as strong as the one we used near Four Crossings."

"But what's *that* got to do with the television?" I asked.

"I'm not certain," Beckin answered, "except that the changes between the timelines are more noticeable in areas of denser population and higher human activity. The number of variables introduced rises. A place this small, a handful of people, might theoretically be nearly the same through dozens of shifts."

"You mean," Farrell asked, "that this spot exists simultaneously both here and in our world?"

Beckin nodded. "I am a warrior, and no scientist, but I believe it's something like that. Our expectations of continuity may keep us in this war-ravaged timeline even as we depart tomorrow."

"You could get us out of here, though, couldn't you?" I asked.

"Certes, though I would have to cast about, back-and-forth, to locate the configuration of my continuum, and Morag and the girls would still be in this timeline. It would be most time-consuming." She grinned at her pun.

"And we would lose the truck," Brone added.

"Oh, well," Farrell said. She grinned at Beckin. "Too bad you didn't spend more time in the books while you were in school."

Beckin's answering smile was cold and pitiless. "Then I would not be such an efficient killer," she said quietly.

No one questioned the importance of that.

"Do you suppose the leftovers are in the refrigerator?" Brone asked, breaking the ensuing silence.

CHAPTER TWENTY-FIVE

CORINNE

We talked for another half-hour or so, then, unable to stand the knowledge that there was uneaten food somewhere on the premises, Brone raided the refrigerator.

"That took long enough," Farrell remarked when he'd returned with a full plate of leftovers, a few minutes later.

"I removed our clean clothes from the dryer in the laundry room and folded them," Brone said. He sat down and carefully balanced his plate on one large knee before digging enthusiastically into the food. "They have a Kenmore washer and dryer, and so is the refrigerator," he said, sticking a large forkful of Salmon *Koxkera* into his mouth.

"Sears survives," Farrell said. Her expression told me she was considering her own trip to the fridge, but Sears sure didn't surprise me nearly as much as that satellite dish and Beckin's explanation.

Eventually, after Farrell hit the leftovers, we fetched three army blankets from behind the truck's seats and stretched out on the patio. Beckin curled up in her chair by the kitchen doorway, in case the children needed anything.

Changelings may not need much sleep, yet it comes easily enough. Even my gnawing anxiety for Quinn and Maren only kept me awake for a few minutes. I drifted off into a dreamless sleep with Farrell spooned up against my back, her breath lightly ruffling the short hair on the back of my head.

Some time well beyond Midnight, I awoke to the stir of movement around us. Musky wolf smell enveloped the patio. The Basques had returned.

I opened my eyes to find a nude Corinne laying facing me, mere inches away. Her family seemed to have disappeared indoors. Smiling sleepily at her, I whispered, "How was it?" Her languorous smile of deep satisfaction required no words. She simply *glowed*, radiating heat and joy.

"That good, huh?" I said. Behind me, Farrell stirred, and I felt her peering at Corinne over my neck. She reached across me and ran the fingertips of her left hand over Corinne's cheek. Corinne shivered at the touch, her smile widening even as her eyes half-closed in pleasure.

"C'mon," I said, putting my arms around her and drawing her into my embrace, feeling the satin smoothness of her thighs and arms and breasts as she moved against me. Her mouth found the hollow below my lower jaw, and she gently kissed me, her tongue flicking my skin with every beat of my heart.

Perhaps Corinne's dual nature made her so receptive and responsive to what took place over the next half-hour, or maybe it was just her sweet eagerness and incredible flexibility. It didn't seem to matter, or need explanation, and her exciting, musky fragrance only added a pleasant focus and urgency to the festivities.

A new meaning for puppy love, I suppose.

CHAPTER TWENTY-SIX

THE VALLEY

Father Ibarra had to say Mass at the Catholic chapel on Warm Springs Reservation early next morning, so dawn found us in the Barinaga kitchen, enjoying coffee, buckwheat pancakes, and Father Ibarra's keen mind. Not necessarily in that order, except in Brone's case, for whom sustenance came first and foremost, at least when there was no imminent danger. For poor Father Ibarra, there was only tea, since he had to hold his fast until after Communion.

Henri, Corinne, and the Garmindia brothers had been already dressed and helping distribute the meal when we'd walked into the kitchen. Marie and Louise were shuffling pans and serving plates at the stove and the adjacent counter. Now the food was gone, and the Basques appeared about ready to head to the sheep pens and begin the day's work. They stood with their final cups of morning coffee, looking out at the long shadows of sunrise striping the tan and green landscape of the new day.

Corinne seemed a bit distracted, standing on the bricks, a smug private smile on her features. Occasionally she'd glance briefly in our direction, and her smile would grow stronger. Getting what she wanted had apparently worked out for her. It certainly had for us, and Beckin had been impressed enough to bitch mildly at being left out.

Bitching was something Beckin'd learned from us. The concept of being displeased with one's lot in life and expressing it had no place in *Siog* society. *Siogi* got what they got and lived with it. Few real problems could not be solved by killing someone, and that was generally first recourse, particularly for a young star like Beckin, whose considerable social stature rested on her abilities to deliver death on demand.

So Beckin cast looks of appraisal at Corinne, speculating perhaps on the possibility of introducing Corinne to the delights of *Siog* sex, which Farrell and I could attest were most extensive. The enhanced senses the three of us shared, coupled with the very different *Siog* life-slant, served to turbo-charge the whole sex act. In the down and dirty, Beckin's natural intensity ignited an upward neuronic spiral that erupted into a maelstrom of synapse-licking pleasure.

Father Ibarra bade everyone farewell, took the small sack of food Marie had prepared for his breakfast, and drove away in his well-maintained Chevy. His mood seemed more ebullient after a night of coursing under the moon with his own kind, and I guessed it must give them release not dissimilar from that which we vamps have when we feed. Without killing. Louis Bergeron had told us that werewolves avoided killing in their wolf forms, for fear of revealing their existence, in case someone recalled the old legends.

We put off leaving until the children came downstairs. When Monette and Paul finally showed at nearly eight hundred hours, the shepherds and their flocks had been gone for an hour or more. Corinne had still looked pretty pleased with herself when they walked off toward the sheep pens, and her goodbyes had been warmer and more wistful than the rest.

"Well, you would hope," Farrell said, when I smiled and cocked an eyebrow at her as Corinne departed, which only shows what a high value my partner places on her sexual prowess. Not without reason, however, I will attest. Oh, yes.

Monette and Paul understood that we had to go, that we hoped to arrive in North Cedar by early afternoon, and they didn't pout or carry on. Brone sat one of them on each of his knees and explained that, while we really had to leave today, there would be other days, and they would see us again.

"They will never forget him," Louise said, standing next to me with her arms folded over her white blouse.

138

Marie was more down-to-earth. "Perhaps next time you could bring some wine," she said quietly, but her smile at Brone and her grandchildren removed any sting from the words.

"Your hospitality to complete strangers was most kind and unexpected," Beckin said, her expression *Siog*-sincere. She is such a dead-pan when thanking people, though better than she used to be, when she'd practically scare them.

"It was our pleasure," Louise said, giving her mother a dirty look.

Brone looked up from where he sat with the kids. "Nothing on earth substitutes for friendship and warmheartedness," he said, as he stood, hugging Monette and Paul to his massive chest, his grin a face-splitter.

I must've sniffed. Farrell glared at me and said, "Don't start," which earned a disgusted look from Beckin.

When Brone disentangled himself from the kids and we'd topped the truck's tank from our gas cans, we loaded up and said our goodbyes, after promises to return with Quinn and Maren in tow.

We were ten minutes to the west on Highway 216 before anyone said anything, and then it was Brone, shaking his head in disbelief. "I never thought werewolves were real, that I'd ever meet any, or that they would be so pleasant."

Beckin chuckled maliciously. "You'd have to ask Megan and Farrell just *how* pleasant, I think."

"Corinne certainly seemed very warm and friendly," Brone replied, picking right up on Beckin's innuendo, but his expression stayed only thoughtful.

"Not naughty and wanton?" Beckin asked, amused.

"Relative terms," Brone said, still thoughtful, "and, like beauty, in the eyes of the beholder. The Barinagas' and Garmindias' lives may be busy and fulfilling, but there cannot be much variation. For a young woman like Corinne, though her lifestyle may be both necessary

139

and protective, that sameness must occasionally chafe. Presented with truly exotic beings such as Megan and Farrell, who can blame her for being attracted?"

I didn't recall ever being called 'truly exotic' in my life, the idea being so foreign that I laughed out loud. So did Farrell, of course, though the term certainly applied to her.

Beckin tried to keep from laughing, pressing her lips together, but didn't entirely succeed. After a tiny snort escaped, she said, "I give up. Megan's Catholic guilting techniques elude me completely."

"You have to be born to it," Farrell observed from behind the wheel, still laughing.

"*You* have no guilt," Beckin replied accusingly.

"Look who's talking, 'Ms. Death Elf of 1994!'" Farrell shot back.

Beckin reached forward from her seat and grabbed Farrell's right shoulder. "I make *no* apology for being skilled at my craft. At least I don't *feed* on my victims."

Farrell was unimpressed. "Sure, climb on your high horse and pick on someone else's innocent little genetic flaw. Typical conservative Republican, labeling the blameless!"

"You *enjoy* it!" Beckin growled, "and take back what you said! I am no Republican!" Beckin knew an insult when she heard one.

"Take it easy, you two," I said, poking Beckin's extended arm. "Remember, in this timeline, *Newt* is the sitting *Republican* President, using his original last name, McPherson."

"Shit," Farrell said, squeezing the steering wheel. "Anyone who sees our military ID will assume we work for Newt. That's depressing as hell."

"Hah!" Beckin said, temporarily ending the argument. She removed her hand from Farrell's shoulder and sat back on her bench, looking satisfied.

Shortly after that jolly little exchange, we arrived at Highway 26, the main route from Portland to Central Oregon over the south flank of Mount Hood. Except for

140

the age of the vehicles, traffic here appeared only slightly sparser than in our timeline.

Beckin's expression became speculative. "Should we turn south here, and travel to Redmond, would we find another John Tierney at his home, I wonder?"

I shook my finger under her nose. "Maybe, but we aren't, just as we aren't going on to Bend to see if my aunts, cousins, and grandparents are there, and we definitely aren't going to Molalla to visit my folks."

"Molalla would be in the Compliance," Beckin replied, matter-of-factly ruling that out. "Redmond and Bend would not."

"Still 'no.' It would only be asking for trouble."

She shrugged. "Of course. I was merely speculating."

Farrell said nothing, just drove across the highway, keeping us on our route toward the northwest corner of the Warm Springs Reservation and then on south into the Lautenbach River drainage. The set of Farrell's shoulders pretty much told me that she was as intent upon seeing Quinn and Maren as I was, though.

The road surface beyond that point became less well-maintained, but didn't slow us significantly as we rose up into the mountains south of Clear Lake. Farrell drove around the larger potholes and through the smaller, and we kept moving, threading between the ends of chain-sawed fallen trees and -- in a few cases -- small rockfalls.

By noon, as we swung around the Rez and dropped down Skyline Road to the east of Peavine Mountain, the unrelenting mix of Ponderosa and Lodgepole pine, interspersed with Aspen, Larch, and Subalpine fir, gradually gave way to predominantly Douglas fir. Soon we were surrounded by big Dougies, two hundred or more feet tall, with dense undergrowth against their bases. The number of varying-vintage tree stumps along the road increased, thirty years of windfall that had been trucked away in sixteen-foot sections to mills

141

somewhere on the Rez or down in the valley, probably to North Cedar or Flint.

Around thirteen hundred hours, Skyline Road hit Highway 46, which seemed in much better shape. Certainly the bouncing and jouncing grew less, and while Brone and Beckin relaxed some, the growing proximity to Quinn and Maren served to key me up more and more. By the time we reached the little hamlet of Lautenbach Hot Springs, forty-five minutes later, passing the usual small stores and older single-family houses, my gut had knotted up nicely.

The fast-moving waters of the Lautenbach River swung closer to the left side of the road as we began the final eleven miles to Flint, then we crossed the river, and I started looking for homes on the outskirts of Flint itself.

"Relax, Megan," Beckin said, smiling at my obvious excitement, "we're nearly there."

My return grin could only be described as wan.

The timber thinned out to our right as the river diverged to the north, and tilled fields began to appear.

Then, up ahead, I saw tents and larger vehicles, among them several M-113 Armored Personnel Carriers, including one with a red cross prominently displayed on its side. Helmeted people in brown stood on both sides of the highway, and, as we got closer, their purpose became obvious.

A roadblock.

CHAPTER TWENTY-SEVEN

BLOCKED

If it hadn't been for the APCs and the pair of V-100 Armored Cars alongside the roadblock, the bunch awaiting us might just as well have been a brown-uniformed UPS picnic expecting a few kegs of beer, and hoping we were it. They were fairly rag-tag-and-bobtail, with sleeves rolled up, pants roughly bloused, and not looking overly-prepared for action. Only about half of the thirty men I could see had rifles and helmets, but the V-100s, both carrying twin M-60 machine guns, lent a certain authority to the proceedings.

"Oh, *fuck*," Farrell said, when our situation became obvious. She let up on the gas, and our little truck slowed.

My heart basically fell through the bed of the truck.

"They may not detain us," Beckin said, seeing my face, "and, in any event, there are not many of them. If we capture the armored cars, we can slaughter them easily."

All that was intended to be consoling in a *Siog* way, and I could tell Beckin was picking out her moves, determining how many long strides would take her to the nearest V-100, how much time to kill the gunner, and which direction to begin firing.

"I can take the group of five on the right," Brone said, his voice casual, "if Megan and Farrell can handle the left, along with the armored car on that side."

"Let's hope it doesn't come to that," Farrell replied, sighing, as the truck rolled up to the bored-looking troops. What a group. Any CO we'd ever had would bust chops on this outfit for lack of focus. In fact, most of them were paying more attention to one of their number on the other side of the roadblock, who was talking with a tall, older guy wearing a campaign hat.

"Looks like a turf squabble," Farrell said, watching them as the truck stopped. The Compliance officer -- he wore Captain's bars -- spoke emphatically, making short, chopping gestures with his hands, and other fellow mostly listened.

"The tall man is local law enforcement, I think," Beckin said. "The jeep parked behind him has 'Sheriff' on the door."

"Where're you folks headed?" the soldier nearest Farrell inquired, still without displaying much interest. Sergeant's stripes adorned his shirtsleeves. Two of the three men with him held rifles, old M-1s, and the third had a sidearm in a closed holster. This close, I could smell their lack of preparedness. The three at least had the brains to eye Brone uneasily, indicating some rudimentary training, but they still looked like unkempt Mormons, a definite oxymoron.

"North Cedar," Farrell replied, her tone matching the sergeant's. Brone yawned heavily, stretching his arms in the air. Beckin did nothing, still sizing up her options, but watching the Compliance men's reaction to Brone's movement.

Her upper lip didn't exactly curl, though I thought I saw an instant's twitch. Meat for the grinder in Beckin's book.

The sergeant nodded, glancing briefly toward his captain in the manner of sergeants throughout history, but, in this case, more slowly. "I'm gonna have to ask you to wait a few minutes, Miss, until the Captain gets done talkin' to the Sheriff." He smiled at Farrell, and started to pat her on the arm, then took a closer look, and decided against it.

He turned away, not really checking Beckin and me out, though in fairness, the half-drawn canvas top shaded us well enough that bright sunlight-adapted eyes wouldn't see much.

Meanwhile, the Captain was not a happy man, trying to make his point with the tall Sheriff, and making no headway whatsoever. "I'm afraid we'll be here until the end of the month, Sheriff Merrill. You know how orders are."

144

Merrill didn't nod, or show any sign of agreement. Instead, he took off his campaign hat and examined the little Compliance encampment, letting his narrow-eyed gaze track the entire group of men and equipment. A very small grin formed on his weathered features, as he brought his attention back to the Captain. "Your Executioner come up with the idea to set up camp here?"

Irritated, the Captain said, "Yes, the *Judge* did."

Ignoring the correction, the Sheriff nodded. "See that big divot in the grass over there?" He pointed to what looked to me exactly like a several-year-old mortar crater, about twenty-five feet off the northern edge of the road.

"Yes, of course," the Sergeant snapped, getting more pissed. "What of it?"

"Well, we did some testing, a few years back, just in case your leaders got a tad ambitious, and sent troops up above the dam. All the places where you might camp between here and the dam'll have one or two of these test spots." He put his hat back on, squared it up, and suddenly looked a lot more serious and formidable. And forceful. "There are three mortars dug into the hillside behind me, Captain, and three Vietnam-vet snipers along with 'em. The plan is to pick off your troops who're closest to cover first, then work back from there. When no one's left standing, then the mortars open up. Sound workable?"

Startled, the Captain looked up at the forested hillside behind the Sheriff, his eyes wide, as though he would be able to spot the three fire-zone points. Of course, nothing showed.

A practical man, this Sheriff Merrill, and gutsy. His smile now turned inquisitive. Not cruel, though. He knew he had the big end of the stick, and he definitely wasn't bluffing, but he wasn't about to rub the Compliance's nose in it, either. I wondered how their leader, who must be in the largest Yurtlike tent, was going to react to the possibility of getting his troops' asses blown away wholesale. Get out of Dodge is what

145

I'd suggest, but you can never tell what loons will do, particularly loons who are on the verge of losing their territory and power.

"You wouldn't," the Compliance man replied. "You'd be the first to die."

"'Fraid not," the Sheriff answered. He rested his right hand on the butt of a .45 automatic hanging from his belt, and his meaning was obvious, though I thought only the brown-uniformed Captain realized it. And the Sheriff was clearly no fooler.

"This man will know the McLeods, our people in North Cedar," said Beckin. She vaulted over the side of the truck, and walked toward the confrontation after tossing her cap on her bench.

Two of the three men with the Sergeant moved to intercept Beckin, but they really weren't prepared to do more than stand in her way. She slipped between them easily and approached the Sheriff and the Captain.

"Excuse me," she said to the Captain, smiling at him, "I need a word with the Sheriff." She removed her sunglasses.

"Young lady..." the Captain began, but Beckin had already turned to Merrill, effectively dismissing the Compliance officer, who stood with his mouth working, and nothing coming out.

The Sheriff looked down at her, fighting a grin. He saw her green eyes, obviously recognized what he saw, and touched the brim of his hat. "You a McLeod?" he asked Beckin.

She shook her head. "No, a distant relative only. Should we be detained here, however, would you be kind enough to inform the McLeods?" At Beckin's side, the Captain continued to splutter, and I wondered for a second time about the reaction of the man in the tent to the snipers and mortars. Their ranking officer -- the *Judge* -- might not be so ineffectual and disorganized.

"Glad to," Merrill replied, and touched his hat again.

Beckin smiled at him, gave a little nod, then thanked the Captain, replaced her sunglasses, and climbed back into the truck. The Compliance men all watched her like hawks, as though she would catch fire or run amok or something.

Meanwhile, the Sheriff had turned his attention back to the Captain, who still hadn't regained his composure. "Well," Merrill said, "why don't I wait while you go explain the situation to your Mister Macklin's girlfriend, see what she wants to do."

The Captain looked unhappy, and not a little angry. "She will not be pleased," he managed to grind out, and I saw that a good portion of his anger was self-directed. He'd probably argued against coming this far east, been over-ruled, and now would suffer for it, for not being more adamant.

"I hear tell she's a real ass-kicker," Merrill added, but kindly, commiserating with the poor guy.

"Know who he is?" Farrell asked, tipping her head toward the Sheriff.

"The Sheriff?" I replied.

"Yeah. Remember when we'd stagger out of Mac Court after wind sprints and sit out in the hall with our water bottles?"

I did. Good times, barely able to stand, laying on the hall floor, sweating like a racehorse. "Sure."

"One of the pictures of teams past in the display case, '60 or'61, Steve Belko the coach, Pacific Coast Conference runners-up, this Merrill was a hot-shooting forward. I'm almost sure. *Virgil* Merrill."

"Really?" I said, trying to see this tall, leathery man as a young dead-eye. Farrell's Change-enhanced memory was apparently better than mine at recalling the Pit's trophy cases. Mostly I just remembered a wet towel wrapped around my neck and sucking water down like a maniac.

"You having a Blonde Moment?" Farrell asked, grinning over her right shoulder. I stuck my tongue out at her.

"History -- other than personal weapons-usage -- will not help us if these ill-trained people attempt to interrupt our journey," Beckin put in from her seat opposite me.

"They don't seem particularly interested in us," Brone said. "The Sheriff has given them something to worry about."

"Aye, truly," Beckin answered, with one of her cold smiles.

The Compliance Sergeant knew he had to go speak to his superior, and quickly, so he decided to deal with us first.

He was *not* in a good mood at this point, caught between his female Judge and the promise of certain death if the Compliance force didn't retreat to the west. "Get out of the vehicle, please," the Captain said to Farrell as he stepped around the Sergeant, his wave including the rest of us. "All of you, please." He didn't want any problems, and probably wouldn't cause us any, but the twist of his mouth and the resigned expression on his features showed he might be pretty close to breaking.

We got out, the Sergeant and his three troopers still concentrating mostly on Brone, and lined up along the left side of the truck, Beckin closest to the front, and Brone to the left of Farrell and me. The Captain gave us a cursory glance, then leaned in the driver's side window and examined the interior of the cab. Finding nothing of interest, he paced in front of us. "I want to *see* you," he said. "Take off your caps and glasses, please." He stopped in front of Beckin and Farrell while we removed our forage caps and sunglasses.

Beckin he'd already seen, and like most of humanity, he found Farrell's disinterested copper gaze intimidating, so he turned to me.

Eyes of a medium brown bored into my grey for a second or two, then suddenly widened. All the color leached out of his face. His mouth fell open. Behind him, the Sergeant gasped, and the three soldiers come instantly alert, the two with rifles bringing them up.

"*God*!" the Captain said, his voice nearly inaudible.

Not knowing what to say, I kept quiet. To my left, Brone stirred, with a soft rustling of his clothing, but Farrell and Beckin did nothing.

The Compliance officer took two steps backward, his knees unsteady for a few moments, as he fought to regain his composure. His comrades looked just as shocked, and I probably looked no different, just not as bad. Did I have something between my teeth, or what? I stood there holding my cap and glasses, and could only stare back at them.

Twenty feet behind them, Sheriff Merrill's features showed only puzzled interest, so whatever the Compliance people saw, he didn't.

Their confusion didn't last, however. The Captain unsnapped his holster and centered his automatic on my midriff. All irritation and uncertainty vanished from his face, and he began to smile. "let's go talk to the Judge," he said, gesturing at the big yurt with his pistol.

"What's the problem, Captain?" Farrell asked. We need to be on our way."

"I'm certain you'd *like* that," he replied, giving me another hard stare as he shook his head. "But I'm afraid it's not going to happen unless the Judge says so." He laughed shortly. "And I hardly think she will, do you?"

This guy thought we knew what he knew, and couldn't see we were clueless. Farrell and I had time to exchange troubled glances, and then the four of us were marched away under the guns of the Sergeant and his men, one of them bringing our ordnance bag from the back of the truck.

"What the fuck is going on?" Farrell whispered, just loud enough for Beckin and me to hear, as we walked across the field.

"They feel Megan is a threat of some sort," Beckin answered, and even from behind her I sensed her continuing assessment of the situation and how to efficiently kill our captors. For once I sort of approved, not having any idea what was going on here, why we were suddenly in the shitter.

Pulling aside the big yurt's hanging hemp-canvas door, the Captain led us into the cooler interior. Inside, there were three rows of old folding chairs, perhaps a dozen in all, and two collapsible tables with three more chairs standing behind them. Behind that, a canvas wall mostly separated this half of the tent from the remainder. The roof was maybe twenty feet high – the thing was *big*.

The Captain motioned for us to wait, then strode around the edge of the partition. "Sir," he said to whoever was there, presumably the Judge. "We have a problem with the locals…and another thing."

The reply sounded definitely feminine, although low-pitched and little more than a grunt, and I heard a chair creak as the Captain seated himself. They kept their voices down, so only about every second word made it out of the canvas-walled room, even to our keen ears, but the Judge readily accepted the need to decamp and head west. She did utter a few bad words directed at Sheriff Merrill, and her voice and its cadence sounded hauntingly familiar, causing the hair on the back of my neck to lift.

Farrell noticed it, too. "I don't like this at all," she said softly, as we watched the Sergeant empty the contents of our ordnance bag onto the table tops. He looked up at us from his examination of our two LaFrances and Beckin's holstered automatic, his expression somewhat more professional than earlier. "No talking," he said.

His professionalism might have increased marginally, but he hadn't thought to check us for knives and back-ups, definitely bad marks.

Finally the conversation ended, and dual creaks came from behind the canvas as the two Compliance officers stood. Footsteps sounded on the withered grass. The Judge was coming to take a look at her mystery guests.

150

She stepped around the partition, tall, muscular, broad-shouldered and narrow-hipped, wearing a crisp tailored brown uniform and spit-shined combat boots. A gleaming competition-matched officer's .45 automatic hung in a well-oiled holster from the right side of her heavy black belt. Her white-blonde hair was no more than a half-inch in length, and only a pair of diagonal slightly-raised scars below her prominent left cheekbone marred her freckled features.

Seeing us, the corners of her wide mouth curved up into a nasty grin, and her grey eyes lit up.

My grey eyes.

Me.

Everyone sees photographs of themselves, sometimes revealing, sometimes embarrassing, sometimes perfect, or with luck, all three. And videos, with similar emotions churned up by the moving figure on a small screen that you know, for better or worse, is you.

Seeing another you is not the same. Not even remotely. The depth, clarity, background, the whole experience, are enormously different. Now I knew how the girls felt, each seeing someone just like themselves every day of their lives.

And she *was* me, before the Change. This close, I could smell her, so there was no doubt.

I saw myself walk to the table, examine the rifles and other weapons from our ordnance bag, picking them up in strong-looking freckled hands, and turn them this way and that. She never really stopped watching me, though, as intrigued with me as I with her, though maybe not for the same reasons.

I figured she'd attribute the LaFrances, obviously evolved M-16s, to research technicians in the employ of the US Government, and we, of course, she likely thought were agents of the hated and nefarious Newton McPherson, though she hadn't said that -- yet.

The Captain had gone back out to speak with the Sheriff and get the troops moving to break camp. We'd provided enough distraction to keep the Judge from reaming him a new one in her anger at being chased out of Flint, and I sure couldn't blame him for escaping while he had the opportunity.

"Now you know how I felt when I first saw you," Farrell said out of the corner of her mouth. I glanced quickly at her, took in her little grin, and tried to appreciate the irony of my situation.

"*I* will not kill her, Megan," Beckin added, as if to reassure me. I knew Beckin expected me to do exactly that, when the time came. And I knew I couldn't, under any circumstances.

"A classic trope of science fiction," Brone whispered, loud enough so that the Sergeant regarded him suspiciously. That *was* funny. I suppressed a giggle, with only a small note of hysteria.

Now the Judge looked at the four of us as a group, speculating as to what we represented. Her interest still drifted back to me every few seconds, and at last she pointed at me. "Come with me," she said, and indicated the other side of the curtain. When the Sergeant started to follow, she shook her head. "I'll be fine, Sergeant. Don't bother," and the look she gave me told me that she didn't consider me even a remote threat.

Boy, could I straighten her out on that score. They still hadn't searched us, apparently thinking that if they didn't *see* a weapon, there wasn't one. Dipshits.

So I followed her into the Judge's mobile inner sanctum, watched her butt under the tailored brown cloth, and smiled to myself at what Farrell had said.

"Sit," she said, pointing at the chair opposite hers. I sat, my hands in my lap, and looked at her closely for the first time. Without vamp mods, she was much paler than me, her stub nose was burned and peeling on its tip, and crows' feet had begun to form around her eyes. And those scars, of course. I don't even have a belly-button.

"You *do* look like me," the Judge said, examining me as carefully as I did her, "but you'd think they'd have sent somebody nearer my age. How old are you, kid?"

"Thirty-three on 17 October," I answered, absolutely the truth.

Her eyes widened for a heartbeat, and she whistled. "They knew *that*, and still left your hair longer, and didn't *scar* you?" She leaned back in her chair, and clasped her hands behind her bristly head. "*Stupid.*"

"Point of information," I said, raising my left hand. "Who are *they*?"

153

"McPherson's people," she replied. "The military, the people you *spy* for, you dumb little shit." She reached down, brought out her .45, and laid it on the table, safety off. "Let's cut the bullshit, kid. We can do this fast or slow, but we *will* do this. Now, what's your real name?"

I grinned at her. "Megan Rose Connolly, born in Oregon City in 1966, raised in Molalla. My parents' names are Brigit and Patrick. I have two younger sibs, Desmond and Mairead." I let my grin expand. "How about you?"

Her eyes seemed to catch fire. She snatched up the .45 and leveled it at my chest. "*You will not lie to me*! Or I *will* kill you right *now*. And I *have* no brother or sister."

"Can I show you a couple of things?" I asked, putting my hands up, palms out. "You need to understand what's going on here. You can keep the gun on me, okay?"

Her curiosity overcame her anger, though it took a tooth-grindingly long thirty seconds. "All right," she said, reluctantly lowering the barrel of her weapon.

First I reached down and unstrapped my little .25 Beretta automatic from my right ankle and laid it on the table, still grinning at her. Then I unbuckled my belt pack and put it beside the pistol, unzipping it and bringing out my military ID and the sealed packet of family photographs that I seemed to be showing everyone these days. I slipped an index fingernail under the edge of the seal and opened it, leafing through the pictures until I found one of just my parents.

"Here," I said, sliding it over to her. "These people look at all familiar?"

She held the photograph in her left hand, the .45 still pointed at me. I saw her knuckles turn white as she stared at it. *Gotcha*! I thought.

"Your...parents?" she asked finally, her voice shaking.

"*Ours*, I think."

"But...they're...*dead*." She squinched her eyes shut, unable to look at the picture, and two tears ran down her cheeks. The .45 sagged from her hand.

"Mine aren't," I replied.

Her eyes slowly opened, bleak and barely seeing me. "I *saw* them die," she said, her voice filled with anguish. I hadn't expected her to be this vulnerable.

"When?" I asked.

"I was seven. Looters came, before Elrod pacified the northern Valley completely. They took over the town and killed almost everyone. They shot my parents, burned our home, and *took* me." She wiped away the tears.

I didn't want to turn over *that* rock. I didn't want to know. The word 'took,' has a lot of meanings, some of them truly awful. I felt terrible, doing this to her. "Look at these," I said, handing her the rest of the pictures and my ID card.

For the next twenty minutes, I watched myself react to a life she'd never known, siblings she'd never had, grandparents she barely remembered, and my heart went out to her in a way it probably couldn't to anyone else.

It ended the way it started, with the picture of my folks. "They're older," she said, after another minute.

"It's been twenty-five years, Megan," I said softly, reaching across the table and touching her wrist.

"Who *are* you?" She looked at my hand.

"I'm you. I don't know any other way to say it. I'm sorry."

"But...*how*?"

"I can't tell you. Maybe if you just thought of us as twins separated at birth?" As I spoke, I removed my hand from her wrist.

She gave me a long and searching look. Pain showed deep in her eyes. "I should kill you and burn these pictures."

"Then you'll never know the truth," I replied, "and how many people saw me walk into this tent? That interesting story would get around."

155

Her wicked smile would have done Farrell credit. "Simple. I discovered and executed a spy."

"When was the last time you uncovered a spy and that spy wasn't taken to Salem to spend time under hot lights and sharp edges?"

She scowled and scratched her chin, something I did on occasion, and I felt an eerie shiver go down my spine. "Good point," she admitted. She picked up my family photos again. Her left hand had never strayed far from them. "These two children. Are they yours?"

"One is. The other is my partner's, the dark woman out front."

"They're as identical as you and me. How is that possible, when they have different mothers?"

"The genetic components of two ova -- hers and mine -- were combined in a lab dish to create a single fertilized ovum. It divided, then was split to make *two* developing ova. One was implanted into each of us, so the girls are identical twins who spent their first nine months in different places."

Now she looked both incredulous and amazed. "Your doctors must have incredible skills," she said, then paused, and I saw the light dawn. "You and the dark woman are..."

"Lovers," I finished for her.

"...lesbians."

"That, too."

She regarded me for another few seconds without speaking, and what passed over her features went from curiosity to speculation. No unease or distaste, which was nice, just good old pragmatic mental slashes of Occam's Razor, searching for some definition of the person sitting opposite her, the person who was so much the same.

"You're my sister," I said, when I thought she'd reached that point in the process, "and it's not catching."

A mild blush appeared on her face. "Most people can't read me that well," she said, and laughed, a little self-consciously. "I learned long ago to hide my emotions."

"When you were seven?"

"Yeah," she said, with a smile of grim satisfaction. "They *all* died eventually. I made it as slow as possible."

"I approve," I said, seeing in my mind's eye a blonde, dirty urchin with an equally dirty, but very sharp, knife. Then I had another thought. "What do we call one another?"

"*Good* question," she replied, grinning as she brought her right boot up to rest on the table top, and crossed her left leg over the right, at the knee. She leaned all the way back in her chair, with her hands behind her head again. "How about Megan with each other, when we're alone?"

"Okay, sure, Megan. And the rest of the time?"

"We need to talk about that." She lowered her voice. "Where were you four going when you got here?"

"North Cedar. Our daughters are there." I kept my voice down, too.

"I need some help. Three years ago, Elrod Macklin wanted to let go the reins of authority, turn things back over to the revived United States government. Anybody with a brain could see that ultimately that would happen, peacefully or otherwise, but some of those in our centers of power didn't want to see their little fiefdoms disappear." Megan looked up at the canvas overhead. "They stalled and put things off, and fomented some small localized dust-ups which distracted him, and gradually removed or discredited the most loyal and sensible of his advisors. I was on the road a lot -- all the Judges are -- and should have seen it happening, but didn't." She shook her head, and turned her gaze back to me. "He's been under virtual house arrest for the past eighteen months, while those he formerly trusted have been free to indulge their basest tendencies. They have created an atmosphere of cruel depravity. Elrod can do nothing. The other Judges either bought into it or had very fatal accidents, and I've been chased around the peripheries of the Compliance to keep me out of Salem."

"Why not start a revolt?" I asked.

"My favorite idea, but not so easy in my case." She chuckled ruefully, and held up a picture of my brother and sister. "You see, I also have a Desmond. He looks very much like your brother. He's only ten. They have him."

CHAPTER TWENTY-NINE

PLOTS

"I'm sorry," I said, after a few silent moments had passed. My head was wrapping itself around the fact that I had a nephew. "Is he actually being held?"

Megan shook her head. "Not yet, but the moment they see me as a direct threat, he'll be incarcerated. They know that my concern for Elrod would hold me back for a time, but I would still act eventually. Desmond is a more overt curb. I won't sacrifice my son, and they know it."

I thought furiously, trying to hatch a workable plot. With any luck the Sheriff would still be here, and I could get word to Morag and the girls through him. Damn my altruistic little heart, I could not abandon Megan and her son.

"I noticed you've got a throwing knife between your shoulder blades," I said, smiling at her. "Hit me."

"What?" She straightened up in her chair.

"C'mon, Megan. Trust me."

She went with it. Hesitated far less than I would have. Her right hand snaked behind her neck and the knife flashed at my face, all in one smooth movement. It's hard to feel pride with a four-inch blade kebobbing your left hand, but I did in her.

"Nice throw," I said, jerking the knife free. I held my bloody hand out, palm up, and let her watch the wound disappear while I did a Farrell, and licked her blade clean. If she'd looked incredulous earlier, it was nothing compared to now. And with all the trauma my bod's taken over the last few years, my healing has accelerated markedly. Fifteen seconds after I yanked out the knife, my hand was whole again.

I handed the blade back to her. "Neat trick, huh?" I asked, as she replaced the knife in its sheath.

Megan reached out and took my hand, turning it over and checking both sides. This was the first time she'd touched me on her own, and an electric tingle seemed to run up my arm. Hers, too, apparently. She blinked. "Interesting. You felt it, too?" she asked, with a tiny smile.

Then, going back to my hand, she said, "Were I a religious person -- and I'm not -- I would probably say you were an angel sent by the Lord to deliver us from our tribulations."

I laughed. "We sure weren't *sent*, and if supernatural forces were involved, they would have gotten the hair and the scars right." I did not say the L-word -- Lucifer -- even though that was the supernatural connection for Farrell and me. Religious or not, Megan likely wouldn't see that as a big plus in our budding relationship.

"Then how do you heal like that?" Megan asked, her grey gaze alternating between my face and my hand.

"Special diet and specific supplements," I replied, our standard answer to that question, much more socially acceptable than telling someone that we basically drink blood until the pump shuts down and then eat the lights and giblets.

"Oh," she said, her eyebrows raising. My ability to read her worked both ways, however. She saw that I was evading her question, but just as quickly decided to shelve the issue for now. "Why did you show me that?"

"You can get me out of here and on the way to Salem, if any interested observers think I'm dead or dying. Shoot me in front of witnesses. I'll *look* badly wounded, it'll take me two or three minutes to recover, and by that time you can have me in our truck and ready to be escorted to Salem."

It was weird to sit there and watch wheels spinning in my own head. Megan thought for twenty seconds, then said, "I read a book something like this when I was a kid, 'The Prisoner of Zenda,' by Anthony Hope." She grinned -- *my* grin. "I'm the prisoner, I guess."

"Close," I agreed, grinning back at her. "Can you get me into your quarters undetected and get uniforms for all four of us? And I'll need a buzzcut like yours."

160

"I like the way you think, sister," Megan said. "With identical bandages on our cheeks, nobody but Desmond and Elrod would know. I just need to figure what advantage two of us would have over one."

"Two places at once, for sure," I answered.

"There's got to be more than that." She regarded me thoughtfully, drumming her fingers on the tabletop. "Do you have other physical abilities?"

I snatched up my .25 on full-vamp speed, and pointed it at her forehead. It must have seemed like magic; her eyes couldn't register the movement. To her, it simply *appeared*.

Her mouth dropped open. She gulped. "Shit!" she said weakly, eyes wide.

Just as quick, the .25 went back in its holster. "I'm strong, too," I said.

Megan gulped again. "How strong?"

"Although I've never tried, I could probably bench-press a jeep."

Another few reflective moments passed. "And the others with you? The same?"

"Pretty much."

Now her grin threatened to split her face. Her eyes glittered like grey ice, and I pitied whoever was in her thoughts. "We can take it *all* back, Megan, make it *all* right again," she said, her fists clenched on the table top.

I waited for her to add Beckin's favorite line, "And we shall kill them all," but she didn't. I wasn't reassured, though. The implication was there, unspoken.

"We were sent up here in hopes," she continued, "that we wouldn't return. Captain Morehouse assured me that was the intention. The locals were expected to react to our presence by blowing us to hell. But I knew North Cedar hadn't become a hub of trade and commerce by promoting violence. So I went along with our temporary banishment."

"You mean," I said, "you went along with this, knowing you might be killed."

Megan shook her head. "No, I went along with it knowing that I could cheerfully kill Major Wachter if he gave me any hint that he knew what was going on."

"I didn't see any Major out there. Just the Captain -- Morehouse?"

The evil grin reappeared. "Major Wachter left to go into Flint and North Cedar just over an hour ago, shortly before the very sensible Sheriff Merrill showed up. What does that tell you?"

"Wachter knew something?"

"Yes." Her grin strengthened. "He expected us to come under attack, after which he would return, in total amazement, and then be able to report my unfortunate demise amidst the carnage."

"How convenient," I replied. "So you'll be in the market for a new Major?"

Megan laughed as she handed me the pictures and my ID card. "Yeah. How about that?"

"Sounds good. And if we're going with you down to Salem, I need to have the Sheriff get word to our people in North Cedar that we're going willingly."

Concern flowed over her features and into her voice. "I could just let you go, Megan, so that you could forget this crap and be back with your kids."

"Yeah," I answered, "but that wouldn't solve your problems, and the girls can wait a few days. We have the time. Besides, I couldn't forget you or desert you. Desmond sounds worth rescuing."

Megan sighed. "I have a feeling, when all this is over, he might be all I have left."

I reached over to her. "Not any more, Megan," I said very softly, laying my hands gently atop hers. "Not any more."

CHAPTER THIRTY

WHEELS IN MOTION

Megan looked down at my hands on hers, and for the first time her smile turned sweet and genuinely moved. Then she lifted her eyes to mine, and her usual cunning reappeared.

"What's your...friend's...name?" she asked.

"Farrell Gray."

"She a Major, too?"

"Yes."

Her nastiest grin flashed on. "Looks like I just found myself a new Major." She stood up, stuck her .45 back in its holster, and shouted through the curtain. "Sergeant! I need you to watch the prisoner while Major Gray and I retrieve her vehicle."

The Sergeant popped around the corner of the canvas wall as if he'd been propelled by springs. "Yes, Sir!" he said to Megan, goggling in my direction.

Megan gestured at me. "Keep your sidearm on this spy, Sergeant. She makes any funny moves, shoot her." She slid my Beretta just out of easy reach, and winked at me with her right eye. Then she walked out to the front of the tent, and I heard her say, "Okay, Major, let's go get your truck and have a few words with Sheriff Merrill." There was the sound of a hearty slap on the back. "And great job ferreting out that spy, Farrell. You were right, too. She *does* look a lot like me, except her eyes are a little too close together." She spoke briefly with the three enlisted men, telling them that Beckin and Brone had helped the industrious and loyal Major Gray, then she and Farrell left.

I wished I could have seen their faces as Megan did her routine. Farrell was now a hero, solidly on the Compliance's side, and I supposed Beckin and Brone would get medals at the ceremony, too. A smart, savvy survivor, my new sister.

I, of course, was set up to be dead meat, but Megan would get Farrell to the Sheriff *and* tell her what was going down, and Farrell would clue Beckin and Brone. When Major Wachter returned, the stage would be set for the next act in our little playlet.

Meanwhile, the Sergeant and I sat in companionable, if nervous -- on his part -- silence, his gaze darting to the holstered Beretta frequently, like I would snatch it up and blaze away any second. Men lead such interesting fantasy lives, particularly involving phallic symbols.

After an interim of ten minutes or so, during which time I put away my pictures, our truck pulled up in front of the yurt. The engine stopped, the doors opened and closed, and shortly the Judge's private chambers became much more crowded.

"Thank you, Sergeant," Megan said. "Go on back out to the front of the tent. Have your men dismantle the roadblock and load up all their equipment. When Major Wachter and Sergeant Cadwell return, I want both you and Captain Morehouse to accompany them in here. Is that understood?"

"Yes, Sir," the Sergeant replied. He saluted and left.

Megan walked to her side of the table, and stood regarding the four of us with eyes which seemed much darker and more dangerous than mine. "I want no slip-ups," she said. "I am going to kill Wachter and Cadwell, and shoot Megan. We'll throw the bodies in your truck, then drive to Salem. The contingent here will thus be several hours behind us, with ample time for all the witnesses to pass the events on to the rest. By the time they reach Salem, our performance here will have passed from rumor to reality. Three secret agents delivered a spy and infiltrator into my hands, she revealed the complicity of two formerly trusted men -- Wachter and Cadwell -- and I did my job." Her hand stroked the butt of her .45. "Any questions?"

During all this, only Brone managed to remain stoic and comparatively blank-faced. Farrell looked like she'd swallowed a number of canaries, and Beckin sported what I'd come to recognize as her 'anticipating fun' expression. Her green eyes were half-lidded and the slight curve of her lips could only nominally be called a smile. Cats look like that just before they pounce. Beckin's pounce might be several hours or even a day or two down the road, but she now knew there would be one. Or, better yet, several.

"How important to them is Wachter?" I asked.

"Fairly," Megan replied. "He's been their lead fireman for the past two years or so, doing first-level dirty work. He and Cadwell have been directly or indirectly linked to a number of deaths that serious investigation would probably reveal were actually murders. Two weasels with sharp fangs, the pair of them."

"So this will confuse your enemies and perhaps make them act precipitously?" Beckin asked, always seeking an edge.

"Definitely."

"They'll know we're phonies," Farrell said.

Megan smiled at her, not a nice smile. "Oh, they'll know that you, Brone, and Beckin aren't *their* people. They won't know that you aren't Elrod's agents who've been working at the borders of the Compliance for many years, secretly doing his -- and my -- bidding. They'll crap."

"And they won't know I exist," I added.

"Right. You will be someone who was supposed to take my place, probably at Wachter's bidding. They're paranoid enough to believe that Wachter would do that without telling any of them. Meanwhile, you'll be in my quarters in the Capitol building itself, learning to be me."

"What happened to the bodies in the truck?" Brone asked.

Megan shrugged, grinning brightly. "Gee, I guess they were dumped somewhere between here and Salem."

"What shall we other three do?" Beckin asked.

"You'll accompany me, one or two at a time. Farrell will go first, become familiar with the Compliance and its hierarchy. Then she and Megan can operate together, and I will train you two."

Beckin nodded, grasping the basic simplicity of what Megan intended. "How many people do we actually have to eliminate?"

"At the top? Only a handful. Altogether, perhaps a hundred, give or take a few. And some will switch allegiance when only one side -- ours -- seems likely to survive."

"Those should die also," Beckin replied earnestly, *Siog* practicality at its finest.

"Does the handful have names?" I asked.

"Scott Lebendig, Lawrence Gorman, Kenneth Berchtold, Thomas Traeger, all members of the Senior Council. A few chief lieutenants who scurry to do their bidding in the Capital. Beyond that, several dozen enforcers and petty thugs, and the usual gaggle of sycophants and toadies. For the most part, people who have carved out their little empires and will resist their dissolution to the bitter end."

"Perverts, too, I bet," Farrell said.

Megan laughed shortly. "And homosexuals..." She didn't quite catch herself in time.

Farrell nodded knowingly. "Lesbians and their ilk." She shook her head. "Such a shame when otherwise good and God-fearing people go bad."

Paler than me, Megan reddened in embarrassment. "I didn't mean..."

"Lick you all over for a quarter?" Farrell said, lifting her right eyebrow and leering at Megan.

Beckin and I snorted. Brone guffawed loudly. Megan glared at us, beet-red. "This isn't funny!" She turned back to Farrell. "I'm sorry..." she started to say, then gave up and sighed deeply in resignation. "I suppose I deserved that."

"*I* have a quarter," Beckin said, holding up a coin, "if you don't."

"I'll pass," Megan replied, laughing drily as she regained some of her composure, her face gradually fading back to its normal color.   She ran her right hand over her short hair, shook her head again, looked at me, and in her gaze I saw a private and personal fondness, including only the two of us.

We had given her hope. Now all we had to do was deliver.

CHAPTER THIRTY-ONE

EXECUTIONS

We waited nearly an hour for Wachter and Cadwell. Apparently the good Major wanted to make certain he missed the fireworks. I figured he'd expected to hear the mortars in Flint, but we were still a mile or so outside of the little town, and the big firs swallow sound pretty effectively. Eventually he'd get curious and return.

So we waited until the only structure left standing was Megan's big yurt. Something like a pre-trip meal was served, to use up the food that wouldn't easily keep. This was a large hit with the newly-anointed Hero Brone. He brought back enough chow for the rest of us, so the condemned woman ate a hearty meal.

Wachter finally showed, a tall stocky, scowling, bluff guy with a neatly-trimmed mustache, trailed by a smaller rather nervous NCO, presumably Cadwell.

Wachter began to bluster the moment he arrived in the rear portion of the tent, with Morehouse and his sergeant in tow. "Oh, thank God, Judge Connolly, everything is all right. *You're* all right. When I learned in Flint that the locals were planning to drive us out by force, or even annihilate our men, Sergeant Cadwell and I returned as rapidly as we could." Cadwell's head bobbed in quick agreement, as Wachter wrung his hands in concern.

It didn't wash. Even though I kept my head down and my hands folded in front of me, trying to look subdued and remorseful, I could still see Megan's smile of triumph as she drew her big .45. "We uncovered your infiltrator, Wachter," she said quietly. "Here she is. She confessed."

My cue to look up at the Major, who was staring at the .45 in disbelief.

As they turned toward me, the expressions on Wachter and Cadwell's faces were perfect. Completely stunned and -- to the designated witnesses -- totally guilty. They didn't know who the hell I was, but they *were* guilty.

Cadwell must've been the one who did most of the dirty work. While Wachter started to protest, Cadwell went for his pistol. Slipping up behind him, Beckin cut his throat.

Even wider-eyed, the Major watched Cadwell sag to the floor, blood fountaining from his neck. "I...he..." Wachter said, his hands fluttering denial.

"Traitor!" Megan said, as hard and cold as stone, and fired two rounds into Wachter's chest, sharp deafening cracks. He snapped erect, stumbling backward, his mouth working silently like a very large goldfish. His back hit the wall, and he collapsed down it to the ground.

Two down and one to go. Me. I stood up.

The tiniest breath of uncertainty flickered over Megan's features for an instant, then her face hardened again. She put two right into my gut, knocking me over my chair and onto my right side, curled up in a heap.

It hurt like hell.

Broke the chair, too.

CHAPTER THIRTY-TWO

SALEM

It's funny how goals change and life flip-flops. We hadn't wanted to go to Salem, for obvious reasons, and, if we had, I personally wouldn't have wanted to travel under a tarp with two oozing deaders.

On the other hand, neither Wachter nor Cadwell were down to heart-stop when we were dumped into the bed of the truck, so the Need got satisfied and I was back up to speed by the time we were over the bridge west of Flint.

"Are you okay?" Megan asked, seeing me moving underneath the tarp, topping off my tanks. I lifted my mouth away from a carotid, and said, "Just fine, thanks. Just trying to maneuver so I can soak up *all* the blood and urine with my clothes."

This seemed almost true. I was a sodden mess, and I stank to high heaven and beyond. Compliance road food apparently ran heavily to legumes and leafy vegetables, and Cadwell had croaked about three minutes after we hit the truck, then lost his anal sphincter and bladder shortly thereafter. Charming.

My little heme-high, plus the endorphins the repair and regeneration process generates to kill the pain, were the only things keeping my outlook on life sanguine. Beckin looked under the tarp once, wrinkled her nose, then let the tarp fall back into place. "Everything's fine," she said sweetly to Farrell and Megan, with a smirk in her voice. Little snot. And people wonder how elves got such a bad rep.

Beckin has a cast-iron stomach. *Nothing* bothers her, but I noticed that Brone -- displaced from the front seat by Megan -- had been silent, and guessed it might be stench-related.

I lay under the tarp for another eight miles or so, mouth-breathing, until we were down below the Flint dam. Then Megan directed Farrell up a side road, I heard gravel beneath the tires, and, after another few minutes, rushing water. Farrell put the truck in reverse, and the sound of rapids grew louder.

The moment the truck quit moving, I flipped the tarp off me, vaulted over the side of the bed, spotted the creek, and marched down the pebbled beach to it. I didn't look at anyone or speak. I just wanted to get something like clean. My boots and socks were halfway decent, so I took them off and waded into the stream, finding the deepest part, then lay down and tried to submerge in ten inches of water.

I probably looked like a salmon struggling upstream, flailing around, rinsing crud out of my hair, and pressing blood out of my very holed T-shirt and intact jeans.

Five minutes later, I stood up and looked at the quartet watching me from the stream's edge. Brone had the tarp folded up under one arm, and I knew he'd taken advantage of this interlude to dispose of my late traveling companions.

"Do I look better?" I asked, and was rewarded with a chorus of very emphatic nods. "Thanks," I said, and sloshed out of the water.

The moment I reached dry land, Megan intercepted me. "Show me," she said, pointing at my midriff. I peeled up the T-shirt, and she examined my restored abdomen, staring in amazement. "Jesus Martha," she said, leaning her upper body around so she could see my back. "Do you have any of those dietary supplements with you?" she asked at last, grinning.

"There is a steep price," Beckin said softly from behind her. No doubt from her tone of voice that she was deadly serious. Megan glanced at her, not understanding.

"No frigging shit," I replied, frowning as I squeezed water out of my hair.

"So how do you do it?" Megan asked, persisting.

I gave my hair a flip up, running my fingers through it as I regarded my twin, trying to say the right thing.

"When this is all over, I'll tell you," I said. "Is that okay?"

"Promise?"

I nodded. "Absolutely." Looking into her eyes, I wondered if mine ever held that level of intensity, that relentless tight focus. Probably not, I decided, or at least not as often. Father Ibarra had been right about different backgrounds creating different personalities.

"I'll hold you to that," Megan replied, looking me up and down with some approval while I got my shoes back on. "Now that you're clean, let's go do the same for the mess in Salem." Her fierce smile included all of us as we headed to the truck. The mission was back on line, and she was eager to get moving.

We pulled the roof tarp all the way back over the truck bed, secured it, and I put my cap and sunglasses on. In a fresh T-shirt, sitting next to Beckin on the shaded bench opposite Brone, no one would confuse me with my aggressive duplicate unless they got me out of the truck.

While I'd been hidden in the truck bed, we'd gone through a large checkpoint by the dam, and Megan was polite with the troops, but still terse. Her exalted status in Compliance society apparently let her do whatever she wanted, within limits we hadn't seen yet. Certainly she had literally gotten away with murder a little over an hour ago.

"Will there be other checkpoints?" I asked her, when we'd re-entered Highway 22 and were driving west at a steady sixty over smooth, sun-dappled pavement.

"Not until we get near the Capitol. About two blocks away, there'll be a mandatory stop, and, even though this is an unfamiliar vehicle, they'll let me through. I'll casually mention Wachter's sad end, and turn that story loose in Salem. By the time you're ready to go out in public, the word'll be everywhere." She chuckled ominously. "We'll see who gets nervous the quickest."

"You think they're all in on it?" Farrell asked.

"Essentially, yes, though Wachter was closest to Berchtold, and without Wachter and Cadwell, the power flow may shift away from their boss. We'll see. Berchtold is still the Council Chairman."

I wondered about all the German names. "Are these people all from old farm families in the north of the Valley?"

"Yeah," Megan replied, sitting sideways in her seat, draping her left arm over the back. "The younger, non-inheriting sons who served in Vietnam and then attached themselves to Elrod's movement. When they found themselves with good set-ups *and* in their late forties, they became concerned over the oncoming integration with the Reunited States. They decided to resist, or at least milk the system for enough to hide somewhere where they weren't known. Maybe set up in northern California with their little hangers-on armies."

"Macklin puts up with this?" I asked.

Megan smiled ruefully, and looked away out the vertical windshield, her gaze troubled. "I don't see much of Elrod these days. He generally has a couple of bodyguards with him. I've suspected for some time that they've got him on something, but I didn't know what to do. Thanks to you four, now I think I do. At least a start." As she finished speaking, any wistfulness her words held disappeared.

"Perhaps we can simply kill them all," Beckin suggested, looking sideways at me, trying to get a reaction.

The reaction she got was from Megan. "That *would* be nice," she agreed, and she and Beckin exchanged conspiratorial grins. "I want you to know, though," Megan continued, "that there are good people still functioning within the government structure. It isn't all bullies and crooks, just most of them at the top. And, of course, they didn't start out that way, so people are reluctant to believe that the heroes of twenty years ago, who brought peace to the region, are now skimming profits, goods, and whatever else they can lay their larcenous hands on."

"Any moral underpinnings?" I asked.

Megan looked sharply at me. "You've heard something?"

"We were told there might be religious justification for some of the nastiness."

"'God's Work' and 'The Lord's Work' are frequently cited as purposes for certain actions," Megan replied, in disgust. "These are good Catholic boys gone bad, Elrod once said, and since they were all his friends, he hesitated to take action." She grimaced. "Hesitated too long, it seems. Decent people have died."

"Are there real troops, a standing force?" Farrell asked,

"Technically, yes," Megan said, "but their officers are allied with one or the other faction within the Council, so they're not precisely a cohesive group. When the Council's in session, which happens every Monday, each Councilman's little faction matches the others in numbers, some on the Chamber floor, most up in the balcony."

"In each other's way," Beckin said, with one of her chilly little smiles.

"Right," Megan replied, then her eyes narrowed. "You're *serious*, aren't you?" she asked Beckin.

Beckin nodded. Her angular face didn't change expression. "It's what I do," she answered, in her raspy voice.

"Like Cadwell..," Megan said, thinking hard. Her gaze bored into Beckin, trying to understand what went on inside Beckin's skull, remembering how swiftly and suddenly Beckin killed. Good luck, sister mine, I thought. You won't find anything originally human in there, just a shallow layer of aftermarket humanity installed by Farrell and yours truly, shed easily enough when the occasion demands.

"We do the same thing," Farrell said. "Beckin just articulates it better and sees the endgame a little sooner."

174

Megan regarded Beckin skeptically for a few moments. "Sounds like the endgame is always the same," she said finally, a note of respect creeping into her words, and a attitude similar to Beckin's lurking in the mind behind.

Watching her, inwardly I shook my head. You're going to Salem to save your people, Megan, you're with a truckload of monsters, and, in your enthusiasm, you're willing to overlook that fact. Because one of them has your face. I laughed silently.

When I refocused on the world around me, Beckin and Brone were both looking at me. I must have laughed aloud. I grinned at them sheepishly.

Except for a few well-repaired washouts where the North Cedar River had gotten winter-wild, the highway seemed no different from our timeline. After Mill City, twenty miles east of Salem, it had been recently resurfaced, but the yellow line still separated the lanes, so the Department of Transportation must be functioning.

The white puffy clouds of early afternoon had given way to almost clear skies, and I saw, high up, a single vapor trail, and heard the muted thunder of a jet engine.

Megan caught my glance, and eyed the faint white track. "They've been going by a lot the past couple of years. The coastal areas of California began coming back to organized life about ten years ago, and the Northwest re-connected in the mid-nineties. Flights in and out of Oakland and Sacramento. That's what got Elrod convinced that the Compliance needed to re-join the Union."

"That's a military jet," Farrell said, peering upward.

"Yeah," Megan replied, "the number of those has been steadily increasing, too, and that's what's caused the frenzy among our greedy councilmen. It's like Chicken Little running around saying 'McPherson's Coming! McPherson's Coming!' The moment any federal troops leave Oregon City moving south, there'll be a quick exodus."

175

"Do you have radio?" Brone asked.

"Sure. There's a station in Salem, three or four in Portland. People listen on early transistor radios, or the old ones with tubes. News and a few local programs, music from the Sixties, almost every evening."

"So you know what's going on outside the Compliance," I said, "other than just word-of-mouth?"

Megan nodded, then cocked her head and looked at me.

"Why do I get the feeling *you* don't know any of these things, like you dropped out of the sky from the Moon? Your ID cards says 'U.S. Army,' Megan. You *are* part of the Federal Forces, for God's sake!"

I'm afraid I just looked uneasy, until Farrell said, "Yeah, how about that, Megs?"

I reached around Beckin and poked the back of Farrell's head. "Why don't *you* explain things to my sister, Major Gray?"

"All right. You see, Judge, we're from a parallel universe where Nixon didn't drop any bombs, where there never was a nuclear exchange, where the Union remains intact and prosperous, and where your President McPherson was -- until he resigned -- the Speaker of the House. *Our* President is a redneck cracker from Arkansas who seems determined to get in the shorts of every really ugly woman in the country."

"Except Elisabeth Ward Gracen," I put in. "She's not ugly."

"Well, yeah," Farrell replied, "she's a mega-babe, but she's the exception."

By now, Megan was looking incredulously from Farrell to me and back again. "You guys are kidding, right?"

"They're not," Beckin said in her dead-serious voice. She hates it when we start going back-and-forth, confusing the issues at hand. "It's true."

I nodded and sighed. "That's why my parents are still alive, Megan, and why I have a brother and sister, both born after nineteen-seventy."

Her eyes went bleak again, and her voice got small. "My mother wanted a boy. She was going to name him Desmond, after my grandfather. That's why I..."

"I'm sorry," I said. "I just didn't know how to tell you. It sounds so ridiculous." And as momentarily pissed as I was at Farrell for just blurting it out, I had to admit that I sure as hell hadn't figured a better way. At least it was done, for better or worse.

Conversation ceased for the next few minutes. The highway and the river diverged, the broader, less-turbulent waters swiftly drifting from sight to the south as the valley spread out before us, green fields of wheat and corn. Fruit formed on orchard branches thick with new leaves. This early in the growing season, produce wasn't going to market, and log truck traffic had thinned out as we left the mills along the river behind. What remained were pickups and cars of less than recent vintage, most of them looking as well-cared-for as those we saw on the other side of the mountains. Not a lot of bright colors, somber greens and dull reds, with fair numbers of 'dump what paint we have in the same pot' hues that defied description.

The vegetation smells up in the mountains had been overpowered by the tannin and pitch of pine and fir. Here the odor of rich old humus underlay the sharper, sweeter scents of new growth, and the thick heavy stench of manure seemed to hover over about every third field.

"Does your...Oregon...look like this?" Megan asked.

"Almost the same," I said. "Vehicles are newer, population is five times higher, and this highway is four lanes from just below Mill City." As I spoke, we passed the crossroads from Aumsville to Silver Falls, here a simple intersection, in our world an interchange congested twice a day. We had paid a price for political stability and prosperity. Our Oregon is a people-magnet. This bucolic and sparsely-settled reality probably looked more like pre-World War II than anything else. A little rot in the political infrastructure,

177

maybe, but basically sound. Well, we had ways to deal with contamination like that. I cracked my knuckles in anticipation. Beckin always says that the Changed -- with the Change -- acquire a genetic imperative to make things right, no matter how cynical many of us seem to get. Even Dierdre, who is cool, pragmatic, ruthless, and totally self-interested, *did* off the first Green River Killer when she had the opportunity, so maybe Beckin is right.

"More people, then," Megan said, frowning, referring to our timeline.

"Lots more," I replied.

Her face clouded even more. "Two of them are my parents," she said quietly.

Beckin turned to me, her right eyebrow lifted a miniscule amount, a question in her gaze. Easy to read that one. Family are very important to *Siogi*. I nodded, and Beckin said, "When we are finished with your task, perhaps you can visit Megan's parents."

Hope blossomed on my twin's features. "*Could* I?" she asked me, as though I would ever want to stop her, or would even consider it.

"Sure," I said, and felt that earlier spark of connection practically jump between us.

"Don't get sappy, now, kiddies," Farrell warned, hearing it in my voice.

"Not a chance," Megan replied, grim again in a heartbeat. She reached over and gripped Farrell's wrist, hard. "*You* understand, don't you, Major?"

As much as she could without putting us in the ditch, Farrell looked at Megan, long and searching. Her voice was throaty. "I think I picked the wrong twin," she said.

I choked back a laugh. Beckin made a little "mmeeph!" sound. Brone bounced on his bench. And Megan, predictably, turned red down to the roots of her hair. She glared at Farrell, a look that promised revenge, her face coloring even deeper as her anger built.

Farrell nodded approval, grinning at Megan as she turned her head back to the highway. "Oh, good," she said. "Our little Judge keeps score."

178

"You *damn* bet I do," Megan replied, grating the words out. "You're helping me with something I can't do on my own. I appreciate that, particularly since it's all volunteer, and it *will* be dangerous. When this is over, though, we might have our day in court, Major. Megan showed me what you can do, the quickness and the healing, and she told me about your strength, but I just might be able to bloody your nose, if I get lucky."

"Probably not," Farrell said, her eyes focused on the pavement ahead, "but I appreciate the sentiment."

Megan subsided in her seat, and her anger slowly did the same. "I've learned a few things about Martial Arts and self-defense," she said. "It'd probably take you five seconds to kill me instead of three, even with all those hours in the Dojo."

Under the frustration of her words, and the throttling-down of her quick anger, I could smell her desire for our physical powers. Desire is one of humanity's strongest emotions, whether it be greed, envy, or overt lust. Megan's was a simple need to be better, and that, of course, was the precise reason I'd so quickly bought into the Change/Need without maybe giving the ramifications sufficient thought. That old devil, jock mentality. Gets you every time. And with the Change, you can't go back again. It's forever until you die.

Farrell wisely didn't reply to what Megan had said. Though neither of us has the mass of someone like Brone, a single knuckled punch into an unprotected temple on a normal human by a Changling and they're dog chow. Limbs and necks snap easily. And don't even think about knives. They were invented for our kind.

We drove up over the I-5 freeway overpass west of Lancaster Drive, and Salem spread out before us, fields for a mile or so west and north, to the edge of a much-smaller city than ours. The Penitentiary, well to the north, seemed the nearest large building, but the golden figure of the Pioneer statue atop the Capitol still towered over its surroundings, gleaming in the sun.

A right turn on Airport Road, then a left onto State Street, and we were pointed directly at the Capitol, moving through traffic that resembled Pendleton's more than a little, except for fewer big farm trucks and a small number of military-appearing vehicles leavening the mix.

"Heads up, folks," Megan said, grinning in anticipation. "Checkpoint's right after we cross the railroad tracks, at the right turn on Twelfth."

"They gonna ask us to get out of the rig?" Farrell asked, as the truck bounced over the north-south railroad tracks. I noticed the rails were shiny with use, so diesel oil must be coming from somewhere to the north. The Alaska oil companies weren't too picky who they sold to, apparently, and the federal government must not control them.

"They wouldn't *dare*," Megan answered, looking smugger as Farrell turned the corner and the Checkpoint loomed ahead.

A pair of V-100s squatted in front of a thick concrete barrier with a heavy yellow-and-black steel railroad-style gate with steel pipe hanging from it. Ten troops were in sight around the gate, all looking more STRAC than Wachter's people up the river. Most of them carried M-16s with newly-machined barrels, rebuilt from basic Vietnam issue. Fairly formidable in this time and place.

"Notice the orange pips on their collars," Megan pointed out while Farrell braked the truck. "These are Berchtold's people, well-trained and loyal."

Watching them as we pulled up, I wondered what 'well-trained' meant here in any kind of fracas. Against Farrell or me, it would probably mean 'lucky.' Against something like Beckin, 'miraculous' might be the better term. With Brone, well, 'dead and indentifiable' would likely be about the best you could hope for.

Loyalty I understood. That was what you did within the job description until the ground opened up and claimed you. Or, increasingly, even in our righteous and moral society, it was what you did until the going got hairy. Then you changed sides or beat feet. For Berchtold's people, I hoped it was the latter. Some of them, though, it probably wouldn't be, and those would be the ones scraped off of walls or buried in less-than-fully-occupied caskets.

Never fuck with an altruistic vampire on a mission of mercy.

CHAPTER THIRTY-THREE

CAPITOL

The men and women -- only two women -- at the Checkpoint were alert and ready, slightly edgy at our unfamiliar truck, military but not theirs, until they saw Megan in the front passenger seat. The sergeant in charge double-timed up to her and saluted. The rest of them stood at ease, curious and interested -- rumor is always a big deal in any military group -- but not real concerned.

"Judge Connolly," the sergeant said. "We didn't expect you back in the area so soon." Lean, clear-eyed, and tanned, with short hair, he looked like any Valley boy who might have served in 'Nam or the Gulf. A nice kid. None of these people were thick-eared goons, for that matter. On the edge of the loop, I figured. Loyal but not fully-informed. The thick-eared goons would be inside the Capitol building.

Megan gave the sergeant a slow, somewhat-pained smile.

"Discovered a problem with Major Wachter, Sergeant Cadwell, and a spy they sponsored," she said. "They sited the unit in a place where the locals would take offence. The spy fell into my hands accidentally, implicated her partners under questioning." Her smile widened. "Weak little slut. I executed all three, then made my peace with the locals. The unit'll be back in Salem by nightfall." She indicated Farrell. "This's Major Gray, just off border patrol, and three of her people. And none of you saw them with me, right, Sergeant Brooks?" Megan didn't quite laugh nor wink, and neither did Brooks, but both knew that we'd be lucky to make it to the Capitol before the news did. Wachter hadn't been the most popular person on the block, judging from the expressions on some of the nearer faces, even though they had Berchtold in common.

And every troop there had one more thing in common: An absolute certainty that Megan loved her work.

The gate raised at Brooks' nod, and we went through the barrier. When we were half a block away, Farrell said, "Weak little slut."

"Made sense on the moment," Megan replied cheerfully. "Now we get you guys into my quarters, get you cleaned up and briefed." 'You guys' again, the classic genderless Pacific Northwest expression beloved by regional linguists.

"This gonna be a sneak?" Farrell asked, holding the truck at a steady twenty-five as she turned left on Court. There was no other traffic, so this must be the official Compliance route into the Capitol area.

"No," Megan said. "We'll use the underground parking, then just walk on in. My quarters are on the ground floor, same level as parking." We were nearly in front of the Capitol now, and I saw that the Capitol Mall, a large open area on the opposite side of Court, was half-filled with semi-permanent troop quarters, canvas over wooden walls.

I hooked a thumb at the Mall. "How many bodies billeted out there."

"This time of year," Megan replied, "with the country largely pacified and subjugated and people busy with their crops, maybe three hundred. But they're all well-armed and most of them have something to lose if their bosses go down."

"Kill them all, then," Beckin put in, scooping out the facilities while we slowly passed. She smiled when she said it, only teasing, but Beckin at night with her knives could probably reduce troop levels by a third, and sow considerable discord in the process. *Siogi* prefer to let their enemies do as much of the work as possible, so Beckin would doubtless clean scattered tents instead of concentrating in just one area. Then perch up in some large tree and watch the chaos, picking off anyone who strayed out from the main camp.

That whimsical scenario reminded me of a very real possibility: drawn by the magnet of potential mayhem, Morag Death's Daughter -- in North Cedar with the girls, and bored half to whatever -- would show up in a day or two with a couple of associates in tow. As the truck slanted down the concrete ramp into the shadows of the underground parking, I figured we had a minimum of forty-eight hours before Morag might arrive, so we were operating on a deadline of sorts.

We had to be discriminate, and we had to move fast. Unless I missed my guess, Morag would be *only* fast.

I put the question to Beckin. "How soon is Morag likely to turn up to see how we're doing?"

She raised an eyebrow. "Ahh, my very thought." She turned to Farrell. "How exactly did you explain things to the Sheriff?"

"Told him two days before we'd be back," Farrell replied. "Isn't that right, Judge?"

"Yeah," Megan said, then frowned. "Who's Morag?"

I laughed. "One of Beckin's relatives. Tall, dark, and deadly. And she won't be alone."

"No," Beckin said, nodding in agreement. "The Sheriff will tell her what he knows of here, and she will bring whoever and whatever she can muster."

"Sounds good to me," Megan replied. She gestured to the far wall of the surprisingly well-lighted parking garage. "Over by that door, Major," she said. "My quarters are less than a hundred feet from it." She swung round in her seat and pointed her left index finger at me, grinning my grin. "*You* are gonna get a haircut."

"I'm droolin'," Farrell said, angling the nose of the truck into the empty spot nearest the door. There were plenty of empty spots, not more than twenty rigs in the sizeable underground garage, and no people. She cut the ignition, set the emergency brake, and we all got out.

"Will there be enough room in your quarters for all of us?" Brone asked.

"With no difficulty," Megan replied, opening the door and beckoning us into the deserted hallway beyond.

We collected all our gear and joined her. Beside the doorway were actual working elevators, which surprised me.

"There are fewer people in residence than there used to be," Megan continued, "so I've got the equivalent of four bedrooms, which should work out about right." She looked up at Brone as we walked down the hall. "Might need some modification to get a bed to fit you, though, and even then, you'll hang over the end."

There was one thing I had to ask. "Where's Desmond?"

Megan looked at her watch, an old stem-wind. "He'll be where I left him, at Lee's Dojo. He'll expect to be there until the end of the month. I'll give them a call and tell them I'm back, and one of the Lees will bring him over after evening meal." She unlocked her quarters' entry door, set in a lath-and-plaster wall that had obviously been added since 1970. It divided a much larger room on the Capitol's ground floor into living area.

When the door was open, Megan slipped her keys back into a pocket, flipped the light switch, and surveyed the large main room carefully before entering. Everything seemed relatively normal to me, and she apparently thought so, too. We went on in.

The place looked fairly spartan, partially because there were no external windows, which made for a lot of undecorated wall-space. Still, there were paintings of pastoral scenes and snow-capped peaks scattered over the white walls of a large main room scattered with furniture. The kitchen occupied the far end.

In the center of the kitchen, on a shiny old Steel-and-formica table with matching chairs, sat a half-completed airplane model, a Piper Cub from the picture on the box. The model had to be pre-nuke, and I realized that when the populace had been reduced by eighty percent, there would be a lot more stuff to go around, whether it was roofing, appliances, or model airplanes. Plus, they'd never really been without fuel or electrical power.

Riots, looting, and disease might have turned more urban environs into self-cleaning ovens, but society hadn't gone completely completely down the tubes. Portland had probably been much worse, but the parts of Salem I'd seen as we'd come into the city didn't seem horribly ravaged. There had been empty spaces here and there among the blocks of homes and small businesses, yet things had generally been tidy.

Macklin and his people had done good things, had brought law and order and kept it. But somewhere along the line, human nature had stepped in, and things had gone haywire.

"You're as neat as Megs, Judge," Farrell observed, examining the orderly room with approval.

"'Megs'?" Megan said, laughing. "I was always 'Meggie.'"

Farrell regarded her for a moment before replying, gauging the situation, then said carefully, "She still is, with her folks." She paused. "That's what you meant, though, wasn't it?"

"Yeah," Megan replied quietly. She pressed her lips together, and her eyes got a faraway look.

"You will see them again," Beckin said in earnest tones, and I considered the irony of the least human of us being so concerned. Maybe Beckin had learned more from our society than I realized, or maybe this was merely another aspect of the *Siogi* family thing. Ascribing human traits to any *Siog* was unwise. On the other hand, I knew Beckin thought of us as family. Megan seemed to have lucked out on the basis of genetic commonality.

"That's a large refrigerator," Brone observed, eyeing a big white Amana on the far side of the kitchen, throwing the conversation in a different, but very Broneish, direction.

"Nearly empty, just now," Megan said. "The Major and I will have to go out and shop after Megan's haircutting session." She looked at me speculatively, her eyes narrowed. "Both of us should get cut, actually, for the sake of uniformity. But first, let's get your belongings situated. Follow me, and I'll show you your quarters."

Three small bedrooms lay in a row along a hallway on the left side of Megan's apartment. The farthest held a bunk bed, with walls covered with line drawings and penciled portraits, and more airplane models hanging from the ceiling. Desmond's room, no doubt, and I was struck with the similarity to my brother's room at the same age. Beside his bed, where he could see it, hung a very recognizable pencil study of his mother, perfectly capturing her expression of pride in having a son who could do this thing.

"He's *good*," I said to Megan, and at my side, Farrell murmured approval.

"He's only *ten*?" Brone asked, eyebrows raised.

"Yeah," Megan replied, her arms folded across her chest, the expression on her features matching the drawing, with a bit of amazement thrown in. "I can't draw my way..."

"...out of a paper bag," I finished for her, then added, grinning, "I know. Join the crowd."

After studying the drawing for another twenty seconds, Beckin pronounced, "It *is* you, and it was done from both life and love." She turned to me. "I am not certain I have ever seen *you* with this precise expression."

"The grubs are only four years old," Farrell stated flatly. "The first time they create something other than problems, Megs'll look the same."

"I'll look forward to that," I said. All too frequently, dealing with Quinn and Maren was like herding cats. Still, I missed them.

While the others oohed-and-aahed over Desmond's talent, I examined the rest of his room. Against the wall nearest the foot of his bed sat a child-sized desk. The drawings tacked above were all portraits, one of them a strong-featured rather grim-faced man who resembled the actor Ed Harris more than a little. I bent over the desk and looked closer at the drawing.

Who could this be? I wondered, then remembered Sheriff Merrill's words about Megan being "Macklin's girlfriend." This must be Elrod Macklin, then, and that probably answered the question of just who was Desmond's father.

Macklin didn't look like anyone who'd let himself get pushed around or talked around. Your best friend or your worst enemy, maybe, but nobody's easy mark.

Except that Megan's weakness -- Desmond -- would also be Macklin's, if I was correct about parentage. And while Megan had reconciled herself to not seeing Macklin much, if at all, that might not necessarily be the case for Desmond's father. Macklin might be keeping a low profile to direct the attentions of the bad guys away from the woman and son he loved.

So, as much as I missed our daughters, I stood in the bedroom of a small boy I had never met, and felt awfully good about being there.

CHAPTER THIRTY-FOUR

DESMOND

Farrell and I ended up with the bedroom nearest the front door to Megan's quarters, which suited me just fine. If anyone came through the door uninvited, we would be the welcoming committee. Neither of us was actually snarly yet, but a little action would be sincerely appreciated, and getting seriously blown away without killing someone always makes me just a bit grumpy, even in a good cause.

Brone got the middle of the three bedrooms, and Beckin would occupy the top bunk in Desmond's room. Megan's room was directly across the hall from her son's, its door set closer to the front of the apartment. Most practical.

We dumped our bags in our rooms, then went back into the kitchen. Megan opened a cupboard and brought out a time-worn set of Oster electric clippers that looked more suitable for livestock than people. Grinning at me, she snapped a grooved guard over the cutters, plugged the thing in, and handed it to Farrell. "Do Megan first to get the hang of it." She stepped up behind me and rested her hands on my shoulders.

"Just relax. This won't hurt at all."

"You don't know Farrell," I replied, grinning up at her.

Having hair the approximate color, texture, and manageability of bleached straw has never been a source of pride for me, but as my already short hair got much shorter,
a sense of loss did make itself felt. Particularly as white-blond clumps fluttered to the floor while Farrell hummed tunelessly.

"You missed a spot behind her right ear," Megan said, trying to be helpful. Beckin sat at the kitchen table and regarded me with unabashed glee, and Brone checked out Desmond's Piper Cub, turning the half-finished model in his huge hands. He looked faintly embarrassed.

When they decided I was done, Megan brushed the remaining clippings off my scalp, examining me carefully. "That seems fine, Major," she said at last. "Now do me."

"Sure," Farrell replied, for once without an innuendo in her words. I stood up and Megan took my place. During the process, watching Megan's face, I saw on her features the pleasure we all get with personal, hands-on attention. She probably didn't get that much hands-on attention these days, and I wondered for a moment who usually cut her hair. Likely Desmond, someone she trusted.

Since her hair was already short, Megan didn't take very long. When she'd brushed her scalp, she grabbed my arm and led me into the hallway to her room. With Farrell and Beckin in the doorway, Megan and I stood side-by-side and looked ourselves over in her big mirror. The same emotions moved over our faces in the same sequence: amazement, uncertainty, and a sort of dawning joy.

"You're darker," Megan observed, her features critical.

"Some," I admitted, thanking the gods that I hadn't been out in strong sunlight much this year. The Change confers extreme tanning ability on even its most pallid recipient. "But no one's going to notice unless they see us together." I glanced at Farrell and Beckin as I spoke, to see if they thought the same, and they both nodded.

"You'll pass for each other," Farrell said.

"Easily," Beckin agreed.

"Well, that's settled," Megan said, grinning at me. "We'll go clean up the kitchen while you shower, and I'll see if suitable uniforms are in my closet." She looked at Beckin. "You're just enough smaller than the three of us so that Major Gray and I will have to go to supply." She shrugged. "No matter, since there's nothing around here that'll even remotely fit Brone."

When they'd left, I collected my kit and clean clothes and went into Megan's private bathroom to shower. Stripping off my grungy clothing took only a few seconds, and I practically leapt into the shower. Warm water cascading over my shorn scalp felt strange, but getting truly clean was a luxury I hadn't had since we left the Cache in the Wallowas, and I gloried in the feeling.

The last of Wachter and Cadwell spiraled down the drain in the bottom of the shower stall, oddly reminding me of the shower scene in 'Psycho.' I soaped and rinsed twice, shampooed, rinsed again, then turned off the taps, stepped out and toweled dry. The new me in the mirror looked quite pleased with herself I thought, as I ran a hand over my bristly head. Then I made a few practice faces, until a cough from the bathroom door interrupted me. Megan had returned to check on me.

Her eyes widened as I turned toward her, and her mouth dropped open. "God!" she said, shaking her head, "if you aren't something." She meant my leanness I guessed, though she was nearly the same, except for me being more muscular through the arms and shoulders.

"Thanks," I replied, draping the towel around my neck. She didn't seem put off by my nudity, but I hadn't had any taboos in that area before I Changed, either. Too many years spent in team showers and locker rooms.

Suddenly I smelled desire again, subtly different. Not just a good healthy envy, or a craving to have the powers I'd demonstrated to her, but a yearning for physical contact. Not horniness, exactly, but a need to be held and comforted, which Megan quite probably hadn't had a lot of recently.

I moved closer to her, watching her, hoping my smile didn't look inviting, but rather merely affectionate. "It hasn't been easy, has it, Megan?" I asked gently, resting the palm of my right hand against her left cheek.

Pain showed deep in her grey eyes. For a few moments, I saw the little orphaned girl whose toughness had protected her from harm as well as insulated her from human contact.

No longer, Megan, I decided. I will give you the world you want and all the things important to you, and I will begin now. What we have is unique, and I'll exploit that to whatever degree necessary. My hand slipped around her neck and down her back.

She moved into my embrace and clung to me. "I'm *not* like this," she protested, and I felt moisture against my cheek.

"I know, I know," I said, stroking the back of her head. "I'm *you*, remember. We're strong, we don't need anybody else to lean on or complicate our existence. But that doesn't mean we don't have each other, Megan. You're why I'm here instead of with my children. I had to be here. You *need* me."

Her hands tightened around me. "I don't know what to *do*!"

I chuckled into her neck. "Beckin's right," I said, still stroking her. "Kill them all."

She tried to laugh, but all that came out was a kind of choked sob as emotions intersected. "I suppose," she said, and gave a hiccuping giggle.

"We *will* win, you know," I said, drawing my face away from hers, leaving grey eyes to grey eyes. "Whatever it takes."

Her mouth twitched, and I took a chance.

Our kiss was long and deep, the only kind I know. I willed my strength and certainty to flow into her, and felt my sister respond. And that's what it was, sister-to-sister, like-to-like. Mairead and I had never done this, for all that we had the Change in common, but Megan was not my little sister. She was me.

"God!" she said again, when we finally broke, after nearly a minute. But that was all she said. In the following silence, we stood holding one another, content, even our heartbeats in sync.

"I almost couldn't shoot you," she said without looking at me, when another couple of minutes had passed.

"I know," I replied, squeezing the back of her neck. "I saw it in your eyes. Didn't stop you, though, did it?"

"Not much does."

"Beckin would say there is no substitute for calculated ruthlessness, and in these circumstances, I agree with her."

I felt her smile against my neck. "This feels so good, like when my mother held me when I was little."

"It's something like that," I agreed, "except we're not little any more."

"I brought you a uniform to try on. And the Lees will be bringing Desmond home soon."

I laughed. "Don't forget the foodless refrigerator while you're coming up with responsible reasons to stop this."

"I didn't mean it quite that way."

I held her away from me, by the shoulders, grey eyes to grey eyes again. "I'm teasing, okay? But you're still right, Megan, and I do understand. Other people depend on us. Brone, for one, will be eating the furniture soon if not fed, and Desmond doesn't need to see his mother in the arms of a nude woman, even one who looks just like her."

"My long-lost twin sister," she said, her eyes wistful. She touched my face as she stepped back from me.

"That's what you'll tell him?"

She snorted. "Unless you can think of something better."

"We could tell him the truth. Will he keep quiet about it?"

"Oh, yeah. Desmond may only be ten, but he thinks of himself as a full-fledged adult, just trapped for now in a small body."

"He'll see this as saving his father?"

Her eyes widened in surprise. "You *knew* that?"

193

"It wasn't a big jump of logic. Sheriff Merrill referred to you as 'Macklin's Girlfriend.' That drawing over Desmond's desk -- is that Macklin?"

"Yes. Desmond's particularly proud of that one."

"He keeps *yours* by his bed."

"If he saw more of his father...they'd both be there." Megan sighed heavily. "As much as anything else, Elrod is a failed priest. The pleasures of the flesh entice him, but he hates the intimacy -- he sees it as weakness."

This sounded all too familiar, all too much like my early relationship with our CO, John Tierney, who loved and lost the enigmatic Dierdre, and reluctantly consoled himself with me -- his relative. Heavy guilt and bad karma. "How old was Macklin?" I asked. "How old were you?"

"I was twenty-two, fifteen years younger. I'd been on my own since I was Desmond's age, and I'd squared accounts with all those who'd destroyed my family and childhood. I knew who Elrod Macklin was, of course. Ten years ago, the mere mention of his name in the northern Valley and heads would bow in reverent thanks. He'd heard of the bunch of snot-nosed kids who provided order and something like law in Molalla. Recruited me personally for the Judiciary." I could hear the pride in her voice at being singled out by the great man. The disillusionment and frustration must have set in later. Yet their tie was still there, and in more than Desmond.

"He loved you, obviously," I said. We were back in her bedroom now, and I slipped into my panties and sports bra and her spare uniform as we talked.

"Do you think of yourself as particularly loveable?" Megan asked, voice and eyes level. She'd sat down in a carved wooden chair with paisley-patterned seat and back cushions, watching me turn into a copy of her.

I looked at her sharply. "That's an interesting question. But, yeah, definitely. Well, maybe not loveable, but appealing and wholesome. Mom and apple pie, the all-American girl, cute as a bug's ear and

194

sweeter than cotton candy at the County Fair. And there are certainly people who love me." I grinned at her as I finished, which provoked a dubious expression. "So, how do you view yourself?" I asked, as I pulled on my socks.

Megan seemed to gather herself. She took a deep breath. "I achieved survival and revenge, and until my late teens, that was enough. I had responsibilities within the community. That kept me busy and distracted, though I did have brief relationships. Then Elrod and his people showed up -- not that someone didn't come by periodically to report back to Salem -- and my life changed."

"He fancied you?"

She nodded, blushing a little. "And I was flattered by his attentions. He was shy and reserved, and *older*, of course. He didn't talk much about himself. I liked that. Most men prattle on about themselves."

Hard not to agree with that. "He was Elrod Macklin, too, after all. Or was that a factor?"

"Sure, everyone's hero," she replied, going into the bathroom and returning with a roll of athletic tape and a scissors. As she cut out two identical small squares, she continued. "He liked me a lot, *loved* even, but he couldn't share enough of himself to keep me satisfied. What I had taken for a becoming modesty turned out to be just the way he was. The ultimate mystery man who always did the right thing, but never said anything about it or revealed any motives. The sex, well, that was fine. He managed that much expression, anyway." Her upper lip curled a degree or two.

"Then there's Desmond," I added.

Sardonic shifted to rueful. "Desmond keeps me going, the best of both of us. A pity his father can't spend more time with him." I recalled my earlier thoughts on that, and resolved to say something later.

We stood in front of the big mirror at that point, each holding a square of white tape. I watched Megan cover her scars, then situated mine accordingly.

195

In the glass she stared at me. "God," she said, "no one will ever know."

She was right. It was seriously weird. Except for my darker skin and slightly younger appearance, we were identical. I brushed a hand over my stubbled scalp. "I'll need a pair of boots like yours, and that'll do it, I think."

"Coming right up," she replied, reaching into her uniform closet, and bringing out another nicely spit-shined pair of combat boots.

I'd just finished lacing the boots up and blousing the bottoms of my pants, when Farrell knocked and stuck her head in the door. Without waiting for a reply, of course.

"Looks like girls' dress-up time's all over," she said, examining the two of us critically as we stood together in the middle of Megan's bedroom. "As long as no one sees you together, you'll be all right. Of course, even if you looked *exactly* the same, that'd still blow the op." She arched an eyebrow at Megan. "Got another .45?"

"Oh, yeah," I said, slapping my empty belt, having overlooked that important item.

"Two of 'em, actually," Megan replied. "My back-up and one I liberated from Judge Compton's quarters after he met with a fatal 'accident.'"

With the pistol on my belt, our resemblance appeared as complete as we could make it. Another minute of scrutiny revealed no significant nits to pick, and Megan's concerned expression mutated into her grim-as-death grin. Watching, I liked that. Maybe I'd given her some certainty.

She took Farrell's arm. "Let's go get some groceries, Major. It's almost six o'clock. We can't all troop down to the common mess, and we'll need at least a couple days supplies. Besides, it's Market Day -- Saturday -- and whatever's left may be picked-over, but it's still fresh."

Farrell looked down at Megan's hand on her arm, blinking, taken aback by a familiar hand that wasn't quite. Then she caught my grin, and laughed. "This may take some getting used to."

"We'll take your truck," Megan said, as we walked back into the main room. Her aggressive certainty seemed to have returned. Any second thoughts or self-doubts had apparently vanished in my arms.

After looking Megan and me over for a few moments, Brone and Beckin decided we'd get away with our masquerade. "I see no problems," Beckin said, "unless someone with a very keen nose notices the difference in odors."

"We *smell* different?" Megan asked.

"Yes and no," Beckin replied. "Basically, you're the same, but Megan's body chemistry modifications provide additional levels of olfactory stimulation. It's quite distinctive. You might even be able to sense it, a very faint cinnamon odor?"

Megan looked at me. "No," she said, shaking her head.

"What if Desmond comes home while you're gone?" I asked, changing the subject before Megan could begin asking questions about our differences.

She pursed her lips and looked thoughtful. "They'll walk over from Lee's Dojo, so Security will bring them down. As long as Security doesn't pass me on the way in as they leave, we should be all right."

"Desmond won't notice anything?"

"Not right away."

"Do you have any sort of ritual after you've been separated for a while?"

Megan laughed. "Well, I don't throw him up in the air and catch him any more. He's gotten bigger, plus he considers that baby-stuff." Her laughter deepened. "And Heaven forbid there should be any public affection between mother and son. No, he'll walk to your right side and put his left arm around your waist. He'll thank whichever Lee brought him home -- that'll probably be Brandon, the oldest. Then you'll smile down at him and tousle his hair -- he *hates* that, so you have to be sure and do it. After everyone leaves, he'll hug you."

"What about us?" Brone asked.

"Since we went through the roadblock, Security will know you might be here. They'll be craning their necks to get as much visual information as they can, but in here they won't challenge you."

"I'll be seated at the kitchen table when they arrive," Brone said. "That way they won't be as threatened."

"And I'll get up from where I've been lying on the couch," Beckin added, "distracting them."

"Sure," Megan said, then looked at me. "Can I borrow your cap and sunglasses? That'd help."

"No problem," I replied. I went into our bedroom, grabbed them off the bed, tossed them to her, and she and Farrell left.

Beckin stood regarding the closed door for a few seconds. "I believe the next thirty-six hours shall be most interesting," she said, her expression again that of a hunting cat. "We must discover all we can about this building and the people we oppose."

"I wish we knew more about Elrod Macklin," I said. "He's Desmond's father."

"Ah," Beckin replied. "So we must keep our Mister Macklin alive while removing his former friends from power."

I explained what Megan had told me about Macklin while we were in the big tent and in her bedroom. Both of them had to go take a look at Desmond's picture of his father. When they were back in the main room, Beckin said, "His face is hard, Megan, hard on himself most of all, I think. A strong and resolute man. They must have a hold on him." She made an angry fist. "Evil men. Betrayers. They have *no* honor." No honor. The ultimate *Siog* denunciation.

Brone grunted quick agreement, and, looking at their faces, I was extremely glad to be on the side I was.

We settled into our positions, Brone at the table and Beckin on the couch. I sat in the chair nearest the door, and watched Brone read the instructions for assembling the little airplane.

Close to a half-hour went by. Beckin seemed to have dozed off, and Brone looked as though he wanted to, when someone knocked on the door. Beckin's eyes snapped open, Brone shifted his feet underneath him, and I opened the door.

Any tiny residual doubts I might have had about helping Megan disappeared when I looked into Desmond's blue eyes and saw total joy and relief at the sight of his mother.

As he stepped to my side, I had a brief impression of a face very much like my brother's, olive-skinned, with hair of the same dark auburn cut virtually like mine. Smiling down at the top of his head, I did notice that his ears were thankfully tucked a tad closer to his skull than my Desmond's.

"How are you?" I asked. With no significant hair to tousle, I simply rubbed his crewcut.

"Fine," he said, simultaneously trying to squirm away and still retain his contact with me.

The young Asian man who'd delivered him grinned at us, tickled at our interplay. "See 'ya, Desmond, Judge," he said, lifting a hand before departing.

"Thanks, Brandon," Desmond replied, and I echoed him, wondering if Brandon's name was just a coincidence. I'd grown used to people being dead here who were living in my world; it hadn't occurred to me that it could just as easily be the other way around. I hadn't seen the movie 'The Crow,' but this Brandon sure didn't look all-Chinese, and our Brandon Lee had a Caucasian mother.

Brandon stepped away from the door, still grinning, and we were left with the Security people, two good-sized guys in brown who were a bunch more interested in Brone and Beckin than they were in Desmond and me. Brone and Beckin were unknowns. We weren't.

"Is there some problem?" I asked the man slightly in the front. There must be a good brain behind his narrow features and brown eyes. He was watching the now-standing Beckin more than he was Brone, trying to assess her. Good luck, I thought, hugging Desmond to my side.

"Uh, there's been some questions about the three people you have staying here, Judge Connolly." He sounded uneasy; he looked cautious. "Some say they might pose a security risk." Paranoid trickle-down, maybe?

"Really?" I asked. "Well, they're just border patrol volunteers who accompanied me back to Salem. I'll vouch for their loyalty and your safety, Corporal." I glanced at Beckin. "You won't hurt anyone, will you, Gilmer?"

"Not until after dinner," Beckin said, with a smile, her arms over her chest, pushing up her boobs, doing elf magic.

That pretty much ended the conversation. Security tipped their caps, thanked us, and left. Brone never did stand up, which was certainly just as well.

Desmond wrapped his arms around my waist and hugged me as hard as he could. "They were going to *kill* you," he said into my shirt, his voice muffled.

"I know, I know," I replied, rubbing the back of his neck. "But they didn't, did they? And how did you know?"

He turned his face up at mine, his blue eyes brimming. "They don't notice me much around the building, they're all so used to seeing me. I sit in places where I can hear, but they don't think anyone can be."

"So you heard something?" I asked, smiling down at him and laying the palm of my right hand against his cheek and neck, just as I had with his mother earlier.

He gulped and nodded. "Berchtold and another councilman. Major Wachter was supposed to see that you died." He clutched me harder, his face red and wet now. "I didn't know what to do."

"Major Wachter tried, Major Wachter died," Beckin said, cold as liquid nitrogen. "Your mother killed him."

200

"You did?" Desmond asked, hope filling his features. "Mister Lee said you would."

Mister Lee apparently had a great deal of confidence in Desmond's mother, more than she did. Still, in the end, he'd been right.

I bent and lifted him by his waist, held him tightly and cradled his face against my neck. "I have something to tell you, Desmond," I said, walking to the chair I'd been in when he arrived and sitting down again.

"What?" he asked, on my lap now, looking at the bandage on my left cheek, seeing it for the first time. "Did Wachter hurt you?"

I shook my head. "No. Look, Desmond, I don't know how to tell you this, so I'm just going to say it. Your mother is fine, she's *okay*, but *I'm* not your mother. I'm kind of like her twin sister."

"What!" Panic spread over his face. Involuntarily, he pushed away from me.

I gripped him by his shoulders, forced him not to struggle, to look at me. "Desmond, it's *okay*. She's just gone for a little while, to get groceries. She'll be back in a few minutes."

"No!" he said, trying to break my grasp and failing.

"Yes." I tore off the bandage. "See. No scars." That *really* freaked him. He got his right arm loose, took a swing at me, missed. I captured his flailing arm. "*Listen* to me, Desmond," I said forcefully. "Your mother is *fine*. Believe me. She'll be back soon."

Beckin knelt down next to us, locking her green gaze with his blue. "We're not Berchtold's people, Desmond. We're going to fool them with two Judge Connollys, then we're going to kill them."

Of course that worked, whereas my approach didn't. It must have been the idea of killing people. Kids always react well to that concept. Desmond visibly relaxed and began thinking again. "How?" he asked finally, his eyes darting between us, wanting to trust us, just not quite certain.

"We're not sure yet," I answered.

"But it *will* happen," Beckin promised.

"After dinner, I hope," Brone said from the kitchen. He shoved his chair back and stood up. "My name is Brone, Desmond," he said, smiling, "and I am here to help your mother." The top of his head nearly touched the ceiling fixture, and Desmond seemed suitably impressed, his mouth and eyes wide. "This is quite a nice model," Brone continued, gesturing at the unfinished Piper Cub on the table top.

The intrusion of familiarity must've convinced Desmond we were telling him the truth. He looked up at me. "She'll be back right away?" he asked.

"Cross my heart," I said, and did so.

"All right," he said, then regarded me with a touch more suspicion. "What's your name?"

"Megan," I said.

"No, really," he said.

"Really. Look, we'll try to explain it all to you when your mom gets back."

"I'm Beckin," Beckin said, holding out her hand.

Desmond shook it solemnly, and gave me a hopeful look.

"Can I go see my airplane?" he asked.

I laughed. "Sure."

He hopped off my lap and went into the kitchen. After introducing himself formally to Brone, he sat down and examined his model, and soon the two of them were happily discussing the little Cub.

"Two four-year-olds don't prepare you for a ten-year-old," I told Beckin.

"He accepted it well," Beckin said, watching events in the kitchen with a -- for her -- warm smile.

"He'd kill Berchtold if he could," I said.

"Ah, yes," Beckin replied, showing even more teeth. "A good and proper lad."

CHAPTER THIRTY-FIVE

KILLING TIME

Desmond may have seemed accepting and convinced of our good intentions and truthfulness, but that didn't keep him from flying into his mother's arms when she and Farrell returned. Beckin and I barely caught Megan's groceries before they hit the floor. Mother and son clung to one another, both trying not to cry and not quite succeeding.

"This Desmond?" Farrell asked me, watching the tearful reunion from behind Megan, after closing and locking the door. She picked up her own bags and went into the kitchen. "The other bags have the chicken," she said to Brone, slapping his hands away from her filled sacks. "This's just vegetables and something for breakfast and lunch tomorrow." She opened the reefer and began emptying bags into it. I saw fresh strawberries, some kind of lettuce, ground meat, a string of juicy German sausage, and tubs of ice cream.

Then I became aware of the aroma of the cooked chicken in the bag I held, the one Farrell had referred to. I headed for the kitchen myself, with Beckin close on my heels.

Seven whole chickens went to the Chicken Graveyard in the next hour, along with a large tossed salad, a gallon or so of milk, and half a flat of strawberries smothered in whipped cream.

"That was quite delicious," Brone said as he stuck chicken bones in the garbage and loaded the dishwasher.

Megan looked at the empty table in mock dismay. "When the Major told me how much to buy, I thought she was kidding. I see now that she wasn't."

Stretching her arms toward the ceiling, flexing her shoulders, Farrell said, "You better hope this operation goes down fast, Judge. This bunch'll put you in the poorhouse on rations alone."

"I can see that," Megan said, giving Desmond a quick squeeze. He'd kept close by her since she'd returned, and only now was he looking like each and every touch, smile and hug might not be absolutely necessary.

Brone closed the dishwasher door and latched it. "Should we run it tonight while we're sleeping?" he asked Megan.

"Now might be better," she answered. "Later, the sound could cover the approach of anyone who might not have our best interests at heart."

"You talk like Megs," Farrell observed.

"You mean my voice sounds the same?" Megan asked.

"Yeah, that, plus you phrase things the way she does."

"It's more complicated," Beckin put in. "All three of you have similar speech patterns, it's when you come into the conversation that differs." She looked at Megan. "You and Farrell are much quicker to respond in general conversation, being, I suspect, more aggressive." She patted me on the left forearm. "*Our* Megan is reserved and considerate of others."

Desmond, I noticed, was hanging on every word of this. We'd explained things to him rather generally, and he'd seen one of the alternate crew episodes on 'Star Trek' from a Portland station -- the Enterprise apparently voyaged on virtually every timeline -- so he caught on fast. It might be a little hard for him to accept that the alternate Megan Connolly was the *nice* one, but there you go.

At Beckin's words, Farrell let out a huge guffaw. "Explain that to yesterday's flying Mormons."

"I watched the entire process," Beckin replied. "I'm certain I heard Megan apologize to each and every one of the three as she threw them from the helicopter."

"Wow!" Desmond said, awed. "You threw guys out of a helicopter?"

"It was them or me," I answered, truthfully but half-embarrassed. "And remember, Desmond, back in Utah there may well be little boys and girls like you whose dads won't ever come home again."

Desmond recognized my tone of voice before I was halfway through my admonition, and his mind reached the end of the sentence before I did. Everyone at the table watched him do it, impressed. Megan smiled down at him, proud that her son possessed that level of understanding. For a moment, looking into his blue eyes, I saw someone much older than ten gazing out at me. "Yeah," he said quietly, and looked down at his hands, breaking our connection.

"Every time one of us kills, Desmond," Beckin said, "it is like dropping a stone into a pond. The ripples go out and out, never-ending, changing lives upon lives, the life of the killer and the lives of the survivors, on and on."

"Tell him how old you were the first time, Beckin," Brone said, his voice as quiet as Desmond's had been.

In answer, Beckin reached down along her leg, slipped her hand under the fabric of her jeans and brought out her Claiming Knife. She laid it on the table. Its worn bone handle -- *human* bone, I knew -- gleamed greyly in the overhead light. The slender eight-inch blade, black-anodized, reflected nothing, swallowing light like Beckin's hair.

We all looked at it, laying there, incomparably deadly in the right hands, yet beautiful for all of that.

"A gift from my mother," Beckin said, "and before that her father, and his mother before him. It is close to six hundred years old. A 'Claiming Knife,' it is called. Most families in my society have them." She paused, her gaze shifted from the knife to Desmond, and her soft rough voice grew even softer. "Go ahead, child, pick it up, feel it, understand what it is."

What showed in Desmond's eyes wasn't exactly fear, but very close. He swallowed, then slowly reached for the knife, his fingers trembling. When he gingerly held it in both hands, he looked at Beckin.

"Hold it in your right hand only," she instructed, and, when he'd done so, she continued. "A tradesman he was, a traveler, who cheated people shamelessly, and stole where he could. Glib of tongue and sleight of hand. He carried his custom on a donkey. A handsome little beast, I remember. It had beautiful brown eyes and a pure white muzzle." She touched the tip of the blade with a fingertip. Her green gaze hardened to jade, her voice flat stone. "My third year at the School of Death, in late Autumn. I was eight."

Desmond understood what he'd heard. Now he tried to grasp the enormity of it. Alternately repelled and fascinated, he stared at what his fingers enclosed. "Eight," he said, that single syllable quivering like a tuning fork.

Megan had the sense and courage not to interfere or say a word. She let Desmond wrestle with the reality of what Beckin told him and what Beckin was.

"When you are constructing your little airplane," Beckin said, "you wish to do it just right, with no mistakes. Perfectly. Correct?"

"Yes," Desmond replied.

"So this is for me," Beckin said, taking the knife from him and sliding it away again, against her ankle.

Congratulations, Desmond, I thought. You just passed Elf 101. And he had, not having run from the room screaming. Beckin smiled at him in approval. His mother put her arm around him. He didn't draw away this time. I wouldn't have, either. Beckin is seriously scary in a way I hope I never am.

"Tomorrow is Sunday," Beckin said, "a quiet holy day. Tonight, just before Midnight, I shall go out to the camp opposite here and reconnoiter." She turned to Megan. "Do they change the guard at Midnight? If not, I can go later."

"No," Megan replied, "they change at Midnight, but you'll never get by them. Five pairs patrol the boundary, and no part of it is out of their sight at any time."

Siog society is excruciatingly polite, its protocols rigid to avoid needless bloodshed. Scorn is unseemly, except between close friends and family, so Beckin only said, "They will not detect me," in her cold certain way.

Megan had seen enough of Beckin to understand how Beckin expressed herself. She shrugged. "It's your neck," she said, and Beckin nodded in agreement. If tonight's little jaunt came down to necks, however, I was pretty sure they wouldn't include Beckin's.

"We can wait for the ice cream until you come back, then" Brone said.

Amusement sparkled in Beckin's lime gaze. "Then Desmond will get none," she said, "and that would hardly be fair."

"Before bed, before you floss and brush your teeth, you can have some," Megan said, smiling down at her son, who smiled back, happy to have the warm familiarity of his mother after the totally foreign experience of Beckin.

Desmond remained in the kitchen working on his plane, while the rest of us adjourned to the living room. Farrell and I sat on the couch. Along the wall next to the door were two tall bookcases filled with books, some old, some newer, most of the latter published by the Willamette University Press.

"History," Brone said, looking over the Willamette titles, "since 1970."

Megan nodded. "Vietnam changed the world. Richard Nixon nearly destroyed us. Moscow, New York, and Washington are radioactive rubble, much of the Northeastern U.S. is uninhabitable, and Southern California still glows at night."

"How about Europe?" I asked.

"The Scandinavian countries caught considerable fallout from our east coast, and they're still suffering. Germany came together again within a few years and has largely rebuilt. The former Iron Curtain countries were freed overnight when Russia melted down. There are literally dozens of little governments there I couldn't even name. France, Austria, Spain, and Italy are much as they were. Their trade with the States goes mostly through Atlanta now, though."

"So the South didn't rise again?"

"No," Megan replied, laughing. "McPherson saw to that. His speeches from the time sound like they'd been written by the Founding Fathers, very Jeffersonian in tone. The South and the Midwest took care of themselves, and McPherson's military maintained order. Reclamation was slow, however."

Brone looked up from the book he leafed through. "What's left to reclaim besides the Mormons and here?" he asked.

Megan shrugged and grinned. "Not a lot. Montana just came back in, along with northern Wyoming. Western Colorado, New Mexico, and what's left of Arizona never really lost contact with the Union. Texas is an economic powerhouse." She shook her head. "McPherson knows exactly what he's dealing with in the Compliance, that the rats will flee, and Oregon will be whole. But the Compliance is small beans. He's got to be more worried about the Mormons."

"Don't blame him," Farrell said. "They've got some serious ordnance."

"Yeah," Megan replied, going to the little television and turning it on. "Well, let's see what's coming down from Portland."

The picture, when it flickered onto the screen, was black-and-white, not a surprise, showing a panel of middle-aged professorial types who were debating the degree of threat represented by the Empire of the Saints. Their military guest, a one-star Army General named Alcover, stood by a large blackboard and diagrammed the disposition of federal forces in Cheyenne, Denver, and El Paso. Then he switched to the Mormon side and showed the probable number of units and troops which could be opposing the feds in any sort of confrontation.

"Not all that uneven," Farrell observed, as the pointer and chalk flew over the board's surface.

I had to agree. Richard's father had wrought well, and both sides likely had nukes. "What's your take on Gregorson, Megan?" I asked.

"Basically not a bad man. Had the power so long he doesn't want to give it up, I think. Doesn't believe anyone else could do the job as well. He'll still lose. Unless they capture the Texas oilfields, the Saints have limited fuel supplies, and McPherson has more bombers. Once a Saint bomber leaves its home territory, it really doesn't have any place to go. Denver is heavily-defended, and the Rocky Mountain Arsenal was untouched in the Exchange. Leaving Utah is suicide. Federal forces can bomb the crap out of the Saints, and even if they lose fifty percent of their planes, there are plenty more where those came from."

Though he couched his words in more guarded terminology, on the TV screen General Alcover had reached the same conclusions. "Then it's up to the diplomats to prevent catastrophic loss of life within the Empire, General?" asked one of the panelists.

The camera zoomed in on Alcover's dark features. He smiled somewhat indulgently, apparently liking the question. Not a blood-and-guts general, then. "Precisely, Mister Wilkins. No matter how efficient any air attacks might be, the Empire has had nearly thirty years to prepare. In any hostilities that might come, there would be a protracted ground war which would be ruinous and devastating to the Saint citizenry. Losses would be high on both sides, but the Mormon on the land would suffer the most." As if to emphasize his point, Alcover slapped his pointer into his left palm.

"Your own family were once Utes, weren't they, General?" another panelist asked, this one as slender as the others, and I wondered if the new society included any fat people. Wachter had been the closest thing I'd seen to pudgy.

"Yes, they were," the general replied, his features sterner now, his mouth set in a grim line. "My grandparents moved to Denver in the Thirties. We

209

weren't Mormon, but my father had plenty of Mormon friends growing up. The Saints suffered terribly in Nixon's War. To destroy their people's splendid efforts and recovery would be a tragedy."

"So you might be considered a Saint sympathizer, then, General?" asked the panelist on the far right, a man wearing a sports jacket and bow tie, and even more gaunt than the others. More snide, too, apparently.

Alcover nodded. "Indeed I am, sir," he said, "and proud of it. I sympathize with all honest, hard-working peoples. And make no mistake. This is what we are dealing with. No one wishes the deaths of thousands of innocents. Our country has seen enough of that. Before we reach for our weaponry, we must first exhaust our supply of olive branches."

"Wahoo!" Farrell said, as the panelists clapped politely.

"What would *you* do, Major?" Megan asked, turning away from the screen, her smile only slightly masking genuine interest. I suspected she was trying to figure out Farrell and just what had brought the two of us together.

"Nuke 'em 'til they glow, and shoot 'em in the dark," Farrell replied, and Beckin snorted.

I reached over and poked Farrell in the ribs. "Bullshit, Gray. Tell us the truth. C'mon."

"Okay, all right, if you insist. McPherson should fly into Salt Lake and meet with Gregorson and the Quorum of Twelve, try to cut a deal. Even *our* Newt would do that."

That answer seemed to satisfy Megan. She switched channels and we watched some sort of College Bowl-type program featuring high school kids answering questions for college scholarships. They really went at it, the studio audience cheering them on, and it was obvious that education here had achieved a higher level of importance than in our society. None of them seemed to be wearing hundred-fifty-dollar sneakers, either, though their clothes were a bit less drab than the adults in the audience. Funny how things change and priorities rearrange when the population drops like a rock, and even survival gets iffy.

The whole scene was very early Sixties-looking, the boys in ties, white shirts and dark pants, the girls similarly dressed, without the ties. There were no skirts, so maybe these were some sort of school uniforms. In Pendleton, a few women had worn skirts, I remembered, but long, below the knees. These kids were aggressive, though, and I reminded myself that this was a studio filled with people and their children who'd been through hell. Aggression wasn't surprising. Here, the meek hadn't inherited the earth. They were dead.

Megan could tell even from our muted reactions to what we watched that our world must be very different from hers, and finally she asked, "How far ahead of us are you?"

Farrell and I looked at one another. "Twenty-five years, you think?" I asked, and Farrell said, "Sure."

"What's different, besides more people?"

"You know what computers are?" I asked Megan.

She nodded. "They've got one at Willamette. I watched them run it once. Amazing how *fast* it does mathematics."

"I have one on my desk at home that's about the size of a breadbox and processes information a hundred times faster."

"No!"

"Oh, yeah," I replied. "Do you remember when Neil Armstrong and company walked on the Moon?"

"No, but I've seen pictures."

I grinned at her. "Well, we were only two at the time, Megan, so you're excused. Now companies hang communication satellites in orbit and beam down television programs. Four hundred channels if you wanta pay for 'em."

She just stared at me. The little black-and-white screen we'd been watching had more reality in her mind than the monolithic whirring mathematical gadget at

Willamette University. Her computer was an oddity; ours were a fact of life she couldn't relate to.

"The satellites also talk to the computers," Farrell added. "If we want to send a message to someone we know in, say, Saudi Arabia, our computer can contact theirs though the satellite link-up. We type in a message, tap a key, and the message shows up in their computer. They see they've got mail, tap their own keys, and read our message. It's called the World Wide Web."

Megan only shook her head, with a bemused smile. Beckin didn't say anything during our exchange, and Brone just listened attentively. In their world were even more amazing things, plundered from a thousand timelines with better stuff than ours, even. Beckin's folks, I remembered, had a ten-year-old Sony HDTV five feet wide and three inches thick, that hung on the wall of their main room. The Siogi brought things back from the places they'd been and turned 'em over to the dwarfs, who could back-tech almost anything. Then they either made their own or sold the concept. Or, if it was art or some other irreproducible thing, paid gold up front and spirited it away.

"And, of course, your world's technology made you what you are," Megan said, looking at Farrell, Beckin, and me, and I scented a repeat of her small surge of desire.

Brone looked up from his book and smiled at me. Hard to do an end run around that question, and I couldn't just roll my eyes toward the ceiling and give her a disarming grin. "No," I said, hoping Farrell wouldn't jump in with the blunt truth. "What we are is something else entirely."

"And I am not the same as Megan and Farrell," Beckin put in. "In fact, were it not for my helpful uncles, we would never have met."

Right, Beckin. You'd still be a virgin, and I wouldn't suffer panic attacks upon seeing a certain shade of green.

212

A frown creased Megan's brow as she regarded Beckin. "You're *not* the same?" she asked. I could tell she believed Beckin, but earlier she might have assumed that Beckin just looked different on the *outside*. The last half-hour had probably convinced her that wasn't even remotely true.

"No," Beckin replied. "Are you familiar with the stories of the Little People of Ireland?"

"Yeah-h-h," Megan said, drawing out the word, looking faintly leery, like she thought her leg was being pulled.

"Also those who live under the *Sidhe* mounds, where one may enter and dance the night away, then discover when they emerge that a hundred years have passed?"

"Yeah," Megan repeated, not so guarded. Irish people love this sort of crap.

"There are likely no Little People, except perhaps the dwarfs, who are generally shorter and stockier than are we, but my people are those under the mounds, I believe. We alone can travel between the alternate realities. Our home timeline is quite different from Megan and Farrell's, much more than here, even. From it we go where we will among the alternate worlds. We are called *Siogi*.

"You're *elves*?"

Beckin avoided grimacing. She paused to select her words carefully. The typical *Siog* who's spent much time in something like the Twentieth Century United States tends to dislike the term 'elves,' with its connection to Santa and the North Pole. "Squeeky-voiced little slaves under the heel of a Capitalist oppressor," Beckin always says, sneering in derision whenever she sees a Christmas program or display, and, "No *Siog* would behave so."

But she gave Megan the benefit of the doubt. "Yes, the tall, stately, and deadly creatures of legend, ladies and lords of another realm, for whom death is life."

A single sentence containing the bare nub of Siog philosophy. Megan looked at me for guidance, a

213

quizzical expression on a face that I'd known for one day and all my life. I grinned and shrugged.

"How about you?" Megan asked Brone.

Brone replied with his warm and open smile. "I am a Berzerker, the Young Champion, an Arena Battler who was fortunate enough to defeat the other regional champions in open combat two months ago."

Beckin regarded Brone with sour amusement tinged with pride. "He is telling the truth," she said to Megan, "but is overly modest. He was the favorite going into the competition, and none came even close to besting him. He could have killed them all. It was no contest." As she spoke Beckin's pride in Brone moved from her face and into her voice. She smiled at him fondly, and he smiled back, basking in the praise of the person who mattered to him most.

"Beckin and I have known each other since we were small children," Brone explained. "She is prejudiced."

"I spoke truth," Beckin said. "It is no exaggeration. Every person in our village who could do so journeyed to Tenbridge for the Championship. All would agree with me without question or qualification." That ended it for her.

"Tenbridge?" Megan asked.

"Portland to you and us," I told her. "And Four Crossings -- their hometown -- is up in the Wallowas east of Pendleton."

These revelations flummoxed Megan some, but I still saw horizons expand behind her eyes. An adaptable person, my twin sister. She shook her head. "This has been quite a day."

"More than just chicken to digest, huh, Judge?" Farrell asked, grinning at her. "So what's on tap for tomorrow?"

"After breakfast," Megan said, "I'll take you and Brone out for a tour of the building and the grounds. That may take an hour at most. Then you, Beckin, and my sister, with Desmond -- who will know anyone you don't -- can do more or less the same thing. Afterward,

214

the six of us will sit down and discuss what to do next."
She cocked her head at me. "How's your memory?"

"Perfect," I replied.

"Whatever you show or tell us will be accurately retained," Beckin added.

"I should have guessed," Megan said, sighing. "Is there *anything* you can't do?"

"Sing," Farrell said, before I could respond.

I gave her a mildly pissed-off look. "Give me a break, Gray! I can sing *circles* around you."

"That is not saying a great deal," Beckin said, snorting. "My family has *wolfhounds* who sing better than Farrell."

Megan laughed for a few seconds. Then her face turned serious. "I shouldn't be enjoying this so much."

"When was the last time you sat in this room and had a good laugh with someone besides Desmond?" I asked.

Serious became thoughtful, and Megan's voice went quieter. "I'm not sure. Years, anyway."

I didn't say anything, just looked at her, and promised myself again that if we got through this okay, I would see to it that her life improved. Beginning in Molalla, with my parents.

The quiz show from Portland had ended by then. There were several commercials for home furnishings and beer, and then 'Bonanza' came on. Beckin immediately looked over at Brone and began to laugh. The big guy appeared shame-faced for about half a second, then devoted all his attention to the screen.

"Looks like we know what Brone's doing for the next hour," Farrell observed.

Megan glanced at her watch before turning toward Desmond and his model in the kitchen. "It's time for ice cream, Desmond." The 'time for bed' part went unspoken.

Quinn and Maren would have belly-ached to high heaven, but Desmond simply finished the wing decal he was applying, then dumped his little cup of water in the sink before giving the Cub a final once-over.

Brone managed to tear himself away from the Cartwrights long enough to join us in finishing off one of the tubs of chocolate ice cream. As we ate, not talking much, I watched Beckin begin to draw inward a bit, readying herself for her trip to the camp on the Capitol Mall.

"Would you show Desmond your family pictures?" Megan asked me, when Desmond had finished his bowl and rinsed it off in the sink.

"Sure," I replied, and brought out the photographs I'd showed her earlier.

While Desmond seemed interested in all the pictures, and spent a great amount of time on each individual one, he kept coming back to Quinn and Maren and my brother Desmond. Holding up my brother and sister's picture, he asked his mother, "Will I look like this when I'm grown up?"

Megan looked to me for an answer.

"I think your face will be shaped more like your mother's and mine, Desmond," I said. "See how my brother's face is a little longer?" My brother's face is an androgynous wonder, saintly, soulful and kind. The family -- particularly my grandmother's generation -- is still hoping for the priesthood.

He looked at the photograph some more. "Is he tall?"

I nodded. "Taller than your mother and me." Six-three, broad-shouldered, narrow-waisted, and seriously graceful, as a matter of fact. Farrell, who's never been too keen on men, secretly lusts after my brother, seeing in his unisex beauty something male she could easily deal with.

The prospect of being tall some day occupied Desmond for another minute or so, then he leafed back to Quinn and Maren. "They're sort of my sisters?" he asked, his brow furrowing like his mother's.

"Your half-sisters, sort of," I said, thinking what a hoot it would be to get the three of them together.

"Aren't they *cute*, Desmond?" his mother asked, winking over his head at me.

Cute hadn't occurred to Desmond. He probably saw only two nasty-looking little brats who would drive him nuts, given the opportunity. His forehead furrowed even more as he tried to come up with an ambiguous inoffensive response.

"They are quite inventive and playful," Brone said, licking his spoon, trying no doubt to encourage Desmond's positive thoughts. Beckin, who'd been around Quinn and Maren a lot, and had good reason to know Brone was full of it on this score, wisely said nothing.

"They look all right," Desmond said finally. "How old are they, anyway?" Typical little boy question, establishing his chronological superiority.

"They're four," Farrell said, "going on twenty."

Quinn and Maren were neither, of course, except in out-of-the-womb years. They would seem average-sized six-year-olds to most people, but what resided inside their skulls didn't compare to their age. Whatever interested them during their short lives had been indelibly etched in brains that gathered information the way Sperm whales gather krill and plankton.

And unless they liked Desmond -- and they probably would, I thought -- they would make his life a living hell. On the other hand, they like Farrell and me well enough, yet manage to make our lives quite interesting, and hellish at times.

If we should get through this mess with whole skins, Desmond and his half-sisters would meet, and, as I watched him search the photograph for indications of some redeeming features, I smiled at Megan and she smiled back.

When the pictures were back in my belt-pack, and Desmond had flossed and brushed his teeth, said his goodnights, and lay in his bed reading, only a little over two hours remained until Beckin's excursion.

Beckin managed to go into Desmond's room and tell him she'd be very quiet when she returned. They talked for several minutes, then Beckin reappeared and went back into herself.

"I've never seen you like this, Beckin," I told her.

She managed the ghost of a smile from where she sat, in an overstuffed Franklin chair, her knees drawn up against her chest. "Going against a few people is one thing," she said. "All that is needed is speed, aggression, and instinctual training. Here, hundreds of people are involved, and perfection is required. They do not expect me. I must commit no errors as I move among them. Since I have time, I can prepare."

"Mister Lee says almost the same thing about my training," Megan said.

"Mister Lee is correct," Beckin replied, and slipped back inside her head.

At twenty-three hundred hours and fifteen minutes, as we four played cards and talked softly, Beckin rose from her chair, went into Desmond's room, and changed her clothes. When she came back out, she wore loose Siog blacks, with black Nike rock climbers on her feet. Her green eyes looked distant and distracted, and her black clothing and pale golden skin made her appear something other than human, imperious, deadly, and remote.

With a single short nod, she slipped out the door.

When the door had closed, Megan looked at the rest of us. "Does she know what she's doing? The terrible risk she's taking?"

"For Beckin," Brone said, "there are no risks. This will be like a game of chess, with three hundred pieces on one side of the board and only one on the other. All the advantages lie with the single piece."

Megan examined her hand, fanning the cards out, shaking her head. "I just hope you're right."

An hour later, Beckin reappeared, flowing into the room through a door which hadn't seemed to open or close.

Brone rose from his chair. "Ice cream?" he asked brightly, and Beckin nodded in silence as she moved

218

through a series of stretches in the area just inside the door. Her angular features were slightly flushed, and her eyes, indrawn earlier, were now bright. Megan stared at her, an expression of disbelief on her face.

Brone went into the kitchen and began filling a large bowl. "Vanilla okay?" he asked, and this time Beckin smiled along with her nod. She walked into the kitchen, and sat down at the table, placing the bowl next to Desmond's model.

Megan, Farrell, and I put down our cards and stepped into the kitchen. When Beckin paused to come up for air, Brone asked, "How many?"

"Thirty-one," Beckin answered. Her eyes flicked up at him for an instant, glowing with an innocent evil.

Megan grabbed my left arm. "What's she saying?" she whispered. "Thirty-one *what*?"

Beckin's inhuman gaze rose to meet Megan's puzzled one. "Both sets of guards," she husked, "first the group coming off duty, then those newly on. Eleven of Berchtold's people in one of the central tents." She looked up at me, a note of apology in her voice. "Two were women. It couldn't be helped." Then her smile strengthened. "As you always say, we've poked a stick in their anthill."

A stick with a hand grenade duct-taped to the end of it, maybe. I could almost hear all Hell breaking loose.

CHAPTER THIRTY-SIX

GRIM TRUTHS

Though Beckin might have caught Megan off-guard, her response time was short. As soon as grace permitted, I found myself back in Megan's bedroom with the door closed. I sat on her bed while she paced back-and-forth in front of me.

"Sorry to drag you in here like this, Megan," she said, "but just what in hell is going on? What *is* Beckin?"

I took a deep breath. "Beckin kills. Her society is about seventy-five percent mercenaries and adventurers, and Beckin is one of the former. Make sense, so far?"

Standing still now, her arms folded over her chest, her gaze locked on mine, Megan nodded.

"*Siog* society is stratified and rigid by our standards. Blood ties and family are all-important, and most children learn the killing arts at an early age. Those judged particularly gifted are sent to one of the Schools of Death at around age five. Four Crossings -- the town where Beckin and Brone were born -- supports *Speirnead*, 'Sky Nest,' the school serving what would be our northwestern United States, western Canada, and Alaska. Words can't begin to describe the place. *Speirnead* is *old*, thousands of years old, built of massive stone, situated on and into a mountainside above the town. Legend says that the blood and sweat from the exercise rooms have penetrated the rock beneath all the way to the molten center of the Earth." Megan had dropped into the chair she'd occupied earlier, and sat with her shoulders hunched, elbows resting on her knees. She didn't speak; her gaze never left my face.

"Somewhere between fifty and a hundred twenty-year-olds graduate from *Speirnead* each year," I continued. "In her class, 1994, Beckin was First."

"The best killer?" Megan asked.

"Exactly."

She looked off to her right, at the carpet. "God, she wasn't kidding!"

"When it comes to her skills, Beckin doesn't. I don't think she can. I've been to Four Crossings, walked the immense ancientness of *Speirnead*. It's too alien to describe. Their culture is so *foreign*. The hair on the back of my neck was half-up all the time."

"She looks..." Megan began, then paused, grinned, and rubbed the back of her neck with her right hand. "I was going to say 'so normal,' but that's not true, is it? But she looks basically human."

"'Looks' and 'is' are worlds apart in Beckin," I replied. "To give you an example, when she saw you and instantly realized who you were, she said, 'I will not kill her, Megan.'"

"Out of respect to you?"

"That's how her head works. For a *Siog*, friendship creates obligations, just as with family."

"God. Thirty-one people dead because I look like you and you committed to my cause!"

I grinned. "It's not quite that simple, so don't even consider blaming yourself. Berchtold and his cronies also have 'no honor.' Beckin can then act in a righteous cause. And she will have done something significant when Morag gets here, a portion of an almost ritual cleansing."

"Morag is a... what, *leader* in their society?"

"Only by example," I laughed. "Morag is over eighty years old, so revered that her name is scarcely spoken aloud. *Morag Death's Daughter*. They say she's the best killer in the last five hundred years."

Now Megan looked confused. "What can an eighty-year-old do? Poke people with her knitting needles?"

"*Siogi* don't age, Megan. Like some wines, they just get better. They also get a little more comfortable in their skins, more human by our standards. Beckin is still rather stiff and formal. Morag is outgoing, wild, and laughs a lot. You'd like her. She's very charming. Still, that particular leopard can't change her spots any more than Beckin can. Morag is their society's equivalent of a top-drawer hired gun, and she's the best of those."

Megan looked briefly thoughtful. "And she'll be here, too?"

I nodded. "No later than Monday, I'm guessing."

She leaned back in her chair and thought for a few moments. "Where exactly do you and Farrell fit with Beckin and this Morag?"

"We met Beckin's uncles a few years back. When Beckin graduated from The School of Death, they felt she was too rigid and inhuman even for their people. They asked us to socialize her. We've tried. And succeeded, to an extent."

Now she looked puzzled. "What do you have in common, that made Beckin's uncles want to do this?"

"Identical line of work. What we do for the Pentagon and what Beckin does are the same basic thing. Wetwork, we call it." I gave her my best grin. "Not to put too fine a point on it, sister mine, but we kill people for Truth, Justice, Liberty, and the American Way. Sometimes in wholesale lots."

"But your physical skills are the same as hers?"

We were getting closer here to the big question and the big answer -- the blood thing -- which I wasn't quite ready to give just yet. "Actually," I replied, "we're stronger, and we might heal a tad faster, but yeah, we're similar critters."

All the things I'd told Megan, or even mentioned casually, began coming together behind her eyes. The memory, the strength, the healing, the lack of aging, it was all adding up.

"How did you get this way?" she asked finally. "You said you'd tell me."

"Not till this's over, Megan," I said, and meant every word.

"Okay," she replied, with a resigned sigh, and took a quick look at her watch. "It's almost one o'clock. We need to get some rest. Sometime between now and the next guard change, the shit is going to hit the fan."

"Sure," I said. We stood up and hugged, and, once again, it was the strangest feeling of contentment and total belonging. As Yogi Berra would say, it was 'deja vu' all over again.'

Sister mine.

CHAPTER THIRTY-SEVEN

MORNING AFTER

Late June means daylight comes early, and even Beckin couldn't hide thirty-one corpses. Probably didn't try. The message would be less effective if the deed weren't obvious. The alarms from the camp went off just after oh-five hundred hours. Deep inside the Capitol and underground, they weren't loud enough to wake Megan and Desmond, but we heard them easily enough.

In short order, the four of us were dressed and waiting just inside Megan's front door, all wearing our official Compliance uniforms, me with my bandage in place, ready to be outraged at the terrible deeds in the camp.

Farrell gave Brone an amused look. "You may be the world's largest UPS man," she said, laughing.

The big man only smiled. "If I knew what that was, I might be insulted," he said, with a brief glance toward the kitchen. To Brone, out of bed meant breakfast.

"Well," Farrell replied, still laughing, "it really doesn't work without the cap."

We sat there until just after six. Nothing happened except ambulance sirens and the occasional faint shout from out in front of the building. Closer, there was Brone's rumbling gut, which sounded like the little men bowling in Rip Van Winkle. Megan and Desmond missed it all. Finally, at six-thirty, Brone and I began to prepare breakfast, and made the horrifying discovery that, not only wasn't there any grinder, there didn't seem to be any coffee, just a pot.

"Jeez," I said, as we frantically searched every cupboard. "Maybe they don't *have* coffee here."

"Yeah, they do," Farrell said from near the door -- Beckin was stretched out on the couch again -- "I smelled it yesterday when we were grocery-shopping."

"Perhaps your sister doesn't like it?" Brone ventured.

"I have some ground and sealed in my go-bag," Farrell said sweetly. "How much are you willing to pay?"

This was desperation. "Lick you all over for a quarter?" I said, with a feeble grin, echoing Farrell's remark to Megan yesterday. Beside me, Brone groaned.

"Huh-uh," she said. "No deal. Free, and taking instructions during the procedure."

"You're harsh, Gray," I said, knowing I was lucky to get off this easily, "but it's a deal."

She grinned at me. "You are such a pushover, Megs," she said, scuttling around the corner, returning thirty seconds later with three packets of her favorite Barcelona Blend, and some nondenominational filters.

"*She* will drink the coffee, too, Megan," Beckin said from the couch. A clear rebuke for both Farrell and me. Me for being too easy, and Farrell for taking advantage. Today would not be a day where any of us would catch much flak from Beckin Gilmer, however. High body counts always make her relaxed for at least a few hours.

By the time we'd adapted a filter and gotten the old percolator up and running, a pajama-clad Megan groped her way around the hallway corner and stood peering blearily at us. "Coffee," she said, slapping her forehead. "Shit! I forgot coffee. I used it all before I left." She came into the kitchen, stuck her nose down by the spout, inhaled, and smiled. "Where'd you find this?"

Farrell looked her up and down. "I brought it. And I gotta ask, Judge. Where'd you get those PJs? Really cute!"

The tight-lipped smile Megan gave her didn't begin to reach her eyes. "I don't usually wear anything, but I wanted to be polite, Major."

"Hey, seen one Megan, you've seen 'em all," Farrell replied, and chuckled suggestively.

Megan glared grey ice-daggers at her. "You know, Major, I *like* you, or at least I *want* to like you. But you take some getting used to. You're a bit too flip for me sometimes. Quick and funny, but this early in the

225

morning, a little too much like being snapped with a wet towel. You know what I mean?"

Once again, Farrell proved she's very good at dodging blame or wet blankets. "Hey, Judge," she said, "I behaved myself during the shopping trip yesterday, didn't I?"

With a sigh, her eyes half-closed in resignation, Megan said, "Yes, you were *fine*. You even distracted people from me." She glanced at me, a 'make-her-stop' look.

"How about you get the first cup of coffee?" I suggested, pouring into a rather mis-matched set of cups that pre-dated the bombs.

That worked. Megan sat down, inhaled, and took a sip. "This's different," she said, examining the dark, pungent liquid. She took another, longer sip. "It's good."

"It oughta be," Farrell said, "at ten bucks a pound."

"Cheap, too," Megan replied, nearly draining the cup. "Ours is over twice that." She grinned through the rising steam at Farrell. "Another cup of this, Major, and I think I'll be able to stomach you -- for the day, anyway."

"Good," Farrell replied, over her own cup, "and I meant what I said about the PJs."

"I'm sure you did," Megan answered, more alert now, as she held her cup up to me for a refill. "Perhaps we can talk about it during our stroll around the Capitol later this morning. Then maybe I can understand what my sister sees in you."

"Other than the obvious, you mean?" Farrell asked, provoking Megan's short laugh and a shake of her head.

"They sound like a couple long-married," Brone observed to me, with a touch of amazement.

"Without physical intimacy," Beckin said from the couch.

"It's unfair," Megan said. "The Major knows nearly everything about me, in a way, and I know nothing about her."

"Except that she's an insufferable smart-ass," I added. "You've figured that out." Farrell was still looking smug.

"True enough," Megan replied. She stood up, cradling her coffee in both hands, smiling at me. "I *have* figured out a few things. Are you ready to shower?"

"Sure," I replied.

"Then let's go," she said, taking my hand.

Farrell's smugness disappeared abruptly.

CHAPTER THIRTY-EIGHT

OUT AND ABOUT

For fear of waking Desmond, Megan and I kept it together until we were in her room with the door securely closed and locked. Then we lost it, me collapsing into the chair, and her on her back on the bed.

"Oh, God," she said, her right hand half-covering her mouth, stifling her laughter. "That was *perfect*!"

"Very close," I admitted, practically gasping. "Did you catch Beckin's face when we were leaving the room? She was about ready to have a cat."

"No, dammit, but the Major..." She kicked her legs up and down on the bed, both hands over her mouth now.

"You know why it worked?" I asked.

"I think so," Megan replied, after another burst of giggling. "I'm probably the only person she can imagine you doing anything with besides her. Right?" She hiccuped twice.

"Yeah, definitely." I snickered. "Poor Farrell!"

She pushed up on one elbow, scowling at me. "*Megan*! Give me a break! 'Poor Farrell' gives you shit whenever she feels like it, and thinks she can do the same with me. She deserved what she got. C'mon, let's shower. The bathroom's right next to the kitchen wall. When she hears the water running, she'll crap her pants."

Well, maybe not quite, but things were very quiet when we came back into the main room, dressed in our matching uniforms, hand-in-hand and trying not to laugh.

From the couch, reading, Beckin looked up from her book and smiled in what I judged to be approval. Farrell, in the kitchen with Brone, gave us one rather stiff glance, then went back to her sausage-laden frying pan. Seeing her reaction, Megan squeezed my hand. Even as my mouth started to water from the smell of sausage, I thought this might be way too much fun this early in the morning.

"Just in time," Brone said, beaming happily, surrounded by unconsumed serious quantities of fresh food. He held up a plate with at least a dozen slices of buttered wheat toast on it. The rest of the loaf sat by the toaster, with another loaf beside that.

As we entered the kitchen, Megan gave my hand another squeeze before releasing it, then winked at me. She went to Farrell's side and put her right arm around Farrell's waist, nuzzling her neck briefly. Farrell stopped moving and her spatula quit shoving the sausages around the sizzling pan. Megan's voice was throaty, suggestive. "You are *such* a lucky woman, Major, to know my sister," she said, kissing Farrell on her left cheek before coming back to me.

For a split-second Farrell almost believed her. The aromas of toast, butter, and sausage filling the kitchen blocked the 'all-in-fun' message Megan's glands projected.

But, of course, that didn't last. She glared at the pair of us, more at me. "Aren't you two just fucking hysterically funny?" she said, waving the spatula in our direction. "Don't think you can fool me that easy."

Megan frowned, then stuck the ball of her right thumb under her chin and the tip of her index finger on the end of her nose. She regarded Farrell for a moment or two before turning to me. "You know, Megan," she said. "I think you're absolutely right. She *is* cuter when she's angry."

"Oh, definitely," I said, nodding. "The best part is, it's not real difficult to keep her that way."

"So I've noticed. Then there's another consideration: Does she taste as good as she looks?"

That almost floored me. Megan had to have heard that line somewhere, not conceived it herself, but it was still perfect, exactly the right thing to say under the circumstances.

Farrell's mouth dropped open in astonishment. Behind us, Beckin began to giggle, and Brone smiled without looking up from buttering the next round of toast.

Before Farrell could attack us with either a few well-chosen words or the spatula, Desmond came around the corner from the hallway, sleepy-eyed and pushing on his nose with the heel of one hand. "You guys make too much noise," he said, the unfocused expression on his features an exact copy of his mother's earlier.

"Did you sleep okay, honey?" Megan asked.

Desmond considered that for a bit. "I think so." He looked at Beckin, his eyes still squinty. "You didn't wake me up when you came back," he said, then, "I dreamt about the donkey in your story. What happened to it?"

"He lives yet with my parents," Beckin replied, smiling warmly, "in a life better than before. We named him Bran, for my rather naughty uncle, and the little creature thinks himself a member of our family. If we let him, he would come into the house. He has grown quite plump and sassy."

Though Brone must know the story, Farrell and I hadn't heard it, and were charmed right along with Desmond and his mother. Any hint of antipathy between my twin and Farrell dissolved in a heartbeat, more so when Desmond went to Beckin and hugged her. In my mind's eye, I saw Quinn and Maren doing the same thing.

"Come have some breakfast, Desmond," Brone said, as he covered a large plate with thick, unbleached paper towels. Farrell off-loaded both sausage patties and links from her frying pan onto the plate, then poured the excess grease into a ceramic mug before loading the pan again.

They'd apparently started their cooking with eggs. Brone opened the oven and brought out a large platter heaped with scrambled eggs. "Which kind of sausage do you want, Desmond?" he asked as he spooned eggs onto a plate.

"Both," Desmond replied, pulling up a chair and sitting at the table, his eyes brighter now, watching Brone.

That seemed a fair answer to me. Megan and I took over the cooking chores while Brone, Farrell, and Beckin joined Desmond at the table. The only thing available to drink involved milk, either straight or as hot chocolate, and there were no reduced-fat versions. California orange juice was practically unheard-of, and the Florida variety too expensive for everyday.

Eventually we all got fed, and by the time the plates were washed and dried and everyone else got cleaned up, it was time for Megan, Farrell, and Brone to go see what was happening in the outside world.

Brone didn't carry any weaponry, Megan had her .45, and Farrell took a minor chance and belted on her ten millimeter Beretta.

Megan looked her companions over briefly. "Okay, first we'll go have a look at the camp, seen how things are progressing there. It's been three-and-a-half hours since they found Beckin's handiwork, so we should be able to receive the initial official word on just what took place.

There won't be any objections to my being there, especially if I act stunned and surprised. When we're done with that, we'll scout out the entire building here, familiarize both of you with it. Any questions?"

Farrell and Brone shook their heads, Megan gave Desmond a kiss on top of his head, and they left.

A very long two hours passed. Desmond worked on his model, Beckin read, and I cleaned both my LaFrance and Beretta on the coffee table, after spreading an old copy of the Salem *Statesman Journal* over the table's glass and wood. The Change doesn't leave a lot of room for jumpiness, tending to keep us vamps on an even hormonal and mental keel, but I used cloth and gun oil to distract any tendencies to fret. Even so, I made sure the LaFrance was finished first and had a round chambered on top of a full magazine before breaking down the Beretta.

When a key slid into the lock sometime later, and the door swung open, no one seemed surprised to discover Beckin spread-eagled with her back against the wall with my Beretta held at eye level, or me on one knee in the darkened bedroom hallway with the LaFrance up and ready.

"How'd it go?" I asked, as Beckin shut the door and locked it after looking both ways down the outside hall.

"Good," Megan replied. "The police, both civilian and military, can't begin to figure out how so many people died without an alarm being raised or any shots being fired." She laughed. "I will say that they've begun to revise the number of probable assailants downward from the original fifty."

"We wandered around and tut-tutted for a half-hour," Farrell added, "and nobody looked at us twice or said 'boo.'"

"They will be looking over their shoulders tonight," Beckin said. Her voice carried an unmistakable edge of anticipation.

Megan regarded her with narrowed eyes. "You're not really thinking of going there again? They'll have guards in every tent!" Desmond had come over to her, and she put her right arm around his shoulders.

"Good," Beckin replied. "A challenge would be pleasant." She turned to me and inclined her head slightly. "Would the eminent Judge Connolly be willing to return to the camp again today, so that one of her subordinates might learn of any proposed precautions?" This was said in normal tones, a touch of humor even, belying the hunger for action I saw in the green depths of Beckin's eyes.

"How about we trot around out there, give the situation a heavy look-see," I said, "and then decide just how practical putting you in harm's way a second time would be?"

"That would be fine. Perhaps I achieved my goal last evening, and even now the honorless brigands are preparing to flee south."

"It didn't look that way," Brone said, shaking his head, "but they are perturbed."

"If not seriously pissed," Farrell added.

"Yes," Brone agreed.

"Go through the Capitol itself first," Megan said, "then inspect the camp. They'll be just that much further along on whatever they decide to do. Berchtold went up to Mount Angel to visit his parents this weekend, so he wasn't there, but Traeger and Lebendig were."

At the last two names, I saw Desmond's face twist, like he was going to spit.

"Which one?" Beckin asked, instantly picking up on his distaste. The *Siogi* celebrate the few children their long-lived culture produces, and child abuse is unheard of. The ultimate betrayal of helpless trust.

"Lebendig," Desmond replied. "He tries to get close to me. I don't let him."

"Wise child," Beckin said. Her shoulder muscles bunched for a moment, swift death's precursor.

"Lebendig's problem is well-known, if left unspoken," Megan said. "Nobody lets him near their kids."

"Perhaps he will be at the camp still," Beckin said thoughtfully, licking her lower lip. "Perhaps I can have a quiet moment with him, with no one nearby. Then he will not need to be concerned about any sudden journey south. Nor will any child again suffer." She exchanged looks with Desmond, two practical minds sharing the same wavelength. The difference was, of course, that Desmond could only *wish* to do something about Scott Lebendig.

"Well," I said, "we may as well go. I'm tired of being cooped up in here. Are you ready, Desmond? You have to be our guide and authority, you know."

Desmond ran off down the hall to his room and came back with a basic tan felt crusher hat, the kind fishermen wear, only without the hooks and flies. When he put it on, carefully adjusting it, even Beckin smiled.

"My dad had a hat like that when I was..." Megan began to explain, then remembered who she was talking to.

"...little," I finished for her. "He still does. Wears it at the most inopportune times. My Mom hates it."

"*My* Mom got it at a flea market," Desmond said, trying to look proud, but mostly looking like a kid wearing a very non-kid hat.

"Do you think they might have one large enough to fit me?" Brone asked, resting his right hand lightly on Desmond's shoulder.

We were all silent. No one seemed willing to comment on that possibility.

"Any other instructions, Judge?" Farrell finally asked.

"No," Megan replied, checking her watch. "It's eleven now. Lunch will be ready by thirteen hundred." She glanced at Brone. "Can you wait until then to eat?"

"If I'm not too active," Brone answered, his features altar-boy innocent again.

Desmond gave his mother a quick, self-conscious hug and we trooped out.

"What's your take on this?" I asked Farrell as we walked toward the stairs up to the first floor. In the distance, on our level, I heard voices, but the tones seemed conversational, not alarmed or angry, just people discussing last evening's excitement in the camp.

"Beckin definitely kicked their pins out from under them," Farrell replied. "Mall duty traditionally's been cush, apparently, with lots of discipline but no danger. The troops probably could've mentally dealt with the guards being picked off. They were on the periphery. The tent in the middle of the camp cleaned, that's what's got them scared. Even in daylight this morning, they looked jumpy."

Beckin, in front of us with Desmond as we started up the stairs, said nothing. Satisfaction radiated off her in nearly palpable waves.

The information kiosk, pale teak or mahogany, stood on the first floor right where I remembered it, close by the smaller south entrance. The grey marble floor of the Rotunda lay beyond, bordered with inlaid Vermont black marble, the bronze State Seal of Oregon in its center. Foot traffic in the building was light, this being a Sunday. Most of the people nodded to me and Desmond, and gazed curiously at Beckin and Farrell.

I walked to the State Seal, Farrell, Beckin, and Desmond at my side. Our footsteps echoed up into the hundred-foot dome overhead. As we examined the Seal from behind its protective ring of velvet cord, Desmond took my hand, doing his part in our little production. I grinned down at him. Smart little guy. My mother and father, perpetually astonished by Quinn and Maren, would easily accept Desmond. For them he would be a more understandable child.

As I thought about my parent's unmet third grandchild, a feeling of peace and certainty enveloped me. We would accomplish what we set out to do, I knew without doubt.

"Can you feel it?" Beckin asked from beside me, her voice filled with more vibrato than usual.

"What?"

She tilted her head down at the Seal. "This building, this *place*, is on one of the most powerful nodes I have ever experienced. Realities flow toward and away from this spot with absolute precision and clarity. I can walk those lines as easily as a breath, should the need arise."

"If we need a way out?"

Her head inclined another few degrees. Her smile scarcely showed. "Yes."

That was comforting, somewhat. I had this image of the group of us standing on the State Seal, firing at the enemy while Beckin spirited us off to our own timeline. Neat in a movie, maybe, but hellaciously exposed in reality. A single thirty-year-old M-16 on full auto could rake the Seal clean in about six seconds. There were

235

plenty of M-16s floating around here, and plenty of people who knew how to use them.

"We need to go look at the Senate chambers," Farrell said. "That's where our initial confrontation will be, tomorrow morning. We go in to give Berchtold the first-hand account of Wachter's demise."

"You and *me*?"

"Sure. If things get ballistic, we have a better chance of getting out in one piece."

As I thought about that, I looked over the Seal, out the tall doors of the Capitol's front entrance. A block away across Court street, the camp on the Mall lay half-shrouded and sun-silvered in morning mist. Brown-clad figures moved wraithlike between the tents, and the scene bore a timeless quality, embodying every camp back to the birth of camps and warring hosts. I could almost hear the battledrums and skirling pipes, and see the skirmish lines forming.

"No objections?" Farrell asked, elbowing me to bring me back on track.

"Not really." I leaned down to Desmond, who still dutifully held my hand. "How many weapons will be at Council tomorrow?"

"Everybody in the gallery. Gorman and Berchtold."

"How many in the gallery?"

He frowned in thought. "More than twenty, usually. Sometimes people with the supplicants. Family."

"Supplicants?"

"People who want favors from the Council, or justice."

"Let's go take a look." I squeezed his hand. "Okay? You can show us all the good stuff."

No kid can resist showing adults something, for them an appealing role-reversal. Desmond was a smart, observant boy, and mature as hell, but he was still a kid. Not letting go of my hand, he eagerly led us up the twenty-eight marble steps to the Senate chambers. Farrell kept on the other side of Desmond, and Beckin stayed a few steps behind, alert for any danger.

At the top of the stairs, just outside the door to the Senate -- here the Council -- Chambers, stood a long bench made of Yellow pine. On it sat a stocky, black-robed monk, his feet crossed at his ankles, reading. His gaze intent on the breviary he held in thick fingers, he didn't notice us.

Desmond pulled me down to whisper in my ear. "That's Father Bernard, the Chaplain. He's really the Librarian at the Abbey at Mount Angel. He just comes down here on his motor scooter on Sunday, to bless the Council on Monday."

While I absorbed the vision of a Benedictine priest on a motor scooter, robes flowing, Father Bernard looked up, hearing the sound of our boots on the marble floor. His dark moon face split into a wide smile, revealing small, white teeth in perfect alignment. He had no tonsure. Benedictines, I recalled, often didn't. Very fine grey-speckled brown hair, shorn short, covered his scalp. Behind thick glasses, beautiful, long-lashed, brown eyes regarded us with genuine pleasure.

"Judge Connolly!" he exclaimed in a high voice, coming to his feet while tucking his breviary into his robe, "and Desmond." From Desmond's expression, Father Bernard was one of the good guys.

"Hello, Father," I replied, smiling down at him as he took my hands in his. I felt heavy calluses, and tried to guess what sort of library work would produce what seemed very much like martial-arts mods.

"I'd understood you weren't to be back until the end of the month," the priest said. "How wonderful that you've come back early. Particularly with the events in the camp last night. All the guards, and a group of Chairman Berchtold's people, I understand." He blinked at me through his thick lenses. "Who could have done such a thing?"

"I'm sure they'll find out, Father," I replied, trying to be non-committal, particularly since the killer stood right behind me. "There were quite a number of investigators going over the area earlier. We'll be heading back out there again in a while. Perhaps they'll have found something."

"We can only hope and pray," Father Bernard said, his features troubled. "Even Berchtold's followers don't deserve death." Then he smiled. "Well, at least not *all* of them."

His last words gave me the information I needed, some inkling of where he stood. "Maybe this will convince him to leave town," I said.

"And take the others with him," the priest said, his voice suddenly low and grim, and Beckin gave a small grunt of agreement.

"Time will tell, Father," I said, and pulled Farrell and Beckin forward. "Let me introduce you to Major Gray and her associate, Captain Gilmer. They came back to Salem with me from border patrol."

As Father Bernard shook their hands, blinking up at them, he asked, "Were you two present when our friend Wachter went to his final reward?" Good news apparently traveled fast, and it was obvious that this *was* good news.

"Yes," Beckin replied, grinning at the priest. "It was very well-done."

"It would be both presumptuous and inappropriate of me to judge, of course," the Benedictine said, "but it I suspect not many rosaries have been said for his immortal soul." His eyes twinkled as he spoke.

I smiled at that, and took his hands again. "I have to show the Major and the Captain the Capitol now, Father. It was good seeing you. Perhaps we'll run into each other this evening, or tomorrow."

"Yes," he said, nodding, "you could come to Stations of the Cross tonight at Saint Joseph's." He reached into his robe and took out an old Pocket Book. "I brought a book I thought you might like, Desmond. People are always bringing old paperbacks to the library at the Abbey."

I looked at its cover as Desmond took the little book from the priest. 'Wasp,' by Eric Frank Russell, not one

238

I'd read, but Science Fiction apparently, from the picture of a man starting up a rope ladder on its front.

Desmond thanked Father Bernard, and the four of us said good-bye and entered the Council Chamber. As the door swung closed behind us, I heard the bench outside creak under the return of Father Bernard's weight.

"Does he give you books often, Desmond?" I asked as we walked up the central aisle, over carpeting showing leaping Salmon and sheaves of grain.

"Yeah," Desmond replied, examining his new book with anticipation. "He always has some with him. Mom says Father Bernard is sort of like Johnny Appleseed, only with books."

"A nice way to put it," I agreed, tallying up the thirty desks along the aisleway, fifteen on a side.

A long, built-in desk lay at the end of the aisle, a speaker's lectern in its center, separated from the Chamber floor by a wooden partition about four-and-a-half feet high. Two doors led out of the area behind the partition, and a mural on the wall above depicted a mid-Nineteenth Century street scene. "Nice field of fire from up there," Farrell said, indicating the galleries on either side. Low wooden walls topped with brass railings served to keep viewers from toppling down into the Chamber below.

"But only wood to protect them," Beckin observed.

Farrell tapped on the nearest desk. "Black Walnut, though, looks like. Pretty dense stuff."

Beckin smiled. "These desks are stout. Good cover. Up there is paneling, providing mostly a false sense of security." She pointed to the tall windows behind the galleries, her smile becoming more nasty. "Back-lit, also, and I have seen no body armor here."

"Beckin," I replied, "may I remind you that, when we're in here tomorrow, Farrell and I won't have any body armor either."

"Everything here is easily within pistol range, and you have your speed and training." Her smile turned arch. "Plus, Brone and I may be lurking about."

Desmond's initial reaction to our verbal exchange had been a kid's, looking from one of us to the other, open-mouthed and wide-eyed. Then he grasped that we were discussing options and tactics in our own loose-jointed way, and began to study our surroundings and consider what we were saying.

"Any thoughts on this, Desmond?" I asked, as he eyed the galleries.

He pointed to the lectern. "The doors behind where the Council sits can't be locked, but they'll have at least one guard by each one during the session."

"Can the guards see one another?" Beckin asked. The doors were set in the curved wall below the mural, about thirty feet apart, at 90-degree angles to each other.

Desmond shook his head. "No. There's little halls."

Beckin slowly turned three hundred and sixty degrees, checking everything again, then cocked her head at Desmond. "The door we entered, are guards also there?"

"Two."

With Beckin leading the way, we checked the doors behind the lectern. Short, narrow halls led to a wider hallway that extended completely across the end of the building. The shorter halls would be easy to defend, but damned difficult to get out of, they were so exposed.

Farrell looked up and down the larger transverse hall, then said, "Best we go out the same way we came in. Otherwise, someone might wonder what we're doing." That made sense.

"We should take a few minutes to examine the galleries," Beckin said to Farrell. "You've seen them, but we haven't."

When we reached the Chamber entrance, the first thing I saw when I stepped through was Father Bernard, apparently talking to someone on my left. The expression on his face, the quick shift from startled to imploring, told me he wanted nothing so much as for me not to be there.

I looked toward my left.

A man wearing a brown uniform. Elrod Macklin.

CHAPTER THIRTY-NINE

SAVIOR

Anger flooded Macklin's broad, angular features when he caught sight of Desmond and me. The skin tightened over his cheekbones. He reminded me of Richard Gregorson in Pendleton. Yet my nose knew Macklin's anger was a hundred and eighty degrees off Richard's, born of concern and caring, whereas the Mormon prince's had been greed and desire thwarted.

"Hello, Megan, Desmond," he said, anguish and despair in every grinding syllable. Like Father Bernard, Elrod Macklin wanted us away from here. Away from here and safe from his former cronies. He wasn't drugged, as Megan'd suspected. Their hold over him must be simply spoken or unspoken threat.

Desmond put his left arm around my waist, forgetting for the moment who I wasn't. He stared at his father, his lower jaw set.

"Hello, Elrod," I replied, and smiled warmly. It wasn't difficult, I felt so sorry for him. He wanted nothing more than the woman and son he loved to be safe and happy. That was the tether that bound him and kept him from acting, but I sensed he might be near its end. He smelled awfully frustrated. We may have come along at the perfect time.

My reaction surprised him. His anger subsided. "How are you?" he asked, shifting his feet, including Desmond in the question.

"Fine," we both answered. Around my waist, Desmond's arm relaxed slightly.

"You should visit," I said. "Desmond and I would both appreciate it. Desmond's getting to be quite an artist. There's a pencil sketch you might enjoy seeing."

The expression on Macklin's face altered to something very close to stunned incredulity. My baggage wasn't Megan's, who I guessed had never said anything remotely similar. Sharp-tongued and resentful, she had probably blistered his butt verbally every chance she got.

"I'd...like that," he replied slowly, and ran his right hand over his thinning blond hair. After another few seconds of regarding me in surprise, he turned to Desmond. "You're still drawing?"

"Yes, sir," Desmond said.

Macklin held out his right hand. "Let's walk around this level," he said to Desmond, then gave me a knowing look, "before my 'bodyguards' discover I'm missing. We can talk."

Desmond took his hand, after giving my waist a sqeeze, and father and son walked off, conversing in low tones, Macklin nodding while Desmond talked.

When they were out of earshot, Father Bernard turned to me and eyed me closely. "Exactly who *are* you?" he asked.

My response was just quick enough.

"Beckin, *don't!*"

CHAPTER FORTY

BUSTED AGAIN

Realizing what I'd meant, without moving any part of his body except his head, the sturdy priest looked slowly over his left shoulder, into the green-eyed face of death.

Beckin didn't blink, and her right hand was inside her shirt. Waiting. In neutral for the moment.

Father Bernard let out his held breath, but didn't take his gaze off Beckin. "Thank you," he said, his voice only wavering a little. "I'm no danger to you, really. Desmond would never behave this way if he didn't trust you completely, so you must be good people. Children are hard to deceive; those like Desmond are virtually impossible to deceive." Only a hint of fear-sweat tinged the air, and we *can* smell a lie. Father Bernard truly was no danger to us.

"That's kind of you, Father," I said, "and here's who I am." I showed him my ID card, while he smoothed the front of his robe nervously. He understood perfectly what Beckin had been about to do. After that close call, his eyes barely widened as he peered at my card.

"Mister McPherson is more interested in us than I thought," he said, as I tucked the card away. "How did his people find you -- a seemingly perfect match? And, more to the point, how did you approach the Judge without being killed outright?"

"I was born with this name. For all intents and purposes, my parents are Megan's parents. We're twins. McPherson and his government have nothing to do with why we're here. Our meeting was complete chance. We drove into her camp on our way to North Cedar, and decided to help her." I tried to keep it simple, never easy for me, and doubly hard in this case.

"This is a matter of faith, then," the priest replied, his right eyebrow raised. "As Desmond and his mother have, so must I have faith in the truth of what you say. How do you intend to help her?"

"We'll attend the Council meeting tomorrow and suggest that Berchtold, Traeger, and Gorman leave town," I answered.

Father Bernard shook his head. "Would it were that simple," he said. "They may balk, though I suspect that Mister Berchtold, at least, has his bags packed and a fast vehicle with a filled tank."

"Then perhaps he will live," Beckin said, with a cream-licking smile, "for at some point it shall certainly be the quick or the dead."

"Just as long as we're the quick," Farrell added.

"We are *always* the quick," Beckin replied, practically purring, on total death-elf mode.

None of this dialogue was reassuring to Father Bernard, who knew full well that he would be in the Council chambers tomorrow, should any excitement begin. He kept looking from one of us to the other, until he decided I was the least threatening. Of course, I had a familiar face, which helped. "How much of a chance do you feel you have?" he asked me. He sounded cautious, but not nervous or fearful. After Beckin, that might be understandable.

I shrugged. "That depends on how many in the galleries are willing to fight. Personally, I hope a high percentage will choose to run. Where will you be?"

"I deliver the invocation at the opening of the session, then read my breviary or observe the proceedings." He smiled in irony. "No one would find it remarkable if I stepped out into the back hallway to meditate."

"Probably a good idea," I said, looking briefly around. Desmond and his father were at the far end of the building, in front of what in our world were the House Chambers. Desmond listened now, as Macklin talked. The floor of the Rotunda stayed almost deserted, only the occasional person crossing the area near the State Seal. No one showed to check on Macklin. The excitement out on the Mall had apparently short-circuited his guards' attentiveness for a time, and he'd temporarily slipped his leash.

245

"If you peeled back that bandage," Father Bernard said, "I wouldn't see a scar, would I?"

"No," I replied. A bright, inquisitive mind looked out of his mild brown gaze, reminding me that monks in isolated monasteries kept the flame of human knowledge burning for hundreds of years during humanity's bad times. Those times when the Elrod Macklins of the world were a bit thin on the ground, over-extended, or occupied elsewhere.

By now, the liberator of much of the Willamette Valley and his son had turned the corner at the far end of the gallery, and were strolling back toward us. Father Bernard watched them with a sad expression. "A good man betrayed by his friends and associates. I hope he finds solace in these few minutes with the son he so deeply loves."

"What will he do when we challenge Berchtold and the others tomorrow?" I asked.

"Support you," the priest replied, without hesitation. As he spoke, he pursed his lips, perhaps thinking that he should support us as well. In his prayers, I guessed. Father Bernard hardly seemed a man of action, though I was still at a loss to explain those calluses.

Macklin and Desmond seemed to walk even slower as they approached us, perhaps subconsciously trying to prolong their contact. Certainly Macklin was more cheerful, with even some spring in his step. His harsh features had softened, and, as he smiled down at his son, I saw the man Megan had fallen in love with. A man who was no politician, no glad-hander, merely someone who gave a shit and had had the leadership and courage to act on it.

"John looks like that sometimes," Farrell said quietly from beside me, referring to John Tierney, our CO.

I nodded. "Since Deirdre re-appeared. He was kind of a sour-ball prior to that, you'll recall."

"Oh, I dunno," she replied. "I thought having me around cheered him up."

"You have an exaggerated sense of your amusement potential, dear," I said, noting that Father Bernard occasionally stole a glance in our direction, though I doubted he could hear any of what we said.

"She was *very* amusing earlier," Beckin said out of the corner of her mouth, her lime gaze simultaneously watching Macklin, Desmond, and as much of the rest of the building as she could see without moving her head more than a few degrees.

Any wise response Farrell might have made was effectively quashed by Desmond and his father, whose obvious happiness in one another was enough to bring a smile to anyone's face.

Grinning as they walked up to us, Macklin tried to hoist Desmond up to his shoulders, apparently forgetting how many years it'd been since he'd last done this. Desmond was not a small ten-year-old, and the lift faltered about half-way up.

"How much do you *weigh*?" Macklin asked, as he set Desmond back down on the marble floor.

"Eighty pounds," Desmond said, his mouth twitching, trying to keep from laughing as he looked up at his father.

"What do you *feed* him?" Macklin asked me, his smile now disarming and open.

I smiled back. "He's a growing boy, Elrod. You remember."

Those simple words triggered more than just memories of Elrod Macklin's childhood. They also brought back what must have been wonderfully happy times with the woman he thought I was. A spasm of pleasure/pain jerked over his features.

"I *do* miss you, you know," I said softly, letting my smile become more intimate.

Again I'd surprised him. He started to stammer some response while I put my arms around him and hugged him tightly. After a moment's hesitation, he hugged me back.

We stood that way for thirty seconds or so, until Beckin growled from behind me, and I heard booted feet running up the steps from the Rotunda.

Macklin and I broke our embrace and turned toward the pair of men just as they reached the top of the steps. We still touched, our hands loose around each other's waists.

Here at last were the expected thick-eared goons. Two mouth-breathers who'd been careless and let their charge slip away. From the expressions on their faces, changing from relief to consternation, they didn't know how to deal with the situation in front of them. They stopped about ten feet from us.

"Uh, there you are, sir," one of them said. Their gazes darted over us, seeing some unfamiliar faces. Seeing the man who probably had been their hero growing up, the woman he'd had a child with, the child, plus the Compliance's head Chaplain. Not to mention two mean-looking women with funny-colored eyes.

Macklin put up his hands, grinning at them. "I'll go quietly, gentlemen," he said, stepping away from me.

"Elrod," I said, grabbing his left hand and pulling him back. I kissed him with as much decorum as I could manage, and I heard one of the guards gasp.

No worse than Macklin. "I...I," he managed to get out, when I let go of him.

"I'll see you at Council in the morning," I said, and winked, knowing Megan was big on winking.

"All right," he replied, still visibly shocked. He turned to Desmond. "Thank you," he said.

Desmond gave him a quivering smile, his lips pressed together. "Bye," he managed to get out, as his father went back down the stairs with the two guards, who, I noticed, kept well away from him.

We watched in silence as the three men disappeared across the Rotunda floor.

"Sometimes," Father Bernard said, his voice filled with approval, "even an aging priest has his wishes granted." He looked up at me. "That was most kind and most brave. Had I scripted that scene for some sort of production, it would have been the same."

"Thank you, Father," I replied. "It seemed the right thing to do." I looked down at Desmond.

A single tear ran down his left cheek.

CHAPTER FORTY-ONE

SECOND NIGHT OUT

I took Desmond's left hand in mine, and would have refused to let go even if he'd wanted me to. But he held on tightly as we went up to the gallery viewing level and scoped things out there. Beckin and Farrell examined the premises carefully, Beckin thumping the hollow wooden partitions and pacing the length of the galleries. "Are there more people on one side than the other, during most Council sessions?" I asked him.

"No," he said. "It's pretty even." He gave me a tentative, self-conscious smile, as if to tell me that, though I wasn't his mother, I made him feel better just now.

"Nice to see your dad, wasn't it?" I asked, while we watched Beckin and Farrell do their thing.

He said nothing, merely nodded emphatically.

"We're going to do our best to make everything right, Desmond," I said. "You know that, don't you?"

He nodded again, his gaze locked on Beckin as she tugged at the brass railing before pacing backward to see if any part of the Chamber floor was visible when one's back was against the tall windows. I could understand his fascination. Watching her was like watching an engineer do a CAD-CAM survey to duplicate an object. Every aspect of a prospective battlezone was committed to memory. And fifty years from now, were Beckin asked to conduct an op here, she would still have all the info on tap. On the other hand, I'd seen her do her tricks spur-of-the-moment, and there seemed little difference. The end was still the same: Beckin standing, everyone else down.

And Morag, of course, was the Grand Doyenne of mayhem, more lethal than Beckin. Tomorrow promised to be an especially fine time.

Satisfied that they had the layout nailed, Farrell and Beckin followed Desmond and me around the remainder of the more public areas of the Capitol. The darker mood he'd displayed after the unexpected interlude with his father gradually lifted, and Desmond discoursed at length over the inner workings of Compliance government. I wondered if Megan knew just how well-informed and observant her ten-year-old was, and I found myself thinking that he was going to be a particularly excellent vampire when he grew up.

That thought nearly stopped me in my tracks and produced a wry smile as we stepped out of the Capitol and trekked down the wide sunlit steps over to the still-congested Mall. During the past eight years, my preferred method of dealing with my personal problems had been a syringeful of vampire blood. First myself with John's blood, then Farrell, then the German WWII vets in Saudi Arabia, and finally my own sister. Saving the world was just ever so much simpler when you could upgrade frail flesh and bone so easily.

The bodies of Beckin's victims had been loaded and gone for hours, so superficially the camp seemed normal. We walked between the tents, which looked a lot like those temporary units featured in many war movies. Wooden-walled and canvas-topped, they were clearly the model for whoever had designed the more-mobile yurts that we'd seen yesterday at Megan's camp.

Troops came and went between the rows. Some looked at us curiously, maybe surprised to see me again after only a few hours. Others ignored us, gripped by fear and nervousness. The air was thick with stale adrenaline, the remnants of earlier fear and panic, and Beckin fairly oozed satisfaction.

Desmond was quieter now. I could tell he sensed the terror and chaos of Beckin's nocturnal killing spree. Even normal noses can pick up the ripe scent of gallons of spilled blood. Down inside me, the Need stirred, and I saw Farrell's pupils widen as we strolled toward the center of the camp, the cook tents and command post. She hadn't fed since the Mormons, and even though we don't *have* to feed regularly, it's still a pleasant distraction.

In front of the command tent stood a group of nine men, two of them cops. Three of the men wore much better-tailored uniforms than the others. Desmond spoke from beside me. "The tall one is Traeger. The one on the left is Gorman." Distaste laced his words. "The other's Lebendig."

Traeger was very tall, slender, elegant, the sort of man who would seem at home in the lobby of the Portland Symphony during program breaks, sipping some nifty Oregon wine and making small talk with his wealthy peers. Gorman, short, beetle-browed, and thuggish, glowered at us, the one thing he seemed physically to hold in common with Traeger being an obvious dislike of Megan Connolly. Traeger's version of glower tended toward the curled lip, with a small frown of disapproval. Much more proper.

Lebendig looked to be another kettle of fish, or can of worms, which might be a better way to put it. Tall enough, about my and Farrell's heights, round-faced, and slack-looking. Even his scowl at us was slack, soft and ill-formed, but his hazel-brown eyes were diamond-bright with interest in Desmond.

And he knew we knew, his scowl changing to a smirk. Our resentment and anger made his overt desire even sweeter. Until he looked into Beckin's eyes, and saw a stronger desire of a different sort. His smirk vanished, and he looked away.

Only Gorman couldn't restrain his displeasure. He continued to stare stony-faced at us, even as Traeger smiled in greeting. "Ah, returning so soon, Judge," he said, his smooth words more relaxed than he smelled.

I didn't smile back. "Any progress?" I asked.

"Nothing substantial," he replied, and one of the cops snorted.

"A few people with knives, then?" I included the cops in my question.

"So it would seem."

"Four at the most, M'am," the older of the two cops said. I had a feeling I should know his name, but he didn't seem to be going to make a point of it, his inquisitive examination of Beckin and Farrell occupying him more at the moment.

"And women were among the dead," Beckin said in her best flat tones, her gaze sliding to Lebendig before returning to the two policemen. Lebendig wouldn't look at her.

"How do you know that?" the cop asked, puzzled.

"I can smell women's blood," Beckin rasped, poker-faced. "At least two. How unfortunate."

Traeger's interest in us suddenly sharpened. He said nothing, letting the two cops ask the questions, but his eyes narrowed.

"That's right," the younger, thinner cop said. Now Beckin had all of them except Gorman interested. He couldn't quite seem to grasp what was happening.

"Who *are* you?" the first officer asked.

"Border Patrol," Beckin replied, smiling at him. "This is my first time in Salem. A fascinating place."

"There *is* no Border Patrol," Gorman said, entering the conversation for the first time, his irritation barely contained.

Beckin regarded him with a good imitation of Traeger's disdain. "Apparently no one felt you needed to know, Councilman," she said, glancing at Farrell.

"Guess not," Farrell said, shaking her head. "We must be a well-kept secret."

Gorman remained pissed, not understanding anything more than that they were being baited. Not so Lebendig and Traeger. We had their undivided attention, and their little heads were working a mile-a-minute. Lebendig looked alarmed, but Traeger was clearly beyond that, his suspicions aroused.

I spread my hands out, palms-up. "I guess I just assumed *everybody* knew about Elrod commissioning the Border Patrol five years ago."

"How are you *paid*?" Traeger asked. The Councilmen all must know where funds went, how they were disbursed.

"Magic beans," Farrell replied. "We put them up our butts and shit gold." She and Beckin grinned at one another, and Desmond giggled. Little boys like those kinds of images.

"*Don't mock me*," Traeger said, stepping forward, displaying a bit of temper.

I let a slow smile spread across my face as I looked up at him. "You don't get it, do you, Councilman? Somebody sent you boys a message last night. Time's up. Get out of town. You're next. One, two, or all of those. You might be wise to pack your bags and go while the getting's good."

Traeger's eyes widened. Smart as he was, that hadn't occurred to him. Behind him, Lebendig looked shocked, and Gorman, dim though he might be, knew a threat when he heard one. His right hand dropped to the butt of his .45.

Farrell did the same to her Beretta. "Think you can out-draw me, Shorty?" she asked, doing a nice imitation of the Duke.

Gorman blinked at her, nonplussed, and Traeger put his right hand up to shoulder level, cautioning Gorman. "That's *enough*. We'll get to the bottom of this after things are dealt with here." He glared at us, his anger capped for the moment. "Is there something more we can do for you ladies?"

I shook my head, still smiling.

Beckin, however, wasn't quite finished. "We understand it was Berchtold's people who were targeted last night." She looked pointedly at the orange pips on Traeger's collar. "Perhaps your own sycophants will die tonight?"

She'd picked her words well. Traeger was probably the only one in the group who knew what the word 'sycophant' meant. He didn't respond, but his gaze darkened.

Message sent.

We sauntered off, Beckin and Farrell real happy with one another. Desmond practically skipped.

Twelve hours later, two tents of Traeger's loyalists died under Beckin's knives.

Message received.

CHAPTER FORTY-TWO

INTERLUDE

On Beckin's first night on the town, she'd gone to bed immediately upon her return. Not tonight. Farrell and I were drowsing in each other's arms after a slow, silent session of love-making -- with me teasing her about Megan -- when Beckin insinuated herself between us and cupped her breasts with our free hands. Under my hand, her engorged nipple felt pebble-hard.

"Eighteen tonight," she whispered. "I know that makes you happy." The entire length of her shivered with delight. "Now you must make *me* happy."

A mission neither of us would ever refuse.

CHAPTER FORTY-THREE

MONDAY

If Sunday morning's racket had been gratifying, Monday's seemed more so. The surprise was that it didn't begin earlier. Of course, Beckin hadn't touched the guards -- she'd mentioned there were twice as many the second night -- and troops were not leaving their tents for *anything*, so that explained why nobody blew the whistle until nearly oh-five-hundred hours.

We squatted by Megan's front door again, listening to sirens and distant shouts. The sounds of heavier truck engines dominated the vehicle noises.

"Much more traffic today," Brone noted.

Beckin only smiled, proud that she'd tilted the Compliance on its axis.

"It's Monday," I said. "Salem's a big farming community in this timeline. People get up earlier, businesses tend to open sooner. Plus, they're on alert from yesterday."

"I dunno," Farrell said, as we listened to the rumbling trucks. "A lot of deuce-and-a-halfs out there. They may be pulling troops in from the outlying areas. Maybe they're thinking McPherson's army could be moving in from the north."

"They'd *know* that," I replied. "There's got to be major personnel and serious communications in Oregon City."

"Makes sense," Farrell agreed. "So they're panicking."

That seemed to sum it up. It was surprising that no one had thought to haul at least Beckin in for questioning, after the confrontation yesterday, but maybe it would occur to them later. The Council session began at oh-nine-hundred, if things ran on schedule. Farrell and I would arrive a half-hour later to sow a little discord and deliver our ultimatum.

At six-thirty, Brone and Beckin started breakfast, and Farrell and I went up into the Rotunda to see what was happening on the Mall.

A *lot,* as it turned out. No one was in the Rotunda, but nearly two dozen empty troop trucks were parked on the grass at the near end of the Mall, and I didn't see anyone without a rifle in their hands.

Farrell whistled. "That damned Beckin."

"Effective little thing, isn't she?"

"No shit." She frowned, peering out the big doors. "They look organized."

I nodded. "If those trucks were up to capacity, there's about three hundred more bodies out there than yesterday afternoon, all of them ready to pull the trigger."

"Well, all of them can't get into the Council meeting," Farrell replied. "What we have to do is clean that end of the building, set up a few barricades, and wait patiently for McPherson to get here. Course, that might take a couple months."

"I don't think we're gonna have two months."

"Or Morag, who's probably more likely in the short term."

That made sense. I clapped her on the back. "Let's get some breakfast. Worry about it on a full stomach."

Megan and Desmond were up and functioning when we got back to her quarters. Desmond munched on a slice of toast as he waited for the first round of eggs and sausage. Megan sipped her coffee.

"How is it out there?" she asked, after we shut and locked the door.

"Beckin really got their attention," I said, pulling up a chair and sitting beside her. "Things are busy. They've pulled in troops from somewhere else."

"That's Berchtold's doing," Megan replied, with a satisfied smile. "His response would be more firepower. He and Traeger must be looking over their shoulders."

Farrell poured herself a cup of coffee, then leaned against the counter top. "When we walk into the

258

Council this morning, they won't have to look over their shoulders any more."

Megan chuckled. "No, I don't suppose they will."

"Unless you can think of any reason not to," I said, "the three of you should probably come on up about fifteen minutes behind us. Unless you hear shooting. Then come sooner."

Megan thought that over for a few moments, then nodded. "I don't suppose it'll make any difference at that point if they know there's two of us."

"If it seems calm in the chambers," Farrell said, "come in the front door. Otherwise, take the gallery watchers down."

Beckin murmured agreement.

The first batch of eggs and sausage were ready. As he set Desmond's plate in front of him, Brone said, "I'll go in the front, regardless. I'll be obviously unarmed, and my Nike jacket has a kevlar liner."

"You don't want a weapon?" I asked him.

He shook his head. "I haven't done much work with pistols or rifles, and I don't need knives." He grinned. "A quarterstaff would be nice, but perhaps a desk will do."

"Just watch your ass," I replied, earning an even broader grim.

Breakfast took quite a while, and showers all around -- *innocent* showers, I might add -- even longer. When we were all dressed and ready, I handed Beckin the .45 Megan had lent me. "Take this and my LaFrance. I'll carry my Beretta. Chances are good none of them will notice it."

"What will *I* do?" Desmond asked.

"You'll stay here, honey," Megan said, reaching over to him and stroking his right arm. "and wait. If someone besides one of us comes in, hide."

Desmond did not like his role one little bit. He wanted to be of some help, even if he understood there wasn't much he could do. Seeing his frustration, Megan sat him on her lap and held him tightly, crooning in his ear, reminding me that if today went well, Farrell and I would be back with the girls soon, maybe by this evening.

By that time, it was almost nine hundred hours. We sat quietly until twenty-five after, then hugged all around and Farrell and I slipped out the door.

There were fair numbers of people in the Rotunda, quite a few of those were civilians, and most of them were looking out the front doors at the goings-on on the Mall. They appeared dissatisfied, talking among themselves in loud voices, and I caught something about the Council meeting being closed. Their angry words echoed off the underside of the dome above us.

These must be some of Desmond's 'supplicants,' people who needed a grievance addressed. Keep your heads down, folks, I thought, as we ascended the marble steps.

The doors to the Council Chambers *were* closed, and two fairly alert-looking lummoxes in brown uniforms stood in front of them. Both had .38s on their hips.

"Sorry, Judge," one of them said as we approached, holding up his hands. "Council meeting's closed today."

"On account of the attacks on the Mall," the other added. They were feeling good about saying this, I noticed, pleased they could shut down the mean lady.

"We don't want these guys behind us, do we?" Farrell asked, her vamp adrenaline rising with mine.

I shook my head, and we simultaneously drove our right fists hard into the mens' voiceboxes. I caught my guy by the back of his neck as he bounced off the wall, and drove him headfirst into the marble floor. Sounded like a cantaloupe being dropped off a two-storey building.

"I wonder how hard it is to clean blood off marble?"

Farrell asked, looking down at the spreading pools beneath the mens' heads, licking her lips. The Need billowed up inside me. I shook my head and pushed it away.

"Let's hope we live to find out," I replied, as we stuck the two .38s in our belts.

"Right."

We opened the chamber doors and went inside.

CHAPTER FORTY-FOUR

COUNCIL

The place went completely silent as we walked down the central aisle. We left the doors open behind us. Judging from the surprise on the faces, the thick marble and heavy support beams must have kept the guards' deathsounds inaudible. That was good. This bunch seemed real jumpy.

Traeger and Gorman sat behind the low elevated partition, flanking a third man, big, blond and wearing glasses, who had to be Berchtold. Elrod Macklin sat in a chair on our side of the partition. His two minders stood behind him. There was no sign of Lebendig or Father Bernard. Nineteen of the thirty desks were occupied by some very nervous-looking gentlemen, all middle-aged or beyond.

It seemed pretty obvious that we were not going to make any new friends in this group. These were something like the landed gentry, after all, with vested interest in the *status quo ante*. Only Macklin looked even remotely glad to see us.

We stopped about twenty feet away from Berchtold. I looked up at the men in the galleries, surveying them. Green pips on one side, orange on the other. "Your boys look a bit drawn, Ken," I said. "Wachter looked that way, too, just before I whacked his traitorous ass."

Berchtold studied me steadily for ten seconds before replying. Up close, there were a lot of silver strands in his blond hair, a slight sag to the flesh around his lower face. The years were beginning to tell. He still looked strong and smart. No fear showed in his brown eyes. He wasn't about to be cowed by a smart-ass kid. "Major Wachter was no traitor," he said finally, his baritone voice similar to Brone's, with an added edge.

"Depends on your point of view," I responded.

For the first time, a spark of irritation glimmered in his gaze. "How did you get past the guards? They had instructions to prevent any entry."

"They fell down and died," Farrell said. She held up the .38 she'd taken from her guard.

Now Berchtold regarded Farrell. "Is this your paramour?" he asked me. He refrained from looking pointedly at Macklin, but I guessed he wanted to.

"We prefer the term 'inamorata,'" Farrell replied.

Berchtold snorted. "*I* prefer the term 'sexual deviant.' The scriptures condemn your evil perversion."

Farrell grinned at him. "Isn't there also something in there about 'Thou shalt not steal?'"

Another spark, this one stronger. Berchtold reached up and tugged on his right earlobe, and two soldiers moved in the gallery to our left, going for their guns.

Nowhere near as quick as Farrell's Beretta on full-vamp, however. In an enclosed space with solid walls, her shots were deafening. One guy flipped backward. The other fell over onto the railing, then slid to the floor, out of sight. Farrell stuck the gun in its holster, her grin even wider. "I just saved your life, Chairman," she said. "Those two were gonna shoot you."

The room was utterly silent. No one moved in either gallery, not wishing to tempt fate. Several of the people on our level were under their desks, however. Headshots being what they are, no one went to their fallen comrades.

In his view, Berchtold hadn't lost anything. Two expendables, that was all. If anything, he'd gained. He now knew that Farrell was at least as dangerous as I was, maybe more so. Unfazed, he laced his fingers together on the podium in front of him and asked Farrell, "What do you want?"

"A few thousand in cash," she said. "You can give it to me on your way out of town."

"You think we will leave." His words were slow and heavy. It was not a question. Traeger leaned over to

Berchtold and whispered in his ear, while the Chairman continued to stare unblinkingly at Farrell.

When he spoke again, Berchtold's voice was lighter. "You are running a weak bluff. Though impressive, you are exposed and vulnerable." He smiled broadly, evilly at me. "Your son will be without a mother, the poor child. His father is certainly in no position to help him." He looked over at Macklin. "Isn't that right, Elrod?"

Macklin's face flushed angrily, and he tried to stand. His guards shoved him back down.

Berchtold laughed, the scornful, arrogant laugh of someone who knows they have the winning hand. "Perhaps little Desmond would be happy with Mister Lebendig," he said, watching me closely. His left eyebrow raised a fraction.

"Do you think they can't kill *you* as easily as your men in the gallery, Ken?" Macklin asked, his voice thick with contempt. He sat with his elbows on his knees. He didn't try again to get up. His gaze didn't leave Berchtold.

That hadn't occurred to the Chairman. For the first time, he looked momentarily unnerved. "Leave now," he said to us, "and I may let you live."

As he finished speaking, a small commotion started up just outside the Chamber doors. I wasn't about to look away from Berchtold to see what was going on, though I had a fairly good idea who was there. A few hard thumps sounded, some short gasps of pain, then silence.

Then Brone. "More unfriendly fellows," he said, brushing his palms together as he came up behind us. From the expressions on the faces in front of me, I knew he must be beaming happily at everyone.

Now Berchtold's surprise showed even more, but I guessed that wasn't just Brone. A freckled left hand squeezed my shoulder as Megan appeared on my right.

"Hello, Ken," she said, grinning at Berchtold.

CHAPTER FORTY-FIVE

IN THE PAN

Of course, Berchtold thought Megan was the fake, and I could tell Traeger and Gorman did, too. After yesterday, I was afraid to look at Elrod Macklin.

"*Who* are you?" Berchtold asked her, genuinely taken aback. Breaths sucked in at the desks around us. Nobody moved up in the galleries, still wary of Farrell and dumbstruck by the sight of *two* Judge Connollys. I sensed Beckin behind Megan, and Brone, of course, was right at my back.

"*I'm* the one you know," Megan replied, pulling off her bandage and turning her scarred cheek toward him. "I see you've met my sister. She's a fed."

"I begin to understand," Berchtold replied, realizing my bandage hid no scar. He sat up straighter, calmer now, a very cool customer. "You'd let us leave?"

Megan nodded. "Clear out and survive. Take what you can carry. Head south or wherever."

Berchtold gripped the sides of his podium. "There are a dozen men above you, all carrying automatic weapons. This podium and the barrier in front of you are armored. If we simply drop down to the floor, we shall be safe. *You* will die."

One of the desk-men spoke up, a note of panic in his voice. "*We'll* be in the line of fire, too, Chairman!" Some of the others joined the chorus, protesting shrilly.

Unmoved, Berchtold only looked at the man blandly. "Perhaps you'll survive. And remember, these people brought this upon you, not I."

"Isn't that another of the Commandments, Kenny?" Farrell asked. "'Thou shalt not kill?' I wanta tell you, your God is gonna be pissed, and I don't think you can buy your way out of Purgatory. Or the other place."

Ridicule didn't set well with Berchtold, any more than it had with Traeger the day before. He looked daggers at Farrell, and started to reply. But the door behind and to his right opened and cut his retort off. He spun to see who it was.

Lebendig entered, a sly smile on his round features. He held a frightened Desmond firmly with his left hand, a small revolver pressed up against Desmond's right temple. "Look what I found," he said, very pleased with himself.

Berchtold turned back to us, his smile oily. "Well," he said, "I see the rules of this engagement have *changed*."

I grabbed Megan.

CHAPTER FORTY-SIX

HONOR

This was more than Beckin could stand. She stepped around Megan and me before Berchtold could say any more.

"You have *no honor*!" She held up her ancient knife, turning to both galleries. "The past two nights, this blade has claimed forty-nine of your comrades' souls." She pointed at Lebendig and the struggling Desmond. "Could I restore their lives for two seconds with this man, I would."

Even in the demented depths of his perversion, Lebendig had never imagined anything like Beckin. He went white as the proverbial sheet, and only Desmond's importance as protection from Beckin stopped him from running.

Except us, everyone in the room stared at her, open-mouthed, as what she said sank in.

Into that absolute silence came a woman's voice, deep and husky, almost chuckling. "A pretty speech, youngling, but do you not know that actions speak louder than words?"

Behind me, Brone began to laugh.

Morag had arrived.

CHAPTER FORTY-SEVEN

IN THE FIRE

It got worse.

Two small voices, in unison. "Mommy?"

Farrell and I whirled around, Berchtold, Beckin, everyone in the room forgotten.

Quinn and Maren stood there with Morag, still in shorts, T-shirts, and wearing their little backpacks, looking hopeful. They ran to us, their arms out.

In a room filled with soon-to-be-dead people, I let go of Megan and gathered my daughter to me, holding her tight. Farrell did the same.

I wanted to kill Morag.

Shit, shit, shit.

CHAPTER FORTY-EIGHT

EASY MONEY

"How *dare* you!" I said to Morag as she paced slowly down the aisle, what appeared to be a walking stick in her right hand. Behind her, facing the door, walked Reen Aith, helm of the *Blood Harvest*. About Beckin's size, very dark and quiet, Reen carried a small *Siog* flechette rail gun, twenty-seven seconds of ripping death. And more in her pack, probably.

Morag laughed at us. "Your *Noslings*? They *wanted* to come, to help their mommies." She surveyed the Chamber with mild displeasure, lowered her voice as she came alongside us. "This looks to be some sort of Shakespearean farce. The children know what to do. Let them. They will be safe, and I will kill everyone who doesn't run." She flashed a bright grin at us. "You may aid me, of course."

Morag rested her left hand on Beckin's shoulder, and addressed Berchtold cheerily. "Good Councilman? May I have a few minutes of your time?"

Berchtold didn't see any weaponry on the tall black-clad Morag, but she was too easy-going and relaxed to suit him. We'd been confrontational. She wasn't, at least not overtly, and that worried him. I saw the pack on her back, knew what her 'walking stick' was, knew he was very wrong if he thought she wasn't trouble in spades. He hadn't noticed Reen, apparently. What she carried was definitely a weapon.

"Yes," Berchtold said cautiously, as Beckin stepped back to my side with a final glare, and let Morag have the floor. Berchtold still felt he had the upper hand, as long as Lebendig held Desmond. And he was curious, wondering just what Morag might represent.

If fear had blanched Lebendig's sorry face, Megan was pale with rage and frustration, fists clenched at her sides. Macklin now actively fought his guards, repeatedly trying to stand and being forced back down.

Seemingly at complete ease, Morag studied Desmond and Lebendig with interest. I knew she could smell what Lebendig was. "So, good sir, you like children?" she said to him, cocking her head. When he didn't answer -- and who *would* answer that question -- she snapped her fingers. "Perhaps these two youngsters might add to your enjoyment."

"Let me down, Mommy," Quinn said. In her hazel eyes shown an alarming combination of anticipation and determination. She pushed away from me.

"Are you sure, baby?" I asked, as I set her on the carpet.

"Morag says we'll be fine," Maren said, always inclined to be the more dismissive of parental authority. Farrell gave me a troubled glance before putting Maren beside Quinn. She looked at the girls. "If anything happens to them, Morag, I'll kill you," she said, just loud enough for the group of us to hear.

Morag chuckled again, deep in her throat. "Should they be harmed, Dark One, I will *fall* on my blade."

Everyone except Reen turned and watched as Quinn and Maren solemnly walked side-by-side up in front of Berchtold and bowed to him. He reacted with perplexed bemusement, giving them a tentative smile.

"Do you hear that?" Morag asked, tipping her head to her left toward the tall windows behind the gallery above.

I listened as the girls headed slowly for Lebendig. And then I heard it, a dull steady throbbing beat, several distinct sources, far away still, but coming closer.

Chinooks. Mormons.

The Saints were marching -- well, *flying* -- in.

CHAPTER FORTY-NINE

DEAD ACTION

Morag had set this up somehow, I was certain of that, and she hadn't lived as long as she had without being a good tactician. I just wished I felt better about the girls being part of her little chess game.

As of yet, only the seven of us could hear the approaching helicopters, but that probably didn't matter. Everyone watched Quinn and Maren, to the exclusion of any outside distractions.

Maren boosted Quinn onto the partition. I watched my daughter clamber up to stand teetering on its top, about six feet from Lebendig and Desmond, her back toward them. Only my fear for them kept me from smiling, what they were doing was so obviously an act, pretending to be normal children.

Quinn reached down, caught Maren's hands, and flipped Maren into the air behind her. Maren's short arc brought her directly down on Lebendig's right shoulder. Before he could react, she had the pistol, and kicked away from him, aiming.

Simultaneously, Quinn launched hard from the railing, right at Lebendig's throat, her arms stiff in front of her, holding a kid-sized knife.

I watched my four-year-old daughter tear out Lebendig's throat, even as her sister put a .38 slug into his right temple.

As Lebendig folded to the floor, fountaining blood, Quinn pushed the shocked Desmond toward the door. "Open it!" she yelled, her left hand in the middle of his back, propelling him forward.

Closest to them, Gorman reached under his desk, snatched up his own pistol and started to turn back toward the three kids.

Morag was quicker. Her 'walking stick' -- a Pulse rifle powered by the Starcore unit in her backpack -- fired a quarter-inch-diameter white-hot beam through

Gorman's forehead. His brains blew out the back of his skull in a pinkish-grey cloud and splattered against the paneling, steaming. His body slumped in its chair.

Maren put two rounds into Gorman's body as the kids disappeared safely out the door.

Then things got hot.

Berchtold threw himself backward as Morag blew the podium to splinters and cut Trager's head off. The nineteen men on our level scurried every which direction. Brone turned desks up on their ends to give us cover. Anyone who got in his path had their heads pulped.

Megan and I shot Macklin's guards. As they fell, the gallery windows started to vibrate from the sound of the Chinooks.

The rattling hiss of Reen's railgun began to clean the right side of the balcony. Men screamed, and unfired rifles dropped down among the desks. Beckin and Farrell methodically shot anything that showed above the rail to our left. Morag joined the three of them, blasting volleyball-sized smoking holes in both railings.

Then everyone hit the deck, as *Easy Money's* M60s sent a storm of glass and metal slashing through the upper part of the Chamber. The tall windows disintegrated into bright razor-sharp shards, spinning away from their frames. Uniformed bodies, some with their hands still clutching weapons, tumbled limply from the galleries.

From the floor, I watched the crouched Morag, moving so fast I could barely see her, coolly pick any glass headed our way out of the air. The white strobes of her Pulse rifle streaked my vision.

Death's Daughter, in-fucking-deed.

CHAPTER FIFTY

REVENGE

With the windows gone, the thunder of *Easy Money's* twin Lycoming engines reverberated through the Chamber, filling it. When she stopped firing, the sound barely diminished. The only way to tell the big gunship had quit was the lack of airborne stuff.

I caught a glimpse of *Easy Money* as she spun up and away from the Capitol, looking like a huge olive drab whale heading for the ocean's surface. I pitied the troops on the Mall, who would be trying to penetrate the heavily-armored monster with only rifles. There were two other Chinooks out there, too, but their engines sounded different. Troopships, likely.

We stood up, weapons traversing the Chamber, looking for signs of life.

Elrod Macklin levered himself out from under one of his guards' bodies, and rose shakily to his feet. A few bloody cuts showed on his face and hands, but otherwise he looked okay.

Megan went to him, her boots crunching on the glass-covered carpet.

As they reached for one another, Ken Berchtold pulled himself up from behind the remains of his podium and emptied his .38 into them.

CHAPTER FIFTY-ONE

SANDALS OF DEATH

Berchtold dropped down just as Morag's answering blast sizzled over his head. Macklin tried to keep Megan on her feet, but she sagged out of his grasp. Having been hit at least twice himself, he wasn't doing all that well. He managed to scoop up one of his guards' automatics and stagger toward Berchtold's last position.

"Mine," I shouted, knocking Morag's barrel up as I sprinted by her. I still had six or seven rounds left in my Beretta.

Elrod Macklin and I went over the partition almost side-by-side, just as Berchtold's feet disappeared through the right-hand doorway. A trail of Traeger's blood marked his crawl through the debris.

Macklin barely kept on his feet. Below his waist, his clothes were half-soaked with his own blood. Something major in his abdomen, I figured. He forced each step, his teeth gritted together, his left hand pressed to his gut. I kept between him and the partially-open door. A man like Berchtold would have more ammo on his person.

He did. A single shot spanged into the door from the opposite side, but didn't penetrate. There was more door than a .38 could manage.

"Megan," Macklin said, and I glanced at him. His face had grown more pale, and his eyes were losing focus.

I eased Macklin to the floor, his back against the wall next to the door. "Wait," I said, "I'll get him." He didn't respond beyond a nod.

From the other side of the door, I heard a high-pitched yell, followed by a very solid crunch. A second yell sounded as I kicked the door open and leapt into the hallway. Just in time to see Berchtold bounce off the wall, both hands to his throat. His pistol lay on the floor, not far from the prone body of a guard.

Facing him, Father Bernard circled Berchtold cautiously, his feet poised for another kick, his hands out ready to jab.

But Berchtold was done. Not being able to breathe will do that. His trachea crushed, he went first to his knees, and then over on his side. His eyes bulged, and his mouth distended, trying to get air and failing.

Father Bernard looked at me over the fallen Chairman, his eyes filled with pain as he realized what he'd done.

"Thank you, Father," I said.

"Thank Mister Lee," he replied, his expression bleak. He sounded lost. He put his left hand over his mouth for a moment, then spoke again. "I have violated some of my vows and a Commandment."

"I believe you have a Sacrament to perform, Father," I said softly. I turned back to Macklin, heard Latin begin behind me. "In Nomine Patris, Filiae, et Spiritu sancti..."

"Megan," Macklin gasped weakly, as I knelt down beside him.

"I'm here, Elrod." Heedless of the blood, forcing the Need away, I took his face in my hands and kissed him. He just managed to return the kiss. Then he died.

FIFTY-TWO

DEATH AND LIFE

I stretched Macklin out on the carpet and closed his eyes. On my knees, I sobbed twice before getting to my feet. Just in time catch Quinn as she jumped into my arms. Behind her, on the other side of Lebendig and Gorman's corpses, Farrell stood holding Maren. Maren still had Lebendig's pistol, and Desmond stood next to Farrell, a .45 in his hands. They must have finished the other guard. But Desmond was unharmed.

Desmond's mother was a different story. I looked out into the Chamber, where Brone had constructed a hasty barricade of desks and bodies near the outer door. He, Morag, and Beckin stood behind it, their backs to us.

Megan lay in the aisleway, her legs twitching, Reen at her side. Reen's gaze rose to meet mine. She shook her dark head. "Hurry!" she said. "We have maybe ten minutes. I have shunts." She pointed at Farrell. "We'll need as much water as you can bring me."

One jump and three steps, and I was at my sister's side. I set Quinn on her feet and lay beside Megan.

Fever-bright grey eyes stared into mine. "It's been fun, Megan," she said, with a faint smile. As she spoke, blood crested her lower lip and flowed down over her chin. "Take care of Desmond for me."

"What do I do?" I asked Reen. Megan had three hits in her abdomen, one in her chest. She gurgled with each breath, drowning in her own blood. I put my right hand in her left, and she clutched it desperately.

Reen gave me a half-grin while she velcroed a nylon wrap around my neck. "Not much for you to do. Just lie here. The shunt tips are ceramic-coated titanium. Your body won't be able to destroy them easily."

As she spoke, she swiftly inserted both shunts into Megan's forearm veins and secured the shunts with wraps. "What lives in your blood will see this woman as you, I believe. A you to be repaired." Reen held the other end of the shunts in front of my face. "I must position these carefully, so as to permit enough flow to nourish your brain. This will sting," she said, and plunged the sharpened tips into my carotid arteries.

I scarcely felt it.

Behind me, I heard Desmond cry out. My shunts in place, Reen looked up at him with a reassuring smile. "No promises, little one, but I believe we are in time. There is old science in your mother's twin, born in the nameless depths of space hundreds of thousands of years agone." She turned her gaze back to me, her grin rueful. "I say science, but it will seem magic to him."

Farrell showed up with the water then, and we poured it in me as quickly as we could, her cradling my head.

Things got a little vague after that. I think I remember Quinn promising to be very good always, but that was probably a delusion.

CHAPTER FIFTY-TWO

GOOD ENDING

Saving Megan took a half-hour, though I think we both missed some of it. After ten minutes, her breathing began to ease, and she stopped bleeding as my viroids and efficient blood bugs repaired her damage. The Need grew *very* confused.

At one point I looked up to see Richard Gregorson and Beckin not more than ten feet away, talking in low tones. Tan-uniformed and stern-faced Mormon troops surrounded them and us. Occasionally I heard Morag's infectious laugh and Brone's deep pleasant voice.

When things gradually came into a better focus, I found Captain Garris hunkered down beside me, smiling and shaking his head. "You just can't quit having adventures, can you, Major? And it looks like we'll have to have that beer here in Salem."

I tried to laugh and failed.

CHAPTER FIFTY-THREE

FINISHES

Elrod Macklin went into the ground the next Friday, Midsummer, in Mount Angel, a cloudless, sunny day. Father Bernard said the Mass for the Dead. The mourners numbered in the thousands, lining the route to the cemetery. The three other Councilmen who died in the Chamber firefight were buried there also, part of the same procession. Sometimes allowances have to be made in the name of human decency, even for Catholic boys gone bad.

Scott Lebendig was buried in Salem, quietly, with no family members in attendance, only Farrell, myself, and the girls at the graveside. That also seemed just. For Quinn and Maren, he was their first kill. Even though they didn't feed, there still needed to be ritual.

I consoled them with the fact that I hadn't fed at my first kill, either. From the expressions on their faces as we walked back from the grave, they mostly still figured that they'd lost out, cheated by circumstance.

Even with a trip to a health food store for minerals and carbon supplements, Megan and I had taken nearly a day to get our bodies up to healthy vamp levels on everything. She'd spent much of that time on sensory overload, as her new vision, hearing, taste, and smell abilities came on line. I will treasure always the grateful look she gave me as we stood after-shower nude in front of her full-length mirror on the day of the firefight. "Migod!" she said, "I'm younger. And my scars are gone."

I'd smiled modestly, poo-pooing my role. She'd find out about the Need soon enough.

Richard and the other Mormons winged back to Salt Lake on the afternoon of the Chamber firefight and one-sided Mall battle. He'd paid his debt to Beckin, and would now deal with his father. We let the rumor spread that McPherson's Airborne troops had staged a lightning surgical raid to cut the rot out of the Compliance leadership, and bring the Valley back into the national fold. Thanks to all the Chinooks being olive drab, that one flew. Tom Garris finally got his wish to go to Portland, for real this time.

Elrod Macklin had died defending his family, of course. No one would believe otherwise, and I have never seen grief like that displayed at his Service.

Enough good, decent, and capable Compliance bureaucrats remained to hold government together during the reintegration with the USA. Salem would again be the State Capital, though the Senate Chambers and the Mall were going to need a lot of work.

Morag and Reen Aith departed even before the Mormons, which was probably just as well. Someone might connect them with Gorman's odd death and the charred holes scattered around the Chamber. I'd thanked them for taking care of the girls. Morag just rolled her eyes and suggested that we enroll them in The School of Death in the fall. "To better employ their true abilities," she'd said, laughing. I said we'd think about it.

Brone, as stalwart and true a man who ever lived, finally sat Beckin down on a bench outside the Capitol and told her how he felt. We didn't see much of them for a couple of days, except at mealtimes.

On Saturday, the day after the funeral, Megan and Desmond gathered what personal things they wished to take, put them in four small boxes, and we drove the truck back to the McLeods in North Cedar. Eight of us filled the little rig almost completely.

Desmond alternated between sadness and anticipation. The latter dominated as we grew closer to North Cedar, as he listened to Quinn and Maren tell about riding in the *Blood Harvest*. "Reen let us steer," they exclaimed proudly. "And we saw a Slash-cat in the mountains!"

We used the McLeod's Shift Point, Beckin taking us in two groups. This time, we took no chances. The girls went with me and Farrell.

Eireann Mor hospitality is comparable to Arab. The McLeods had gone out with their wolfhounds and taken two elk, enough for the crew of the *Harvest* and us. Their place was stone, a huge combination of an English manor house and junior-grade castle. The walls of the main hall were covered in weaponry and the skins of fauna our world hadn't seen in thousands of years. Brannoc McLeod, the head of the family, who looked thirty-five despite being over two hundred, sat below the McLeod tartan and presided over the doings.

The beer was good and the stories were better, Morag's best of all. I don't think Desmond's mouth was closed except when he was chewing. He even got a tour of the *Blood Harvest*, its cabin all polished wood and brass, dominated by the centuries-old wheel that Reen used to maneuver the big zeppelin. Enough excitement so that he stopped missing his father for a time, I hoped.

On Sunday morning, Beckin shifted us to our world, one of the younger McLeods drove us into North Cedar proper, and the six of us rented a Dodge mini-van for the drive to Molalla.

I phoned Mairead, my Desmond, and our folks, telling them what time we'd be there, and to expect a surprise.

Surprise was an understatement.

CHAPTER FIFTY-FOUR

HOME

Molalla was both different and the same as Megan remembered, mostly the same as her childhood. I drove slowly through the small town, letting her take it all in. She couldn't seem to look enough directions at once.

Quinn and Maren were bored, wanting to get to their grandparents and exploit that relationship. Farrell and I had explained that this was Megan's visit, that her needs were paramount, and their new half-brother was next in line. They were to keep in the background initially, or get their little butts blistered.

A new wing had been added to the house in 1975, bedrooms for Mairead and Desmond, but it didn't show from the street. I pulled the mini-van up in front and stopped behind Desmond's white Honda CRV and Mairead's cute red Miata.

Megan only stared at the modest white house. Flowers bloomed in beds and hanging baskets, reds and yellows bright in the late morning sun. Recently-washed windows sparkled. My mother's watering can sat on the edge of the wooden porch, a circle of moisture around it. Middle-class, middle America. "It's the same," she said, gulping.

"Yes," I replied, trying to guess what must be going through her mind. I took her hand. "C'mon," I said. "It won't get any easier. I'll be right with you."

We climbed out. I kept Megan and Desmond on either side of me, Farrell and the girls just behind us. Megan's hand shook in mine.

I took a deep breath and rang the doorbell. Mairead, always the most aggressive of us, answered the door. Her hazel-brown eyes went wide. "Oh, wow," she said, and stepped aside to let us in. As we entered, Megan sort of slipped behind me.

My parents stood in the middle of the front room, wearing puzzled expressions, older than Megan

282

remembered, going grey. Desmond leaned against the kitchen doorway with a beer in his hand, nonchalant as usual. I waved to him. "Hi, bro."

"*Megan*!" my mother said. "You've cut your *hair*!" The second Megan didn't register on her immediately. We'd deliberately dressed differently, me in shorts, her in jeans.

"Yeah," I replied. "Look, Mom, Dad, Des, Moy...there's someone here you need to meet." I pulled Megan alongside me, put my left arm around her. She still shook, worse now. The girls shoved their half-brother forward, anxious to get this over with.

Dad and Desmond were quicker to realize what they were seeing than Mom, though Desmond damn near dropped his beer.

"Megan?" my mom said, staring at *two* of me. "What *is* this?"

Megan could hold her emotions back no longer. She burst into tears, her body wracked with deep sobs. "*Mommy, Daddy*!" she wailed, clinging to me.

I patted her on the back, held her, let her weep, and tried not to cry myself. "It's a long story," I said.

CHAPTER FIFTY-FIVE

TRIPS

After we got to Redmond, clued John, and settled in, trips were taken, some together, some just me.

We went to Pine Grove, less than fifty miles from our home -- our *crowded* home, with Megan and Desmond in the guest room -- with Beckin and Brone in tow, and discovered that Beckin had been right. The Garmindias and Barinagas were the same as in Megan's world. They remembered us, were overjoyed to see us, and we had a great time. Little werewolves were a bit overwhelmed by little vampires, but it all worked out. Corinne seemed *very* happy with our visit.

I checked out Hosea Gregorson. Nice that he had such a distinctive name. He ran a dental studies center in Salt Lake, and traveled all over the country giving lectures and testing dental restorative materials. He'd graduated from the University of Washington Dental School in the late sixties. His son Richard was in his junior year in Portland, at Oregon Health Sciences University, following in his dad's footsteps. *Dentists*, for shit's sake! How the mighty had fallen.

In late July, visiting our folks, Megan and I drove up to Portland and checked out the Vietnam War Memorial in Washington Park. It didn't take long to find what we wanted to know. Elrod Macklin had been killed in Vietnam in the fall of 1968. We stood together and stared at the letters chiseled in the gleaming stone, but this reality didn't change. No Elrod Macklin who might learn to love her lived somewhere down in the Valley. Desmond would have to be enough memory for Megan. We sat on the grass under a young elm tree, and I listened to her talk about Macklin. Then, after a time, we left.

Tom Garris' name was nowhere to be found on the wall. On a hunch, we went out to east Portland to the Air

National Guard Unit field. I showed my ID card, and asked if his name rang a bell.

"Oh, sure," the young sergeant at the desk said. She pointed the way down a side hall, smiling. "The Colonel's on leave now, Major, but his office is the third door on the right. It's open. You can leave a note, if you want." We went into Garris' office, leaving the door slightly ajar. I sat down at his desk, flicked on his desk lamp, and examined the pictures on his desk and the wall above it. Helicopters and their pilots. Colonel Garris in flight togs, his two daughters dressed the same, both Captains. His daughters beside their own ships, standing with their husbands and Garris' grandchildren. Three Blackhawk helicopters flying in formation, all in line, with little doubt who they must be. He and his wife, a handsome couple almost my parents' age.

I put my head in my hands and wept with happiness. For at least one person, in one of the timelines, things had worked out well.

Of course, things had worked out well for me. I had saved who I could, made some things right, gained a sister and a nephew, and made them as happy as possible.

Closure, I figured, or close enough.

It is early August, at Dierdre's Birnbaum Enterprises ranch, northeast of Lakeview in eastern Oregon. Farrell and I sit up in the second floor balcony, the great hall floor thirty feet below us. She reads, I sip a Doctor Pepper and watch out the enormous windows.

John and Dierdre are off somewhere. Since we have only been here two days, and they haven't seen each other for some time, I can guess what occupies them.

Tremaine is up at the shop, situated above the old underground drug labs. Occasionally she kicks her KLX 330 over, and the air vibrates with mellow four-stroke sound while Tremaine adjusts the carburetor and pops the throttle.

Megan, November, and Desmond have been watching Tremaine. Now they walk slowly across the asphalt down from the shop. Megan's hands are in her pockets, November gestures with teenage enthusiasm, and my new nephew hangs on November's every word.

Desmond has discovered girls, or rather, girl. He is too reserved to say much, or pester November, but vampires can have no secrets of that sort from one another, so she knows.

Desmond is one of us now. There could be no choice on that issue.

His mother smiles as she listens to November. Both victims of childhood horror, they have commonality. I look at Megan's tanned youthful features, and consider what I have wrought. Nothing bad this time around.

Then Quinn and Maren, who I think are in the kitchen snacking, run out from behind the ranch house yelling and spring over the trio's heads. They land in front of Desmond, and, from their waving arms and animated faces, I know they are enlisting him for some kid adventure. Running coyotes, probably, one of their favorite pastimes here.

Desmond turns them down, preferring to use his mother to be near November. Inwardly, I applaud him.

I remember Morag's suggestion that we send the girls to the School of Death. Farrell and I must address that issue soon, if not this year, the next. A guarantee of two Morags from that fifteen-year investment of time may possibly be worthwhile. But miss most of their growing up, so perhaps not.

Trying little monsters that they are, Quinn and Maren are still ours. I cannot imagine life without them.

There are other issues. Dierdre's joint venture with the Japanese is bearing fruit. Their spaceplane has made several trips into orbit. Soon the space station will begin to come together. Some time after that, Deirdre plans to commence orbital manufacturing and the acquisition of a nickel-iron meteor for a laser iron refinery and smelter.

Deirdre needs vampire personnel for her ventures in weightlessness. Only we can survive unscathed in those conditions. She also knows that eventually the attention of
those who watch over the Solar System will surface. She seeks to tweak the noses of our creators, to force them to open trade with us. With Dierdre, actually. Yet another issue, the Dierdre-monopoly. Something else to think about.

For now, though, I am content. I finish my drink, give Farrell a kiss, and go down the broad staircase, past the old Indian blankets with their colorful swastika designs.

This is our safe haven, our Changling refuge from the world outside. I smile to myself as I reach the bottom of the stairs and see my sister and the others coming toward me through the front entrance.

I have everything.

ACKNOWLEDGEMENTS

Mental illness takes many forms, and writing may well be one of them. A goodly number of people kicked my can down the road to something like cohesive storylines and words in some degree of order. Not quite there yet, but maybe someday.

John H. Quiner – Married to my mom's older sister and the son of Thomas Quiner – the real-life Uncle Tom in Little House on the Prairie – he found me reading his college geology textbook when I was seven, gave it to me, then provided me with material more suitable for a kid, mostly Burrough's adventure stories. Still have them all.

Sister Mary Thaddeus, SJM – my home room sister my Junior and Senior years of high school. She encouraged me to write. Didn't show me how, exactly, but was very supportive, particularly when the stories were about the religious life. The sisters loved to laugh.

Mike Contris – my English instructor at St. Martin's College. Way smart and helpful, pointing out things like syntax, punctuation, and plot. A good and kind man, deserving of every honor he ever received.

Steve Perry – one of the bright lights in Oregon writing, read most of my crap, occasionally drawing attention to plotlines which went nowhere and the lamentable fact that most of my protagonists are sociopaths. As though his never are.

Keith Tittle – a far, far better writer than myself, just brilliant. Helps greatly and doesn't lord his superiority over me. Read his stuff!

The Lucky Lab Rats Writers' Group – John Bunnell, David D. Levine, Jim Fiscus, and Sarah Mueller. All thoughtful, fair-minded, even-handed, and charitable, seldom screaming at me. Yeah, even Jim.

Sandra Hazard – a great name for a female action hero, but in reality a brilliant, bicycle-riding, nature-loving dentist, who for some odd reason approves of my efforts, which is a bit of a mystery.

Maryann Congreves – the mistress of good, effective communication and as funny as anyone can be. Any skill my characters have in their verbal exchanges is due to her. A true word guru.

www.ingramcontent.com/pod-product-compliance
Lightning Source LLC
Chambersburg PA
CBHW021218250626
47155CB00008B/2853